FALL OF HOUSTON SERIES BOOK ONE

NO WAY OUT

T.L. PAYNE

Contents

1. Will — 1
2. Betley — 13
3. Will — 18
4. Cayden — 28
5. Savanah — 32
6. Will — 40
7. Will — 48
8. Cayden — 55
9. Will — 58
10. Will — 62
11. Savanah — 70
12. Will — 77
13. Will — 84
14. Will — 92
15. Will — 99
16. Savanah — 106
17. Will — 112
18. Will — 126
19. Will — 131
20. Betley — 136
21. Will — 141
22. Savanah — 148
23. Will — 154
24. Savanah — 159
25. Will — 165
26. Will — 176
27. Will — 184
28. Will — 192
29. Will — 203
30. Will — 208
31. Will — 219
32. Will — 224
33. Will — 230
34. Savanah — 236

35. Will	242
36. Will	249
Also by T. L. Payne	255
About the Author	257

NO WAY OUT
Fall of Houston Series, Book One

Copyright © 2020 by T. L. Payne
All rights reserved.

Cover design by Deranged Doctor Design
Edited by Melanie Underwood

No part of this book may be reproduced in any form or by any electronic or mechanical means, including information storage and retrieval systems, without written permission from the author, except for the use of brief quotations in a book review.

Don't forget to sign up for my spam-free newsletter at www.tlpayne.com to be among the first to know of new releases, giveaways, and special offers.

Check out other Books by T. L. Payne

The Days of Want Series
Turbulent
Hunted
Turmoil
Uprising
Upheaval
Mayhem
Defiance

Fall of Houston Series
A Days of Want Companion Series
No Way Out
No Other Choice
No Turning Back
No Surrender
No Man's Land

The Gateway to Chaos Series
Seeking Safety

Seeking Refuge
Seeking Justice
Seeking Hope

Survive the Collapse Series
Brink of Darkness
Brink of Chaos
Brink of Panic
Brink of Collapse
Brink of Destruction: A FREE Novelette

Desperate Age Series (Coming soon!)

Although much of this story takes place in and around Houston, Texas, some aspects and locations have been altered to enhance the story. Most of locations within Calcasieu Parish, Louisiana, are fictional. Thank you for understanding an author's creative license.

"Texas is a blend of valor and swagger." — Carl Sandburg

❀ Created with Vellum

ONE

Will

DAY OF EVENT

"It's just a house," Will told himself as he nailed the last piece of plywood over the window. It was just wood, bricks, and concrete. That's what he told himself, but Will Fontenot knew better. It had been a home—a real home—the place where he'd been happy once—where his wife and son had been happy.

Will studied his house. He'd done all he could. He hoped the sandbags and boards over the windows would be enough. The door slammed, and Will saw his son, Cayden, round the corner carrying his suitcase. It wasn't just a house to Cayden, either. It was written all over his face as he stared back at their boarded-up home. Will wanted to reach out—to comfort his son, somehow—if only Cayden would let him.

"Do you think the water will reach my bedroom?" Cayden asked.

They were the first words Cayden had spoken to him all week. Will kept track—for the therapist. Cayden's—not his. She would ask Will about it at Cayden's next visit. His son suddenly seemed so small, much like the little boy that he'd been that night, two years before. Will looked away, unable to face him.

"Maybe," Will said. He couldn't lie to him. He wished he could. He would love to tell his son what he wanted to hear—that their house would be spared the damage from the incoming hurricane, but he couldn't. At thirteen years old, Cayden was way too smart for that. He knew what a category five storm could do.

"Will you grab my backpack?" Will asked. "It's just inside the door."

Cayden grunted and dropped his suitcase near the back of the 1978 Jeep Wagoneer. Will had opted to take the old SUV rather than his truck. The truck was insured. He could get another, but the Jeep was irreplaceable. It had been his grandfather's and would be Cayden's in another three years.

Will placed the hammer and nails back in the garage and pressed the down button on the remote. He knew the next time he saw his truck or his tools, they would be underwater. The house had been spared during the last few hurricanes that had hit the Texas coast, but this time, the monster storm was heading straight for them.

Even though Cayden wouldn't articulate it, Will knew what was on his mind. Will felt it too. If the house still stood after the storm passed, instead of opening his closet and smelling the scent of his wife's perfume, he'd smell the stench of stagnant floodwater. Where they'd sat and enjoyed breakfast on Sundays, there'd be a foot of mud and debris. His hands balled into fists. Will cursed the storm that threatened to erase the last bit of his wife from their lives. He turned to face the Jeep and sucked in a breath. It wasn't the storm that was to blame for that—he was. It was all him. He was the reason Cayden no longer had a mother. Will bowed his head and placed a hand on the side of the SUV.

"Here," Cayden said, walking up behind him. Cayden dropped the backpack into the back of the Jeep and walked around to the passenger side. "I locked the door too," he said.

Will nodded and stole one last look before climbing in and putting the Jeep into gear.

No Way Out

On the freeway heading north, Will let the Jeep roll forward a few more feet, coming to a stop behind the loaded-down pickup truck he'd been behind for the last several hours. It seemed all two million residents of Houston, Texas were attempting to evacuate at that moment. He ran a hand across his close-cropped brown hair and wiped the sweat from his brow.

Cayden hadn't said a word since he'd plopped into the front seat and stuffed earbuds into his ears. There'd be no conversation on this trip. They had a lot of one-way conversations. Will kept trying, hoping eventually for the forgiveness that he feared would never come.

In the six hours they'd been on the road, traffic along Eastex Freeway had moved less than ten miles, many times coming to a standstill for several minutes before inching forward only to stop again. Will was about to lose his mind. They were still eighty miles from Point Blank and his family's house on Lake Livingston.

Will's phone rang, and Cayden retrieved it from the cup holder between the seats. "It's Aunt Savanah," he said, handing the phone to Will.

"Put her on speaker," Will said.

Cayden connected the call and placed the phone down between them.

"Hey, Sis," Will said.

"Hey, yourself. Are you two on the road?" Savanah asked.

"For about six hours already."

"Six hours? How far have you made it?"

"About ten or fifteen miles," Will said.

"That sucks. I told you that you should have left earlier."

Will said nothing. They both knew she was right. The last thing

Will needed was a lecture from his younger sister. Yes, he should have left yesterday. He would have avoided most of the evacuation traffic, but he'd been trying to arrange to pick up Cayden's birthday present early. He'd hoped that getting the puppy would make staying up at the lake house more tolerable for Cayden.

"How's Cayden?"

"Ask him yourself. You're on speaker."

"Hi, Aunt Savanah," Cayden said.

"How's it going, bud?" Savanah asked.

"Okay," Cayden replied.

Will knew the one-word response was only because he was listening. Cayden didn't have a problem talking to Savanah.

"Well, I called to wish you a happy birthday. I wish I could be there," Savanah said.

"Thanks," Cayden said. "I know. Maybe we can come to see you soon."

"Yeah. The kids would love it. Tell that brother of mine he should just come here instead. You know you both are welcome."

Cayden glanced over. "He heard you."

"Well, I'll be here, if you change your mind."

"Thanks, Savanah," Will said.

"Love you guys," she said.

"Love you too," Will said.

Cayden placed his earbuds back into his ears, and Will turned his attention back to watching the truck's brake lights in front of him. He glanced at the fuel gauge and then toward the back of the vehicle. At this rate, they would run out of fuel before they even reached the city limits of Humble. There'd be no way they'd make it all the way to Point Blank before having to refuel. After hours stuck in traffic near downtown Houston, they were forced to leave the highway searching for gasoline. Will pulled off at the next exit, only to be greeted by a long line of vehicles waiting their turn at the gas pumps. After finally filling up, Will pulled away from the fueling island.

Will saw the vehicle careening toward them a second before the impact. A waterfall of glass cascaded down around him. The metallic groan was deafening. Past and present collided in his mind. Stunned, Will searched for the door handle.

He heard screaming.

Melanie?

Coppery blood pooled in his mouth.

There's smoke.

He had to get out. He had to get his wife out.

No! No! No!

"Melanie!" Will yelled.

"Dad!"

"Cayden?" *No. This is wrong. This is all wrong.*

Shaking off his stunned confusion, Will looked around. A midsized sedan had jumped the curb and gone airborne, barreling sideways through the parking lot, and narrowly missing an older gentleman standing outside his truck. The vehicle had rammed into the line of cars waiting at the fueling island, then continued past them and slammed into the side of the Jeep. This was not one of his nightmares. This was real. And this time, it was his son's life at stake.

Will strained against the seatbelt and reached for Cayden. "We have to get out of here."

His gaze shot to the cars shoved together in a jumbled mess of metal just outside his door. There was smoke.

The fuel pumps!

He had to get Cayden away from there before the gas pumps exploded. Reaching down, Will quickly turned the key, shifted the old Jeep into gear, and punched the gas. The Jeep's heavy-duty grille guard clipped the bumper of the car blocking his path, pushing it aside. Will's heart raced as they sped across the parking lot. Blood filled his eyes from a gash above his brow. He couldn't see.

"Dad! Stop!"

Will stomped on the brakes. He and Cayden were flung forward by the inertia. The seatbelt dug into his shoulder. The vehicle stopped inches from the concrete wall that separated the parking lot from the building next door. Will wiped the blood from his eyes and turned to his son. "Are you hurt?" Will asked as he ran his hands over his son's torso and arms.

"I'm fine. Dad, I'm fine," Cayden said sharply. "What happened?"

"That car jumped the curb," Will said, turning his attention to the chaos outside the Jeep.

Cayden unbuckled his seatbelt and stared out the shattered window. "Is anyone hurt?" he asked.

Will glanced at the wreckage. "Maybe."

"Shouldn't we help?" Cayden said, reaching for the door handle.

"Wait here," Will said, opening his door.

He examined the dent in the side of the old Jeep Wagoneer, surprised that there wasn't more damage. Images of his wife's mangled Volvo flashed before him. He quickly pushed the memory aside.

"Lock the doors," Will said, shoving the keys into his pocket.

"I don't think it will do much good," Cayden said, pointing to the broken window.

"Stay in the car," Will said.

As he ran around the side of the building, Will could see that the careening car had shoved an SUV overtop of the pump. Will weaved between cars and stopped in the parking lot. The vehicle burst into flames. In seconds, smoke rose from its back window. Mothers and fathers snatched small children from their cars and ran from the burning wreckage.

"That woman's trapped," a man yelled as he ran from the scene.

Without thinking, Will ran toward the burning SUV.

"Someone, turn off the pumps!" a woman yelled.

Another shouted for someone to call 911.

As Will ran, he reached into his pocket and retrieved his cell phone. The screen was black. He pressed the button over and over, but his phone was dead.

"My phone's dead," a twenty-something man said.

"So is mine," another replied.

As Will approached the burning SUV, the heat coming from the gas pump was intense. The back half of the car that sat on top of the pump was now fully engulfed in flames. Will expected it to explode at any moment. His stomach tightened. He had to act fast, but time seemed to slow. Voices stilled as Will focused on the driver slumped over the wheel.

He raced to the driver's door. The interior of the car was full of smoke. Yellow flames flickered between the twisted metal. Will sucked in the rancid, smoke-filled air and coughed. His eyes stung and tears streamed down his cheeks. Will shielded his mouth and nose with his shirt and pulled on the door's handle. It was locked. Will pounded on the glass, trying to rouse the woman. The back seat was now in flames. He had to do something. He couldn't just stand there and watch this woman burn to death.

Panic gripped him. His heart raced. He felt his mind slipping, detaching.

Not now. Not here.

Images flashed through his mind. The sights, sounds, and smells of the night that had changed his family forever nearly paralyzed him. He was back there watching his wife as she lay trapped in the mangled, twisted metal of her Volvo. Her screams pierced his soul as the heat from the flames melted the fabric of her synthetic clothing. Will fought to shake off the overwhelming guilt and shame that hit him like a tidal wave. Screams jerked him from his fog.

"It's going to explode!" a woman screamed.

Will reached into his pocket and found his car keys. On the ring was his car escape tool. He pressed the device against the window in one fluid motion, punching a hole in the glass. A rush of heat and smoke hit him in the face. He coughed violently as he reached in and yanked open the car door. The flames, now fueled by outside air, intensified and spread to the front passenger seat. Will grabbed the woman by the arm and yanked hard. She screamed but didn't budge. Will reached down and felt for the seatbelt across her waist. For a moment, it was Melanie's frightened eyes that stared back at him, pleading with him to save her. Will pulled and tugged, but the belt didn't budge. He turned the tool around and used it to slice through the strap.

"I'm getting you out," he said as he pulled her from her seat.

Will dragged her away from the burning vehicle. Not taking time to stop and assess the woman's injuries, he scooped her up into his arms and ran toward his Jeep. He hoped the building would shield them from any fiery debris that might be propelled into the air by an explosion. No sooner had he placed her on the grass by the road than the car, then the pumps, exploded, sending a ball of flames into the air. Will kneeled next to the woman, gasping and coughing as he tried to suck in oxygen. He felt a hand on his back.

"Is she okay?"

Will glanced back. A petite Asian woman, clutching a green duffle bag to her chest, bent over the injured woman. "She's in shock. She needs a hospital," the woman said straightening. She looked like she needed medical attention herself. Blood dripped from a gash above her eye. Her lip was split, and her pants were torn.

"An ambulance should be here any minute," Will said. "You're injured. You should sit down."

Even without calling 911, surely the fire department or police would see the massive ball of flames shooting into the air. People were standing in the middle of the parking lot, staring at the burning wreckage.

"Get back behind the building. There could be more explosions," Will said, pointing to the side of the store.

Will turned his attention back to the injured woman on the ground. She stared back at him, wild-eyed. Will could see blood in her long brown hair. He wiped it from her face and examined the bump above her brow. She had abrasions on her left cheek. Her right forearm was burned. It looked like her wrist might be broken as well. She needed medical attention right away.

Cayden appeared by his side. "Is she all right?"

"Run to the Jeep and get the trauma kit from the back," Will said, tossing him the keys. "Get the one in the red and yellow duffle. Grab a bottle of water too."

Will hoped that emergency services would arrive before he'd need the trauma kit. After his and his wife's accident, he'd vowed to never be caught without one again. He'd taken a first-aid class and made sure to carry the bag in his vehicle at all times, but he'd never had to use it. Will looked up, searching for fire trucks, ambulance, or police. He saw none. What he saw were vehicles piled up in the intersection. Smoke was coming from one of the buildings downtown.

What in the world is going on here? Something wasn't right. The lights had cut out, the phones all stopped working, and cars just died all at once. This was no storm. This was something else entirely.

"Do you know what happened?" Will asked the Asian woman still standing over them.

"My car died. I had no brakes. The car would not steer. It was an accident," she said in a thick accent.

"I understand," was all Will could say.

It wasn't his place to absolve her of her guilt. He certainly couldn't exculpate himself from his own. That day, two years ago, he'd been the one to run the red light. It was his carelessness that had left his son without a mother, and there was no taking that back. There were no words that could undo what he'd done. No, there was nothing he could say to ease this woman's guilt.

"Where are the ambulance and fire department? Where's the police?" Will asked no one in particular.

"There are wrecks everywhere. They're going to be very busy," a middle-aged man standing nearby said.

"What happened?" the woman from the burning car asked.

"You've been in an accident," Will said.

She raised her burned arm and looked at it. She squeezed her eyes shut.

"What's your name?" Will asked.

"Isabella D'Angelo. My emergency contact is Kevin Arnold. He's my boyfriend," she said.

"Well, Isabella, I think you're going to need a stitch or two in that gash above your eye."

The woman tried to sit up.

The petite woman's shoulder-length brown hair was matted to the side of her face. Blood had dripped onto her pink top and her blue jeans.

"I need to get up. I have to get home," Isabella said.

"Is she okay, Dad?" Cayden asked as he dropped the trauma kit on the ground next to the woman.

"She'll be fine. She has a little gash above her eye. They tend to bleed a lot. Why don't you go start the car and get the air conditioner going? We might have to drive her to the hospital," Will said.

"None of the cars will start," the woman parked next to them said as she exited her vehicle.

"None of them?" Will asked.

"Something's wrong. No hurricane knocks out phones and makes cars not run," a man in his fifties said as he approached Will.

"None of the cars will start?" Will asked as he hurried toward his Jeep. Just before he reached the door, Cayden turned the key, and the engine roared to life. Will turned back to the people gathered around the injured woman. "Mine started fine. Maybe you're just out of gas."

"Why is your car working when no one else's runs?" one of the men asked.

"I have no idea." Will looked around. All the other vehicles were newer model cars, SUVs, and trucks. His grandfather's Jeep was over forty years old. That was the only explanation he could come up with at the moment.

"I just filled up. I should have fifteen gallons of gas in there. It just won't start for some reason," a stocky man said.

"Mine too," another man said.

"It's the aliens. I told you, Betty. Didn't I tell you they were planning something big?" said a balding, paunchy man wearing a black cowboy hat and scuffed boots.

It wasn't long ago that Will would have dismissed that idea as crazy talk, but after the Pentagon announced that it was establishing a task force on the subject, Will had actually stopped to consider it for a moment. It wasn't that he believed that little green men from Mars could be behind whatever was happening at the moment. It was more his concern about unidentified flying objects of more earthly origins. The Russians, Chinese, and even North Korea all had technologies that the general public wasn't aware of, Will was sure of it. If this was something of manmade origins, it would be from one of them.

"Don't start with that crap again, Herman. This ain't the time for your alien conspiracy theories. This is real. That hurricane churning out there in the gulf ain't gonna wait for the mechanic to fix our truck. We gotta get the hell out of here now," the short, pudgy woman standing next to him said.

The people huddling near the intersection, watching the cars near the pumps burn, seemed as clueless as Will was. The electricity could be explained. If the hurricane had spawned tornadoes or dumped early rain on a substation area, that could cause an outage. The loss of cell service during a storm could be as well, but there was barely a cloud in the sky, and that wouldn't cause phones to not power up at all. Cars suddenly dying and not restarting, Will didn't know how to explain that.

TWO

Betley

DAY OF EVENT

As FBI Agent James Betley turned his dark blue sedan onto Interstate 610, he pressed the phone icon button on his steering wheel and said, "Hello."

"I have to go today," a female voice said.

"No, that's not possible. Just hold on a few more days and I'll pull you out," Betley said.

"I can't. They know. I have to go today."

Betley exhaled hard. Dealing with informants was never easy. He'd spent months developing this contact, and he wasn't about to let her slip off the hook now. Not when they were so close to blowing open the biggest corporate espionage case of his career.

His partner, Agent Nico Rodriguez, pointed to the dash and mouthed, "Mute it." Betley pressed the mute button on the instrument panel.

"We have to bring her in and calm her down. If she's compromised, it could bring down the whole investigation. Rybeck has been itching to give this case to the task force investigating the breach at the Texas power grid ever since the CIA alerted us to what the Chinese Communist Party has been doing at their consulate in Houston."

There had been a lot of activity with the CCP lately. It wasn't anything unusual to have multiple investigations swirling around the consulate, but Betley didn't see any connection between his corporate espionage case and the investigation into the Communist Party's unusual interest in the nation's energy sector.

Betley hadn't been read in on the case, other than being told to pump his sources for any information about anyone snooping around power plants or oil refineries. What information the seventh floor had received from the Central Intelligence Agency, Betley didn't know. He'd give his left nut to get on that task force. With the contacts he was making in the Chinese community, he'd be a valuable asset to the team. Not to mention how it would help his career.

"Okay, I'll insist," Betley said, depressing the button to unmute the call.

"You still there?" Betley asked.

"Yes. Are you going to get me papers?" the informant asked.

"Meet me," Betley said.

"It is too risky. I think they are having me followed."

"Where are you? I'll come to you," Betley said

"No. You're not listening. I have what you want. I need you to keep your promise and get me papers, or I am out of here."

"I'm on the six-ten. I can meet you at the usual place in about twenty minutes," Betley said.

"What if I'm being followed?"

"Call me when you get close. Stay on the line and drive around the block twice. I will be able to tell you if you have a tail," Betley said, glancing over to Rodriguez and shaking his head in frustration.

"All right. I'll turn around and…." She paused. "Oh, no. They are following. What do I do?"

"Act normal. Don't let them know you suspect they're back there," Betley said.

He heard the screech of tires on pavement.

"Slow down. You don't know for sure that they are following you," Betley said.

The line went dead. Betley's gaze dropped to the dash's instrument panel. It was blank. The sedan had died. Betley mashed the brake.

"What the hell!" Rodriguez said.

As Betley attempted to steer the vehicle onto the shoulder, another car rammed into him from behind. Luckily, they weren't going very fast, and Betley was able to coast to a stop well off the roadway.

Betley put the sedan into park and pushed open the car door. As he climbed out of the vehicle, he saw other cars veering to avoid a collision and steering to the shoulder of the road.

He turned and stared down the eastbound lanes. Cars were stopped in the roadway as far as the eye could see. Immediately the silence struck him. It was an unearthly experience in the middle of a city that over four million people called home.

Rodriguez exited the sedan and came around to join Betley on the roadway. Others had left their vehicles and were milling about along the shoulder. Betley walked back to the car that had struck him. He leaned down and peered into the driver's window.

The driver sat rigid in her seat, staring straight ahead. He tapped on the glass. When she turned to look at him, he motioned for her to roll down her window. She reached over and pressed the button, but nothing happened.

"It won't roll down. I think my battery is dead. My car just died right there in the middle of the interstate," she said.

Strange.

"Are you all right? You're not injured, are you?" Betley asked.

The woman felt her head.

"I don't think so," she said.

"Rodriguez, why don't you go ahead and call nine-one-one just in case," Betley told his partner.

A moment later, Rodriguez returned, holding up his phone. "It's dead."

"Use mine," Betley said.

"I tried. It's dead too."

"It can't be. It's been on the charger all morning," Betley said, walking back to the sedan. He reached in and grabbed his phone from the console. Betley pressed the button to wake it up and nothing. He stared at the black screen as the realization seeped into his brain. He cursed under his breath and threw the phone onto the seat. Betley turned and leaned against the sedan, running both hands through his black hair.

"What's up?" Rodriguez said.

"We're freaking screwed, that's what's up."

"You don't think?" Rodriguez said.

"You tell me. What the hell else can simultaneously kill all vehicles and phones over a wide area?"

Rodriguez leaned back against the vehicle, bent over, placed his hands on his knees, and retched.

"Exactly. They actually set off an EMP on us," Betley said.

"I can't believe they really did it, knowing that we'd respond," Rodriguez said.

"I can't believe we weren't able to stop them in time."

"You think they fed us that information about the refineries as a distraction?" Rodriguez asked.

"It must have worked," Betley said.

There had been chatter about a plan by the Chinese, Russians, and Iranians to release a nuclear bomb high in the atmosphere over the Midwest, creating an electromagnetic pulse capable of destroying the US power grid, crippling most of the United States. But there had been chatter for years. As far as Betley knew, there hadn't been any credible proof of them attempting to implement such a plan. Obviously, there was a lot he didn't know.

"So, now what?" Rodriguez asked.

Betley turned and looked south. "Now, we get the hell to high ground."

"Shit, I almost forgot about the hurricane." Rodriguez scanned the highway. "And how are we supposed to evacuate now?"

"Walk," Betley said, flatly.

"Damn. Now I wish I hadn't moved out to The Woodlands. That's one hell of a walk," Rodriguez said. He stepped into the roadway and took a deep breath. "What are you going to do?"

Betley looked back over his shoulder. There was no way he was attempting to hump it all the way to Clear Lake. They were less than three miles from the safe house where he was to meet his informant. Betley reached into the sedan and retrieved his keys.

"I'm heading to Midtown."

"You're crazy. You need to head north. You're welcome to join me. You can crash at my place. Julia won't mind. You can sleep in the kids' room," Rodriguez said.

"No, that's fine. Besides, she might still show up there."

"Will it matter now?" Rodriguez asked.

"It might. It depends on what she has," Betley said.

Betley waved goodbye to his partner and opened the back door of the sedan. He retrieved his gym bag. He was grateful that at least he wouldn't be walking in his dress shoes.

THREE

Will

DAY OF EVENT

Long minutes passed with no sign of help from emergency services. The heat bearing down on them was relentless. Will held out a bottle of water to Isabella. She appeared to be more alert, and Will hoped the shock was wearing off. The burn on her arm looked terrible. She had to be in a great deal of pain.

The store clerk had passed out what drinks the store still had in the stockroom as they waited for help to arrive. Will was beginning to think it never would. Isabella sat on the curb, holding a can of Pepsi to her head and handed the Asian woman a can of beer.

"Hi, Kim. I'm Isabella."

A surprised look spread across the Asian woman's face.

"Your badge," Isabella said, pointing to the University of Houston identification badge hanging around Kim's neck.

"Are you from Houston?" Isabella asked.

"No," Kim said.

"I'm new here too. I'm from a little town south of Oklahoma City. It's in Oklahoma," Isabella said.

Kim wasn't paying attention. Her focus was on the people in the intersection. She turned her head to the left and right, scanning the cars stalled in the street. She clutched her green duffle bag tighter. Will's suspicious mind wanted to speculate about what could be inside that bag. Whatever it was, she wasn't letting it out of her sight.

"What about you, Cayden? Are you and your dad from here?" Isabella asked.

Cayden glanced at Will. He'd been taught not to give out personal information to strangers. It was evident that this woman didn't have children or hadn't been taught about stranger danger. Cayden hadn't spoken much to anyone lately. Since his mother died, he'd withdrawn into the fantasy world of his science fiction books.

"We're from here," Cayden said, earning him a glare from Will. "Well, I am. But my dad's from South Louisiana."

Isabella's head snapped toward Will. "You're a Cajun?"

Will was surprised that Cayden had chosen now to become chatty. Will breathed in slowly, trying to think of a polite way to shut the woman up. He decided that saying nothing was his best move, taking the "if you can't say something nice, don't say anything at all" approach his mother had taught him.

"I think we should at least put a dressing on that gash, Kim," Will said, changing the subject.

Will unzipped the trauma kit and was about to pull gauze pads from a pouch when Kim snatched it from him and began dressing her wounds. She placed butterfly bandages over the gash above her brow like a professional. When she'd finished, she zipped the kit and pushed it away without so much as a thank you.

Will was having a difficult time reading the woman, but there was something about her that made him uneasy. Not being able to put his finger on it made him even more uncomfortable.

"Where on earth is the fire department?" Will asked.

A moment later, Kim began vomiting, showing the first signs that the gash on her head may indicate her injuries could be more severe than they appeared. Head injuries and burns were nothing to take lightly. Both Isabella and Kim required immediate medical attention—much more than his trauma kit could provide.

"Can you help me get her to my car?" Will asked the two men beside him. "I need to take her to the hospital."

"I think I am all right. I can walk," Kim said, trying to stand on her own.

"Let us help you," Isabella said, sliding her arm around Kim's waist.

He wasn't in the habit of giving rides to strangers. Most people around here never even made eye contact with others. They didn't stop and exchange pleasantries like the small parish where he'd grown up. Neither of these women looked like much of a threat, but you could never know for sure.

Will closed the back passenger door and ran around to the driver's side of his vehicle. "Okay, let's go then."

Isabella climbed into the back seat next to Kim.

"I am sorry. I have insurance," Kim said.

"It's all right. No need to apologize," Isabella said.

As Will pulled onto the road, he looked at Isabella in the rearview mirror. "Where's the nearest hospital?"

"Turn right there and then make a left. It's a few miles south of here," Isabella said.

"Cayden, try your phone. See if you can get a signal to call nine-one-one and let them know we're coming," Will said as he pulled from the parking lot.

"It's still dead," Cayden said.

"What's up with the phones not working?" Isabella asked.

"I have no idea," Will said.

Kim stared out of the side window. If she had any thoughts on the matter, she wasn't sharing them.

"This is all too strange. I'm still shaking like a leaf. I can't believe my car plowed into a gas pump like that."

"I am sorry," Kim repeated.

"Oh, that's okay. It happens," Isabella said. "Everyone makes mistakes."

Will swallowed hard and ran a hand across the top of his hair. He knew all too well about careless mistakes. He glanced at Kim in the rear-view mirror. She didn't look remorseful. In fact, she wore no expression at all.

Will tuned out everything else Isabella said as he tried to concentrate on weaving in and out between all the stalled cars. Sometimes he resorted to hopping the curb and driving on the sidewalk. Will was grateful for the old Jeep's ability to go in most any terrain. He could still recall, as a kid, he and his sister, Savanah, piling in it with his grandfather and going out for ice cream every Sunday. He missed those simpler times.

After Hurricane Rita had flooded their home, he and Melanie had fled to Houston. He'd eventually found a job at one of the chemical refineries and worked his way up the ranks. Melanie earned her teaching certificate and began teaching third grade. Before long, Cayden arrived, and they'd settled into their suburban middle-class life together.

Will's heart broke for Cayden. It was hard enough to be a lanky teenaged boy without having to do so without his mother. Will had wanted to tousle Cayden's brown hair and pull him into his arms to comfort him, to tell him somehow it would all work out, but he knew that would be as unwelcome as having fire ants in your sleeping bag. Cayden blamed him, but not as much as Will blamed himself.

Will had to backtrack twice and find new routes around the stalled cars blocking the road to the hospital. Some of the vehicles must have crashed into buildings nearby. Will couldn't tell which buildings were on fire, but something was. Thick black smoke rose in the direction of the Toyota Center, the home of the Houston Rockets basketball team. He'd taken Melanie there to see Garth

Brooks and Trisha Yearwood a couple of years before their accident. He'd planned to take Cayden there to see a Luke Combs concert. The memories of her and their lives together were everywhere.

An uneasy quiet settled in as Will maneuvered the vehicle through the crowded streets. Will glanced into the rear-view mirror. Isabella had quieted and was chewing on her fingernails. The previously stoic Kim now looked nervous as well. Kim repeatedly turned and looked behind them every few minutes. It was apparent she was afraid of something. Will just didn't know what.

Will's mind was still whirling, trying to make sense of what was happening. He was likely reading things wrong. Now wasn't the time to make mistakes. This was serious. He needed to be able to read a situation and react quickly, but everything was turned upside down. The patterns and body language he'd usually use to judge things were now influenced by all the craziness of the strange event that had occurred. Will hoped that someone at the hospital would have some answers for them. Someone had to know what the hell was going on, right?

It was taking much longer than he'd anticipated reaching the hospital, and after several more detours through parking lots and alleyways, Will pulled the Jeep back onto a four-lane street. Almost immediately, people began flailing their arms, trying to flag him down. There was nothing he could do for them. His vehicle was full, and his cell phone wasn't working to call anyone to help, so he swerved and continued past them. One man raised his fist in the air and cursed them. Will could understand his frustration. It was an unsettling time, and everyone was on edge.

Will glanced into his rear-view mirror to make sure none of the stranded motorists were following them. Kim was half turned in her seat, staring out the back window.

"You see something?" Will asked.

Without a word, Kim turned back around and stared straight ahead.

Will slowed before approaching the next intersection, trying to determine his best route around the stalled traffic. On his left was a side road, but he wasn't familiar enough with the area to know if it was a dead-end or not. There weren't many cars along its curbs, which likely meant it wasn't a through street. He scanned the crowd to his right. They noticed him, and some were approaching the Jeep. Will made the left-hand turn onto the side street. A middle-aged woman in business attire and heels stepped off the curb and into his path with her hand in the air as if she were hailing a taxi.

Not again.

"Dad!" Cayden yelled, pointing at Will's side window.

Before Will could even register what was happening, his door flew open. Hands were on him, dragging him from the vehicle.

"Dad!" Cayden screamed.

"Cayden!" Will yelled.

Will was shoved to the ground, and the man jumped into the driver's seat. The Jeep was rolling forward as two cops ran up. The officers struggled with the man inside the vehicle.

"Cayden!" Will screamed, fear stretching his voice high and tight.

He scrambled to his feet. Long tendrils of panic seized his chest, threatening to paralyze him where he stood. His mind searched for what to do to save his son.

"My son's in there," Will shouted at the officers' backs. "Cayden!"

Panic seized his gut, twisted, and then yanked hard as Will ran alongside the rolling Jeep. He reached for the back passenger door handle, but the vehicle sped up, knocking him off balance. Will tripped and went down hard onto his right knee. Pain shot through his body, causing everything to momentarily go dark. He felt bile at the back of his throat. Smoky black rage yanked him back to his feet in pursuit of the vehicle and his son. The Jeep jerked to a stop as one of the officers pounded on the carjacker's head. Will tried to open the back driver's side door, but it was too damaged to open.

"That's my car, man! Get him out of my car!" Will yelled.

As Will started around the back of the Jeep, the back passenger side door opened, and Kim and Isabella jumped out. The Jeep began to roll.

"Cayden!" Will shouted. "My son's in there."

Kim shoved Isabella aside and yanked on the passenger door. A second later, she pulled Cayden from the slow-moving vehicle.

The vehicle lurched and stopped several times as the carjacker tried to pull away. One of the officers had a hold on the steering wheel. His feet were dragging the road as the carjacker accelerated and then sped away. "Stop the car. You're dragging him," the second officer yelled as he took chase after them.

"Dad!" Cayden said. "They took the Jeep."

Will ran to his son and wrapped his arms around the boy. "Are you hurt?" He ran his hands up and down the boy's arms and legs, searching for injuries.

"No, but they got the Jeep," Cayden said.

"I know," Will said. "Are you sure you're okay?"

"I tried to stop them. I tried to get the keys, but the cop pulled his taser, and I didn't want to get shot."

"It's okay. I'm just glad you're safe, and you weren't hurt," Will said. Tears welled behind his eyelids as he wrapped his son in his arms. He closed his eyes and thanked God that they'd all survived.

Will moved Cayden to the sidewalk next to the two women. Isabella was crying uncontrollably with her arms wrapped around herself. Will couldn't blame her. It was a normal response after what they'd just experienced. It was terrifying. Kim, on the other hand, was seemingly unfazed. Was she in shock? Maybe her head injury was worse than he'd thought.

"Are you two all right?" Will asked.

"We are fine," Kim said. Her eyes were flat, and her face expressionless.

"Thank you for getting my son out," Will said.

Kim bowed her head slightly. Will watched as her head rotated, scanning the parking lot near the corner. He looked, but all he saw were more confused, stranded motorists.

"What are we going to do now?" Cayden asked.

Will turned and scanned the street. There was no sign of any other police officers. Half a dozen people were standing around gawking at them now.

"Does anyone have a working vehicle? We have injured women here that need to get to a hospital," Will yelled.

"My car's dead," a man dressed in business casual said.

Everyone else just shook their heads.

"Does anyone have a working cell phone then?" Will asked.

"That died too," the man said.

Being on foot in the heat of summer was bad enough, but being on foot in downtown Houston was even more dangerous.

"How far are we from the hospital?" Will asked.

"The hospital is about six blocks that way," a stocky man said.

"Thanks," Will said. "I guess we're walking."

Will turned to Kim. "Do you think you can make it?"

"Yes. I can make it from here on my own. I do not want to put anyone to trouble," Kim said.

"No," Isabella snapped, regaining her composure. "You're injured. You shouldn't be on your own." She wiped tears from her cheeks and straightened the hem of her shirt.

"Are you sure you're up to it?" Will asked Isabella.

"I think I'm okay. I can walk a few blocks. It's probably faster than taking a vehicle anyway." She smiled and let it fall. "I'm sorry about your Jeep. It was a cool old car," Isabella said.

Cayden's shoulders slumped. "It was my great grandpa's. I was supposed to get it when I turn sixteen."

Isabella bent and placed her hand on Cayden's shoulder. "I'm so sorry. Maybe the police will get it back to you. They've probably stopped that jerk by now."

"Maybe. I hope they don't wreck it. The paint was original," Cayden said.

Now Will regretted driving it. He hadn't wanted it to get damaged in the storm. It meant so much to Cayden. Besides, the trunk of his two-door sedan wouldn't hold all their go-bags and supplies to survive up at the lake house for weeks if everything flooded again.

Will looked to the south, checking the sky for signs of the storm. It was the first time since the lights went out that he'd had time to consider how dire their situation was. Downtown was not where he wanted to be stranded during a hurricane.

When Hurricane Harvey had stalled over Houston, dumping more than fifty inches of rain, Interstate 45 was submerged. The Buffalo Bayou flooded and flowed into downtown inundating over a hundred thousand homes and many people lost their lives.

As adrenaline and stress hormones flooded his brain, Will struggled to control the rising panic that threatened to seize hold of him and cut off his ability to think his way out of the situation. How long did they have? Eighteen hours? Twenty-four at most? How far could they walk in that amount of time? Far enough, he hoped. But they needed to leave now. Hundreds of thousands of people who'd been evacuating away from the coast were now stranded on the highways. Not all of them would be friendly. Most would be frightened. Before long, they might become desperate. Only a few blocks away was a large homeless camp. Houston, like most large cities, had a homelessness problem. You couldn't even take your kid to the zoo without being confronted with it.

They were on foot without water or a weapon to defend themselves in the fourth largest city in the United States, with over two million people in it; not all of them model citizens. Will shook his head. What choice did they have? He needed a plan. He needed information. The hospital would have radios and security guards.

They'd be in contact with emergency services and would have kept informed about the approaching hurricane. They'd have information about where they needed to go to be evacuated away from the storm.

Will grabbed Cayden by the arm. "All right, let's stick close together. We don't want to get separated in the crowd."

FOUR

Cayden

DAY OF EVENT

Watching his dad attempt to give first aid to the woman he'd pulled from a burning car had given Cayden a new sense of respect for his father. Lord knew he hadn't given him credit for much of anything lately. But he had to admit, the way his dad ran toward the burning car as everyone else was running away was pretty badass.

Cayden scanned the crowd of people standing outside their stalled cars. It was all pretty crazy. The Asian lady was the only one that didn't appear completely freaked out by it all.

After hours sitting in the car waiting for traffic to move inch by inch out of the city, he'd been glad they'd pulled off to get gas. Who knew they'd find themselves in the middle of all this? It was undoubtedly the most excitement he'd had in a long while.

Mostly, he and his dad stayed at home these days. Cayden remained in his room, mainly to avoid talking to his dad. In the beginning, he just didn't want to have to talk about his mom, but later, it was just too painful to watch his dad mope around the house missing her. Cayden never knew what to say to him. What could he say?

He called her name. When that car slammed into them, his dad had called out his mom's name. Cayden hadn't been there when his mom and dad had their accident. But he'd overheard bits and pieces from relatives, mostly after the funeral. It was pretty bad. That's what made his father running to help now so amazing. He had to have been thinking about that night, but he put that aside to help save a woman's life.

He could tell by the way his dad looked at him that he believed Cayden blamed him. He didn't, of course. He'd told him so—right after. How many times did he have to say it? He'd even made Cayden see a shrink. It helped some, maybe. But mostly, they spent the hour talking about books, music, and video games. He couldn't tell that to his dad.

His dad was several paces ahead. He was walking too fast for the injured ladies. He was doing his best to clear their path through the crowd. Everyone seemed as in shock about what was happening as his dad was. Some appeared in a panic to get somewhere. Cayden didn't know what to make of it.

"My boyfriend has some friends who are Cajun. I loved it when they invited us over to supper," Isabella said.

Cayden nodded, not quite sure what to say.

"Your dad was really brave to pull me from my car," Isabella said in a low tone. "You should be very proud of him."

"I am," Cayden said.

"Do you have any kids, Kim?"

Kim shook her head.

Cayden tried to read Kim. She seemed distant and lost in thought. Maybe that was just how she processed trauma, as his therapist called it. Isabella, on the other hand, seemed to freak out like his mom used to. It used to drive his dad crazy when his mom talked too much when she was nervous. Maybe his dad should be the one in therapy. Maybe it would help him move on. Not that Cayden wanted to see his dad with someone else. He definitely didn't want a step-mother, but he would like to see his dad get out more and enjoy life. He knew his mom wouldn't want them to be sad for the rest of their lives. His gaze fell to Isabella.

Something about her reminded him of his mom and how much he missed her.

Kim dabbed at the gash above her eye with the back of her hand. It was still bleeding despite the butterfly bandage. Blood had dripped down the side of her head and onto her shirt and pants. The sight of blood used to bother Cayden. In his dreams, his mother would stand with her arms outstretched, calling his name. As he drew close, he could see that she was covered in blood. He hadn't told the therapist about that dream. He didn't want to talk about it.

Cayden pulled his phone out to check it one more time. The screen was still blank. Maybe the old guy back at the gas station was right, but he hadn't seen an unidentified flying object or little green men. Whatever it was, it couldn't last very long. If it did, things were about to get really, really bad, especially if the police vehicles weren't working.

Will led them around the stalled cars and back onto the crowded sidewalk. Cayden wondered where all the people had come from. He glanced up at the skyscrapers overhead. As far as he knew, everyone was supposed to have already evacuated the downtown area. Obviously, a lot of people had waited until the last minute.

He and his dad would have left sooner, but his dad's work had needed him. He had to stay and shut down the chemical plant so it didn't erupt when the hurricane made landfall.

The fear on people's faces troubled Cayden. A lot of times, he thought grown-ups overreacted to things. But this many freaked out people had him getting concerned now.

Up ahead, a homeless man sat with his back against the wall and his legs outstretched outside the doors to a coffee shop. A woman in her thirties tripped over him and fell into the man in front of her. He spun around and punched the woman causing a fight to break out among several bystanders. Cayden moved to the side near the building, trying to get a better look.

Will grabbed him by the arm and motioned for Isabella and

Kim to cross the street. Halfway down the block, Cayden heard the sound of gunfire. He looked back, and people were running in every direction. He stopped in the middle of the sidewalk. The homeless man was slumped over the curb, his body half into the street. "They shot that poor old guy," Cayden said. "We need to help him."

His dad grabbed the back of his shirt and spun him around. "Don't look. We need to keep going. It's getting dangerous out here."

FIVE

Savanah

DAY OF EVENT

Savanah Fontenot pulled her minivan to a stop in front of Broussard's bakery. Twice a month, she drove into her small hometown of Vincent, Louisiana to drop off herbal teas and candles at the local bakery. She was fortunate to have several local businesses that had offered to sell her locally-made herbal teas and homemade candles. Between that, and the farmers' markets, and her on-farm sales, she was doing pretty well with her herbal business.

As usual, she'd printed out flyers to place in the store windows announcing her on-farm classes. Savanah grabbed the brochures and stepped out of the vehicle. She glanced up the street toward the courthouse before pulling open the van's door. Her stomach tightened as it always did when she came to town. She needed to hurry. She needed to make her deliveries and get back to her four children.

Savanah reached in to retrieve the boxes she needed to deliver and noticed that the van's interior light hadn't come on. She made a mental note to check the bulb when they got back home and picked up the box.

She glanced down Main Street toward the barbershop. Usually, there'd be several older gentlemen sitting outside, sipping sweet tea, and playing checkers or something. Vincent, Louisiana, looked like many other picturesque small southern towns. Growing up, Savanah had always felt safe there. She'd always believed that the close-knit community was filled with good people. But now she knew better. Savanah knew firsthand about the corruption and dirty dealings of the city officials. She knew, and there was nothing she could do about it. The mayor had made sure of that.

Maryann, who owned the florist shop, stepped out, scanned the street, and then went back inside. Savanah could hear her engage the lock. She watched as Maryann turned the sign on the door from open to closed. Savanah checked her watch. It was a little after two. It was a bit early to close up.

Savanah entered the bakery. An old-fashioned bell above the door rang as she opened it. It was dark inside, and Savanah stopped for a moment. She stepped back outside the door and checked the sign. The neon light was off, but the one on the door was still turned to "open." The lights were out.

"Paul," Savanah called out to the dark.

"Back here, Savanah. The darn lights just went out. I was trying to see if we'd blown a breaker or something," Paul said as he entered the room. He pulled his white apron over his neck and headed toward the door. "I tried to call the electric company, but the darn phone's out, too."

"Must be something on the power company's end then," Savanah said.

"That's what I was thinking. You got a cell phone I could use to call them. Mine's dead at the moment."

"Let me run out and grab mine from my handbag," Savanah said.

A moment later, Savanah returned with her phone in hand. She swiped up to wake it, and nothing happened. She pressed every button on the cell phone and still nothing. "That's strange. I had a full charge five minutes ago."

"That is strange," Paul said.

"I can stop on my way out of town and let the folks at the electric company know your power's out," Savanah said.

"Would you? That would be great," Paul said. "Just leave those boxes there. I'll get you a receipt." He turned to go around the counter and stopped. "Wait. The computers are down. I'll have to write you one the old-fashioned way."

"That's all right, Paul. You can give me one next week when I bring by that plantain salve we talked about," Savanah said.

She had no reason to mistrust Paul. He was one of the good guys. Savanah wondered if he knew. Of course, he did. It was a small town. Gossip ran as free as the southern sweet tea he served. Did he know and look the other way? Or did Thibodeau control him too?

"You sure? It's no trouble. I just need to find my pad and pencil," Paul said.

"I'm sure. I trust you, Paul."

"All righty then. You drive safely. If the lights are out in the rest of the town, those intersections with traffic lights will be dangerous. When the thing is flashing, people just plow through. Folks don't seem to know how a four-way stop works."

"I'll be careful," Savanah said.

Paul picked up a bundle of cookies and held them out. "Give these to those precious little ones of yours."

Savanah knew that her children would be thrilled to receive cookies from Broussard's. People drove from miles away to stop in and have a pastry or cookie in the garden out back. Savanah glanced down at the smiling face cookies covered in artificially colored purple icing. She almost cringed but didn't want to offend the man. She'd taken her kids off sweets and artificial colorings years ago.

"I know Sweetpea loves purple," Paul said.

Savanah nodded as she stuffed the cookies into her handbag and headed back to the van, waved at Paul, who was standing in the doorway of his shop, and turned the key to start her van. Nothing. The engine didn't rev to life. There wasn't even a click.

"Something wrong?" Paul asked.

"My van won't start. I think it's the battery." She tried her best not to panic. It has to start. It just has to.

She glanced back toward city hall and cranked it again. The engine didn't even sound like it was trying to turn over.

"I noticed that the interior light was off before I came into the store," Savanah said.

"I've got some jumper cables. Let me run out back, and I'll pull my truck around and give you a jump," Paul said, disappearing inside the store.

Savanah jumped out, opened the sliding door, and retrieved her backpack. Tossing it onto the front seat, she unzipped the front pouch and ran a finger over the pistol's grip. She let out a long breath trying to control her rising panic.

A moment later, Paul reappeared in the doorway. "My truck won't start either," he said. He pulled the door to his shop closed. "I'm gonna walk down to Earl's Garage and see if he can come to take a look at both our vehicles."

"Okay, Paul. I'm going to run some stuff over to Peggy's Boutique."

She couldn't just sit there like a trapped animal—exposed, vulnerable, and waiting for Wade or one of Tibdough's other henchmen to drive by and see her sitting there—alone.

Paul threw a hand in the air and waved over his shoulder as he walked down the street toward the auto repair shop. Savanah prayed that her van only needed a jump. She needed to hurry and get out of there. She never stayed this long.

After what seemed like an eternity, but was likely just minutes, Paul reappeared at her driver's side window.

"Earl's fancy new wrecker truck wouldn't start either," Paul said.

"What on earth is going on?"

"I don't know. Sunspots, maybe?"

"Sunspots?" Savanah asked.

"You know, solar flares and such. I heard there was a small one a while back," Paul said.

"Solar flares can knock out cars? I thought that was just satellites and radios?"

Paul half shrugged. "That's all I can come up with."

Snake-like panic coiled its way around her heart and squeezed. Breath caught in her throat. Her worst nightmare had become a reality.

"Are you okay, Savvy?" Paul asked.

She looked up at him with tear-filled eyes. "I don't know how I'm going to get back home to my kids without my van. It'll take hours to walk home."

"I wish I could help. You're welcome to wait at the store and see if things come back on."

"I appreciate that, but I have animals that will need tending to. I milk the goats twice a day." Savanah couldn't tell Paul her real reason. She'd have loved to have someone to confide in. But she didn't dare. She knew the consequences if she did.

"I understand. You be safe walking out on that road. I'd walk you home if my knees weren't so bad," Paul said.

"I appreciate that," Savanah said as she reached the back of the van.

She was anxious about the kids. They'd be worried sick when she didn't make it back right away. Since her home was off the grid, her children would be fine. They had their homework and chores to occupy them. At fourteen, Kendra had more responsibilities than some adults. As a single mother with four children, Savanah often had to rely on her to help with her younger siblings.

Reaching into the passenger seat, Savanah grabbed the backpack that she always kept in her vehicle. In it were water, dehydrated food, and a change of clothes for herself and each of the kids, along with copies of their birth certificates and other important documents. It was one of four that she kept. The others were located by the front and back doors of her house, and one was hidden in the barn. Her grandfather and brother had thought she was behaving paranoid. They'd chided her for scaring her children. But they didn't know her true reasoning. It was her responsibility to protect her children. She certainly couldn't count on the law to do it. Not when the person she feared the most was the mayor.

Mayor Clarence Thibodeau was the most powerful man in Vincent. As far as she was concerned, he was the most powerful person in all of Calcasieu Parish. He was also the most corrupt. A fact that was well known, yet he'd retained his office for over ten years, even amid all the accusations of abuse. Some of those girls were no longer around to testify. All the others were too scared.

She'd been eighteen years old when she made the unfortunate mistake of marrying his son, Derek. Four kids later, she'd discovered her husband was stealing drugs from drug dealers and selling them to a man in Beaumont, Texas. She'd gone to her father-in-law, but that had been the biggest mistake of her life. She should have never told anyone. It not only ended her marriage, but it made her a target of Thibodeau and the rest of his crooked staff. They'd made it clear they'd do anything to keep their little secret.

Thibodeau came around occasionally just to remind her how powerful he was. Once, she'd arrived home and found him sitting in her kitchen. She'd blown a gasket and demanded he get out, but he just sat there, tapping his fingers on the table.

"You know, *mon cher*, marijuana is still illegal in Calcasieu Parish. I could have the police haul you in and lock you up in my jail. You'd do time. Serious time."

She didn't have any pot, but she knew that wouldn't matter. Thibodeau could say she did or plant some in her house. He was a god in that town, and there would be nothing Savanah could do about it. It was such a helpless feeling.

"What do you want?" she'd asked him.

"Now that is more like it, *cher*. Come to think of it, there is something you can do for me." He stood and walked to the back door. "I'm gonna have one of my employees drop off a bag here tomorrow sometime. If you could drive that over to Beaumont and deliver it to my accountant, I'd be eternally grateful."

The next day, one of the street department employees dropped off the bag, and she'd delivered it to the accountant. She'd thought that would be the end of it, but it hadn't. She'd made that drive every week for two years. She wanted to leave and take her children far away from this place, but she was sure he'd find her. She'd considered confiding in her brother, but after both their father and grandfather passed, Will drifted away from her and Calcasieu Parish. He had a kid. She was afraid to involve him in her mess. Besides, she hadn't wanted him to know just how badly she'd screwed up her life.

So, after her grandfather died, Savanah had moved to the family farm. Being away from town had put her out of Derek and the mayor's bullseye. They rarely came around anymore. She did her runs to Beaumont, and they left her alone—for the most part. She'd still had to deal with Wade Melancon's unwelcome advances when he dropped off the bags and the unspoken threats left in her mailbox from time to time. She'd had to obtain a post office box in town to keep her children from finding the dead rats.

Savanah worried that her children suspected something. They were smart kids, and they noticed how nervous she was when Wade dropped off packages for her. She was sure that at least Kendra had been able to put things together. How would she explain it to them? How could she tell them that not only was their father a good-for-nothing scumbag, but their mother was involved in illegal drugs and money laundering as well?

Savanah unzipped the backpack and tossed in the cookies Paul had given her for the children. If it took longer than a few hours, she might be grateful to have the sugary cookies. Savanah zipped the pack and slung it over one shoulder as she thought of Karson, her youngest. She didn't like being away from him that long. Karson was small for his age. He'd been born premature and struggled to survive his first year of life. Now, apart from some stomach issues, he was a healthy four-year-old boy. But she was still worried.

As she crossed the street, Savanah looked back and scanned the side road leading toward city hall. For a moment, she wondered if the city's vehicles would run. If they too were dead, perhaps now was the time to get her children away from Calcasieu Parish, maybe even out of Louisiana. Savanah took two steps toward city hall and stopped. There was no way of finding out whether city vehicles had been affected without exposing herself. The idea was foolish. Everything was likely to come back online before they could get far enough away. Reluctantly, Savanah turned to her left and headed toward home.

SIX

Will

DAY OF EVENT

Reluctantly, Cayden walked close to Will's side as he and the two women set out on foot for the hospital. He'd heard Cayden speak more than he had in months. Against Kim's protests, Isabella insisted on holding Kim's arm as they walked. Kim seemed to need the assistance. The gash over her eye was still bleeding, and she seemed a bit disoriented. He was torn. They were heading south when they needed to be heading north, away from the city. But he'd committed to taking the women to the hospital. He hoped he wouldn't regret being a man of his word.

The sidewalks were packed with people who'd found themselves on foot. Men and women in business attire trudged with their heads down. A middle-aged man draped a suit jacket over his shoulder. His expensive dress shoes made a clicking sound on the concrete. None of the windows of the buildings downtown were boarded up. Will shuddered at the thought of all that glass raining down on them if the winds blew out the windows.

He didn't want to push the women too fast, especially without water to stay hydrated, but Will's insides were screaming, Hurry! Hurry! as they sidestepped slower walkers. Guilt racked him as his thoughts replayed the scenario back at the Jeep. But with everyone on foot and desperate, it had probably been only a matter of time before someone took it from them. He wished they'd gotten a little closer to the hospital.

"What are you studying at the university?" Isabella asked Kim.

Kim looked shocked.

"Your badge," Isabella reminded her, pointing to the student ID hanging around Kim's neck.

"Chemistry," Kim said.

"What type of chemistry?"

"Biological."

"Oh, okay," Isabella said.

Kim had been purposefully vague and Will wondered if it was part of her Asian culture, her nature, or if she had something to hide. He wondered if it might have something to do with the duffle bag she still clung on to for dear life.

"Do you like it?" Isabella asked, not giving up. "It sounds interesting."

"Yes."

Will wondered if maybe her vague one-word answers could be from a language barrier, but she spoke very clear English.

"I wanted to be an archeologist when I was a little girl. I was fascinated by ancient civilizations and discovering how people lived thousands of years ago."

Kim said nothing.

"Did you have to go to school long to be a chemical biologist?" Isabella asked.

Kim didn't answer her.

Will bumped into a petite woman in front of him, almost knocking her over. His eyes were scanning the road ahead. The flow of people had stopped. The foot traffic had backed up at an intersection. Will heard shouting. He glanced to his right, looking for a way around whatever was going on. Spotting an opening in the crowd, Will pulled on Cayden's arm and stepped off the curb.

"This way, ladies."

Will led them across the street. There were fewer people, but they all seemed to be heading north. That was the direction he and Cayden should be heading. North, out of the city and away from the incoming storm.

Isabella picked up the questioning where she'd left off. "I'm curious, how long have you been in the United States?"

Will was getting the impression that Isabella was more than curious. She was nosey. Folks in Texas were generally friendly, but that didn't fly in a city the size of Houston.

"Four years," Kim replied.

"Do you have family here, or did you just come to attend school?"

Kim hesitated before answering.

"No family," she said.

Will detected a note of sadness to her tone.

"Do you like it here?" Isabella asked.

"Yes."

With all that was going on, Isabella's questions were grating on his nerves. He needed to concentrate. He needed to think and come up with a plan of action. Nothing that she was asking would put them in a better position to deal with whatever the hell was happening.

"My boyfriend and I plan to visit China someday. I want to visit the Great Wall and see panda bears in their natural habitat. We visited the Chinese Embassy, not that far from here, to see about getting visas," Isabella continued.

Kim said nothing.

It was obvious to Will that Kim wasn't going to divulge much personal information. He wondered how long before Isabella got the hint that Kim did not want to be friends. Her chatter reminded him of Cayden, back before he'd lost his mother. Cayden had been full of questions and never met a stranger without chatting, despite Melanie's strong admonitions. He'd strike up a conversation with people at the grocery store or in restaurants. Cayden had been an avid reader and loved to make up stories. He was curious and imaginative and would spin wild stories about random things. He'd once made up a whole conspiracy about a postal worker and their neighbor being part of the KGB and running a spy ring from their garage. He claimed all the packages the guy received were secret surveillance equipment. His endless chatter used to irritate Will. Right now, he'd give anything to hear one of his tales.

"My boyfriend isn't going to believe what a day I've had. He's waiting for me at our apartment. I just ran out to see if I could find more bottled water and snacks for the party," Isabella said.

"Party?" Will said. As soon as the question left his mouth, he realized how judgmental it sounded.

She looked back at him and smiled. "The hurricane party. My boyfriend is a musician. He and his band are going to ride out the storm at our apartment." She glanced back at Kim. "I'm going to Oklahoma City to stay with my sister. I rode out the last storm. I'll never do that again."

Oklahoma City was nearly five hundred miles away. Will was pretty sure she wouldn't be riding out the storm there. Under the circumstances, he and Cayden wouldn't make it up to Lake Livingston either. They needed to find somewhere else to stay during the storm. But where? If whatever had caused the cars and phones to stop working couldn't be fixed soon, they'd need something more permanent. He imagined things were about to get really ugly in Houston.

"How far away do you live?" Will asked.

"About ten miles. I live over on the east end," Isabella said.

"Did it flood in Hurricane Harvey?"

"Hell, yes. It's right there by the bayou. Our apartment didn't flood. We're on the third floor, but our cars flooded, and we were trapped inside and had to be rescued by the Cajun navy in boats."

"And you went back there?" Cayden asked.

"I had no choice. They wouldn't let me out of my lease. When the waters receded, they said we could return as our place was dry.

The first-floor apartments were empty for months as they ripped everything out and remodeled them."

"Where do you live, Kim?" Isabella asked.

"Sharpstown," Kim replied.

"Oh, in Chinatown?"

Kim said nothing.

This time, Isabella didn't press her for more information. Maybe she'd finally picked up that Kim didn't want to talk about herself.

As they approached the intersection, Will spotted the holdup. There was a brawl outside the coffee shop. Will wanted no part of that. He turned to motion for everyone to move across the street, but couldn't find Cayden. For a moment, he was about to panic, and then Cayden slid under some big guy's arm and stood on his tiptoes, attempting to get a view of the fight. As Will hurried Cayden and the women away from the scene, someone shot a homeless man, leaving him bleeding in the street. Will wanted to somehow shield Cayden from what was happening. This wasn't something a thirteen-year-old boy should be going through. It made Will's desire to get away from the city that much more urgent.

As they crossed over and turned onto the next street, two men were playing tug of war with a shopping cart. Items spilled onto the street as each man struggled to gain control. A young woman raced over, grabbed a bottle of water from the ground, and ran away. One of the men suddenly released his grip on the cart and took chase after the woman.

"Stay close," Will said, stepping back and allowing Kim and Isabella to walk in front of him. He wanted to be able to react quickly if someone bothered them.

Will pulled his T-shirt up and used the hem to wipe sweat from his forehead. He ran his hand across the top of his head, wishing he had a hat and some sunglasses. The Texas sun was brutal. They'd only walked a mile or so, but his mouth was dry and his shirt drenched in sweat. He glanced around, trying to see if there was anywhere that they might find water. There seemed to be nothing. Will could think of no other way to find water than entering one of the businesses or restaurants and seeing if they had any bottles left, which given that everyone had been snatching up water in preparation for the storm, he doubted.

Will stopped in front of a restaurant. It was dark inside. He couldn't see if anyone was even in there. He considered trying the door. As he reached out to try the knob, shots rang out, and he jumped, pulling Cayden onto the recessed steps of the restaurant. People around them dropped to the ground, some taking cover behind abandoned cars.

"This way," Kim yelled to him as she grabbed Isabella's hand and pulled her toward the alley ahead.

Will pushed Cayden in front of him, shielding him with his body. "Follow Kim."

With his hand on Cayden's shoulder, they followed her down an alley between two apartment buildings. Will looked up at floor after floor of balconies overhead. He spotted two bicycles, and an idea formed. He was in the middle of working out how he'd get them down without destroying them or killing himself when he heard Isabella scream.

"Let her go," Cayden yelled as he broke free from Will and took off running.

Isabella was bent at the waist, face down, struggling to free herself from the grasp of the naked woman who had both her hands wrapped up in Isabella's hair. Will was taken aback by the woman's crazed laugh as she swung around, putting Isabella's body between her and Kim. Cayden ran around and jumped on the woman's back.

"No! Cayden, get away from her," Will yelled, sprinting toward them.

The woman spun, and Cayden fell backward. Will reached

down and grabbed hold of him, hauling him to his feet a second before the woman stepped back.

"Angel!" A woman's voice rang out behind Will. He pushed Cayden behind him and turned to face her. An elderly African American woman wearing a bright yellow top, long floral skirt, and a colorful headwrap stepped from one end of the alley. She pushed her shopping cart to one side and approached the crazed woman.

"Angel, baby. You let go of that woman's hair. You know you're not supposed to behave like that." Will thought her accent was likely Haitian or African, but he wasn't sure.

Kim had her hand on the back of Angel's neck. She squeezed, and the woman dropped to her knees, nearly taking Isabella down with her.

"It's okay, Angel. You relax now, child. Everything will be all right. Come to Fahima," the elderly woman said. Instead, the crazed woman jumped to her feet and took off running down the alley.

Will turned his attention to Isabella. "Are you all right?"

"That woman ripped my hair out," Isabella said with tears welling in her eyes. She held out a clump of hair.

"I'm sorry, child. Angel's just not been herself today. She wasn't able to get her meds," Fahima said.

Kim turned and started back down the alley in the opposite direction to which Angel had run.

"Wait up, Kim," Isabella said, running to keep up with her.

"Thank you," Cayden called back as he too set off after the women.

"Cayden, wait!" Will yelled after him.

Just as they reached the street, more shots rang out. They were closer this time. Too close. Kim ducked and then dove to the ground. She rolled and hurried to her knees, crawling to reach cover behind a concrete half wall. Isabella stood frozen. Cayden turned back and ran toward Will.

"This way, children," Fahima said, waving them over. "You'll be safe in here."

Will ran over and grabbed Isabella by the arm, dragging her back into the alley. As they neared the elderly woman, Will grabbed Cayden by his shirt, nearly ripping it off his son, and followed the elderly woman down a blind alley. When he realized it was a dead-end, he turned, but Isabella and Kim blocked the exit. Three-round bursts bounced off the brick wall near the entrance of the alley. Are they shooting at us? Why? Why would they shoot at us?

"This way," Fahima said, pushing open a door. Will stood to one side and allowed Cayden, Kim, and Isabella to enter first before stepping inside and slamming the door closed.

SEVEN

Will

DAY OF EVENT

Will looked up at all the pipes running overhead. They were hiding in the apartment building's mechanical room. Normally all the systems that ran its heating, ventilation, and air conditioning systems would be running, and the sound would be deafening. From the relative silence in the room, it was obvious that the generator hadn't kicked in. Candlelight flickered along the walls and ceiling in one corner of the room. On the floor was a mattress and what looked like someone's personal possessions. It was obvious that the elderly woman had been sleeping there.

As Will tried to locate something to secure the door, the elderly woman took Isabella and Cayden to the back of the room. Kim yanked open a side door and looked back.

Fahima turned and took two steps toward her. "Where are you going?" she asked.

"Up," Kim said.

"That inner door is locked," Fahima said.

Isabella whipped around. "We're trapped in here?" Her gaze flicked to Will. The color drained from her face. "I don't want to die in here."

"No one's going to die. We just need to wait until it's safe outside, and then we'll hurry and get to the hospital. There will be help there," Will said, trying to sound much calmer than he felt.

The last thing they needed was for everyone to panic. That wouldn't do any good. Fahima wrapped her arms around Isabella and led her over to the mattress on the floor. Kim gave the door one last tug before turning to face them. She looked up and met Will's narrowed gaze.

"What's going on here?" Will asked.

"I do not know," Kim said, returning to the door they'd just entered by.

"How long are we going to wait in here, Dad," Cayden asked. Will hated seeing the concerned look on his son's face. He was supposed to protect him from the world. That was his one job. The only job that mattered. In the space of just a couple of hours, Cayden had seen more blood and violence than any boy should in a lifetime.

"Just a little while longer. We'll let things die down out there, and then we'll get on our way," Will said.

He wasn't sure how they'd know if things had calmed down or when it was safe to get back on their route to the hospital, but he knew one thing; he needed a weapon of some kind. Will looked around the room, hoping there'd be something they could use. At the chemical refinery where he worked, their tools were all huge and pneumatic, but maybe he'd get lucky, and this place would hold a regular pipe wrench.

Will ran around the room, searching for a tool cabinet. Along the back wall was a pegboard with belts and hoses. On a roll-around cart, Will found only pneumatic tools—nothing that would make a good bludgeoning weapon.

"What are you looking for?" Isabella asked.

"Something to use as a weapon," Will said, pulling one of the hooks from the pegboard. He held it between his fingers. He might be able to use it to poke an eye out, but he sure hated the thought of getting that close to a bad guy.

Kim walked over, tugged on the handle of the tool cart, and set about removing its bolts by hand. A moment later, she held it in the air. Will took it from her and felt its weight.

"That's pretty light. I'm not sure how much damage it will do."

"It is not the tool, but how one uses it," Kim said.

Will sat with his back to the cold cinder-block wall, staring at the metal handle. He turned it over and over in his hand, trying to think of some way to turn it into an effective weapon. Cayden, Isabella, and Fahima were huddled together on Fahima's mattress. They were talking about Fahima's life back in Nigeria. Isabella was full of questions, as usual. Will was just glad she had someone else to grill for a while. She looked up. The corners of her mouth tilted up in a weak smile. Will looked away, not wanting to attract her attention. When she returned her gaze to Fahima, Will studied her.

She was petite and pretty. A dangerous combination out on the mean streets of Houston, even before everything went to shit. Her brown hair hung straight down, framing a heart-shaped face. Her hazel eyes were lively and expressive as she spoke. She was slim but not as slim as Melanie had been. He pushed the image from his mind and focused on the handle. Will stood and walked back to the tool cart. He rummaged around, finally finding what he was looking for. Will placed the hook next to the end of the handle and wrapped a length of duct tape around it over and over, securing it in place. He studied it. He'd keep his eyes open for something more lethal, but in the meantime, the makeshift dagger was better than nothing.

Now they just needed to get back out there and get where they were going. Time was ticking away. Time they didn't have. His mission had been to get Isabella and Kim to the hospital. That seemed impossible now. If he hadn't gotten involved, he and

No Way Out

Cayden would be halfway to Lake Livingston by now. Isabella and Kim were not his problem. His responsibility was to his son. He had to do whatever it took to get Cayden away from the city before that hurricane made landfall. After that, if things didn't return to normal, they'd need to find a way to Calcasieu Parish to his sister and her kids living on his grandfather's farm. He and Cayden could ride it out there.

Will stared at Cayden. He needed to get his son away from there. But how? Think, Will. His mind whirled as he ran through several scenarios, including finding an older model car and taking it. Could he do that? It could mean death to the car's owner. He'd be no better than the thief that had stolen his Jeep. There had to be another way. There just had to be. Images of the bicycles on the balconies came to mind. He began calculating how Cayden could possibly ride that far and how long it would take to reach Lake Livingston that way.

Fahima handed Cayden a bottle of water. She smiled, and her skin crinkled into crow's feet at the corners of her eyes. Will wondered for a moment how the woman had come to be on the streets of Houston, Texas. She didn't look like an addict. She wasn't behaving like she had a mental impairment. What calamity had befallen her to leave her alone and homeless? Where was the woman's family? Was anyone looking for her? Did she have a husband and children desperately wanting her to come home?

Despite her circumstances, Fahima seemed to still genuinely care about people. She'd tried to help the naked woman that had attacked Isabella. She'd trusted them enough to bring them into her makeshift home in the maintenance room when the shooting started. He admired her ability to not become bitter and untrusting, but he wondered if that made her a target out on the streets. How long could someone like that last out there?

Isabella chewed her thumbnail and shifted uneasily on the mattress. She was traumatized and in pain, that was obvious. Could he abandon her and Kim to head off on his own? Will placed his hand on his abdomen where an acidic knot had formed just below his breastbone. Why was doing the right thing so difficult? He needed information. He needed to find someone with answers—a police officer, fireman, someone with FEMA. FEMA. They'd have someone at the hospital preparing to take in casualties from the storm, possibly they'd have a way of evacuating people.

Kim had finally settled in on the floor next to the door. She sat with her arms crossed over her chest, her face impassive. Her eyes were dark and watchful. She looked up and caught Will staring at her. His face flushed. He wanted to look away but didn't.

"How's the head?" Will asked.

Kim touched the bandage above her eye. "It will heal."

"Where do you plan to go? After the hospital, I mean. Do you have somewhere to evacuate to?" Isabella asked her.

"I was on my way to the airport," Kim said.

Up until now, Kim had been so vague that Will was surprised she'd revealed that much information.

"What now?" Isabella asked. "Will you go back to Sharpstown?"

"No," Kim said.

Will glanced at Kim out of the corner of his eye. He detected something in her one-word answer but couldn't put his finger on it.

"What about you, Fahima?" Cayden asked. "You can't stay here. The building might flood."

Fahima placed her hand on Cayden's knee. "I'll be fine. Don't worry about me, child."

"You should come with us, Fahima," Isabella said. "They'll have help at the hospital—or you can come home with me. It looks like I'll be riding out the storm from my apartment after all, now that my car is ashes."

"I don't think so. I'll be fine. I don't walk so good anymore. I'll just slow you down," Fahima said.

"You have to come," Cayden said. There was such a pleading to his tone, almost desperate. It was a flash of the tender-hearted boy he'd known. Will had forced him to see a counselor, and he'd been starting to open up to her, and then this happened. How many years of counseling would it take the poor kid to work through all he'd seen in this mess?

"What about you, Will?"

Will was lost in thought, recalling happier times and his life before the accident. He didn't hear her question.

"Will?" Isabella said. "Are you and Cayden going to return home since you lost your car?"

Will glanced at Cayden. He was torn whether they should head the twenty-five miles back home to Friendswood or head toward the lake. If they headed north, even traveling the twenty miles or so to Humble, they would at least be out of the worst of the floodwaters. If they somehow were able to get one of the bikes down from the balconies or find a couple somewhere else, it would still be a hard trek on bikes to go the rest of the distance, but the way things looked, he'd much rather be at the lake than trapped in their flooded house.

"I haven't decided yet. I'm leaning toward continuing on up to Lake Livingston," Will said.

"How?" Cayden and Isabella both said at once.

"Bikes. Did you see all the bikes people had left out on the balconies of this building? If we were able to get a couple, we could travel ten, maybe twenty miles in a couple of hours. By dark, we could be out of the potential flood zone," Will said. Saying it out loud made the plan sound even more plausible.

He wished they still had their go-bags from the trunk of the Jeep. They contained everything they'd need to camp for the night. It would be a hard night sleeping on bare ground with the fire ants and giant, Texas-sized mosquitos.

The most important items were their Ferro rod and a water filter. Without good drinking water, they'd die out there. Dehydration would be what did them in, not the hurricane. Food would be an issue as well. He'd packed protein bars and dehydrated meals in their bags. Even those wouldn't have been enough to provide the energy they'd need for riding ninety miles in the heat. Food needed to go on his list of items to keep an eye out for. Fire, something to filter water, food, a tarp would be great, some rope or paracord, a flashlight, and a weapon of some type—a rifle or pistol that is what they needed.

Will's plan was coming together in his mind. Get the ladies to the hospital, find out what the hell was going on, see if they were evacuating people from the city. If not, steal bicycles and head north. But first, he needed to go on a treasure hunt. First things first, he needed something to carry supplies in when he found them.

Will stood. The waiting was killing him. Every minute wasted hiding in that mechanical room was a minute he and Cayden should be getting away from there. He stared at the door leading into the apartment building. "Fahima, is there another way into the building from here?"

EIGHT

Cayden

DAY OF EVENT

Cayden stole quick glances at his dad. The deep furrows in his forehead told him how worried he was. They'd lost Papaw Fontenot's Jeep. That had to have upset him. His great grandfather meant a lot to his dad. Papaw had practically raised his dad and Aunt Savanah. Besides that, they'd lost all the stuff they'd packed to take up to the lake. Dad was fanatical about those go-bags.

His cousin, Kendra, had told him about how his mom and dad had gotten trapped in their house during a hurricane. Cayden imagined that's where his obsession with having a go-bag ready all the time came from.

"How long have you lived in Houston?" Isabella asked Fahima.

Cayden's mind drifted off as Isabella and Fahima talked. His interest was in Kim. She intrigued him. He tried to imagine her life in communist China. He'd read a little about their crackdown on Hong Kong and attacks against protesters there. Cayden wondered what Kim thought about it. As a scientist, did she favor free expression?

"Don't you have any family to stay with, especially now, with the storm coming?" Isabella asked.

"My family were all killed. Extremists burst into the church where we were worshiping and killed everyone. I was homesick, or I would be with them now," Fahima said.

"I'm so sorry, Fahima," Isabella said.

"I came to the United States to get away from the violence in my country. I found I could not escape it," Fahima said.

Cayden listened for the gunshots that had sent them running in there for cover. He'd often heard about the violence on the news, but the shooting in broad daylight with all those people out on the street, that was crazy. And then there was the woman that had attacked Isabella. Cayden didn't know how Fahima could stay out on the streets.

"So, you and your dad are heading up to Lake Livingston?" Isabella asked.

"Yeah," Cayden said. He knew if his dad overheard him giving out personal information, he'd be pissed. His dad was private. Cayden wasn't sure what he was hiding or what difference it made if anyone knew where they were going, especially now. It wasn't like the woman could jump into her burned-out car and follow them there.

"That's pretty cool. Do you get to spend a lot of time up there?" Isabella asked.

"Not really. Not anymore."

They used to go up all the time. His mom had loved the lake house. They also used to visit the beach and go kayaking with relatives in Arkansas. They used to do a lot of things. But not anymore.

"My boyfriend and I went to Lake Charles a while back. His friend's parents have a fish market there."

"My family is from that area. My aunt lives in Calcasieu Parish," Cayden said.

"That's really cool."

Cayden liked the sparkle in her eyes. It had been a while since he'd spoken to an adult that didn't treat him like an injured bird.

Even his teachers at the middle school treated him differently because he didn't have a mom anymore.

"Everything's going to be okay, you know. Your dad isn't going to let anything happen to you," Isabella said. She glanced over to his dad. Her expression changed. Sadder, like she knew he was broken somehow.

"I know. He'll get things sorted out when we get to the hospital," Cayden said. "How's your arm and stuff?"

"It hurts a little still. I think my ankle is swelling," Isabella said, showing him her foot.

His dad looked up and then quickly looked away. His dad didn't want him to know he'd been checking her out, with swift glances here and there. Like Cayden wouldn't notice. He didn't have a problem with his dad being human. He doubted his dad would ever act on it and Cayden wasn't sure how he'd feel if he did. He was torn actually.

"Maybe you should elevate it. It would be better if we had ice to put on it. That's what my mom used to do when I hurt my foot playing soccer."

"Here. Put your leg up on this," Fahima said, pushing a milk crate in Isabella's direction. "Let me see what I have to wrap it up and stop that swelling."

Isabella and Fahima dug through the trash bags containing Fahima's belongings. Cayden was grateful Fahima had distracted Isabella before she could start asking questions about his mother. He didn't mind talking about her really, but it would make his dad sad if he overheard them. Today wasn't a good day to remind him that his wife had died—or how.

NINE

Will

DAY OF EVENT

Fahima led the group to the back of the room and pointed to an oversize crate wrapped in plastic.

"What is it?" Cayden asked.

"I don't know. It was just delivered yesterday. The movers parked it there to be out of the way, but it blocks the door into the loading bay area," Fahima said.

"The door to where?" Isabella asked.

Fahima pointed. "Up."

Pushing past Fahima, Kim quickly moved to the door. She put her back against it and turned the knob slowly. She pushed it open, just a crack.

"See anything?" Will asked, moving toward her. Cayden tried to follow him, but Will stuck his hand out and stopped him. "Wait here. We need to make sure it's safe."

Kim nodded and pushed the door open wider. She looked to her right and left and then stepped out into a hallway. Will joined her. The only light came from candlelight in the mechanical room. Will began looking for a stairwell or door leading to an elevator; he found the elevator at the left end of the hall.

"Here are the stairs," Kim said. "No electric for running the elevator."

"Right," Will said. He wasn't thinking clearly enough. He had to do better. Mistakes like that could be devastating.

"It is clear. I will go up. Wait here," Kim said, heading up the stairs.

Gripping his makeshift weapon tight in his hand, Will followed her. "I'll have your back."

When they reached the top of the stairs, Kim eased open the door. "It is dark, but I do not hear or see anyone."

"Dad?" Cayden called up.

"Cayden. Stay with Isabella and Fahima. Kim and I need to make sure those guys with the guns aren't in the building."

"But, Dad, I—"

"Cayden, just do as I say," Will said, sharply.

When he turned back to the dark hallway, Kim had disappeared. "Kim?" Will whispered.

He listened but heard no reply. Stepping into the hall, Will squinted, trying to adjust to the blackness. "Kim, where are you?"

"I am here. Go to your right," Kim said.

At the end of the hall was a large set of metal double doors. "I bet these lead to a loading bay for moving furniture in and out to the freight elevator," Will said.

Kim pushed on the bar, and the door opened. Light flooded in. The ramp down to the alleyway confirmed Will's assumption. Kim cautiously stepped outside, scanning the alley from her right to her left. Will followed her gaze. He saw no one. He listened. He was struck by the lack of noise. The absence of mechanical noise was eerie and unsettling. In the distance, Will heard screams. His first instinct was to see where they were coming from, but he refrained. They had enough trouble without taking on someone else's. He momentarily felt bad for thinking that way.

"What do you want to do?" Kim asked.

Will turned to face her. Their eyes met, and she averted her gaze. "Honestly, I know you and Isabella need to get to the hospital and get treatment for your injuries, but I'd like to take just a minute and have a look around. We need things, Cayden and I, things for our trip out of the city."

"I understand," Kim said. "You need a better weapon. It is not safe out now."

"It never was," Will said under his breath.

Kim glanced from her left to her right again.

"I'll understand if you can't wait for us," Will said, half hoping she wouldn't and that she and Isabella would choose to go off on their own. He hated being responsible for other people. He sucked at it.

"No. I need a weapon too," Kim said, brushing past him and walking inside.

Will stopped at the door to the stairwell they'd come up. He could barely make out Cayden, Isabella, and Fahima in the faint light below. "We're going to have a look around. It might be a few minutes. Go back inside and close the door." Will didn't wait for their reply.

His stomach twisted at having to rely on the two strangers to look after his son while he searched the building, but right now, it was the lesser of two evils. If he and Kim ran into trouble, he didn't want his son caught up in it.

As Will and Kim made their way back down the hall toward the elevator, Will tried every door. They were all locked. A storage room in the back corner on the opposite side of the elevator stood slightly ajar. The light from the loading bay doors barely made it that far down the hall. Will could hardly see into the room. He pushed open the door and instinctively reached for the light switch on the wall. He flicked it, and nothing happened. He cursed under his breath. He needed a flashlight. This was going to be an impossible task without one. He could leave behind valuable supplies that might mean the difference between life and death for him and his son.

After stepping into the storeroom, Will felt along the shelf to his left. He felt spray bottles and towels. He stopped to consider how he might use them. If he tied enough towels together, could he make a carry pouch? He grabbed them up and stuffed them under his arms. Further along the shelf, he found a box of trash bags. "Bingo," Will said

"What?" Kim asked.

"I found trash bags."

"Trash bags? You need trash bags?"

"Yeah! They're not only good for carrying stuff, but they can be used as a rain poncho, a ground cover to protect you from the wet ground, to wrap around your shoes to help keep your feet dry, just lots of stuff," Will said, grabbing a handful and stuffing the towels inside one and continuing on his quest.

Will heard a loud crack and spun around. "What was that?"

"Broom," Kim said, handing Will a broken broom handle.

"Okay," Will said, tentatively.

"Feel the point. We can sharpen it on concrete to make a spear," Kim said.

Will felt the splintered end of the broom handle. It wasn't much at the moment, but he could see how they might be able to fashion it into a sharp instrument. He liked the length better than his cart handle. Will dropped the cart handle into his bag and hung onto the broom instead.

"Thanks," he said, returning to the shelves. He stooped and searched the bottom shelf. On it, he found a plastic paint drop cloth. He dropped it into his trash bag and pumped his fist up and down. He had a bag, a better weapon, and now a plastic cloth to make a shelter. Things were looking up. He was feeling hopeful for the first time since the lights went out.

TEN

Will

DAY OF EVENT

After completing the search of the maintenance supply closet, Will and Kim moved to the first floor of the apartment building. Will went from door to door, knocking to see if anyone was home. Only a few people still occupied their apartments. Kim went behind him, trying the knobs of every door where they didn't get an answer. They were all locked tight. Several minutes later, Will and Kim stepped out onto the rooftop and stared out at the Houston skyline. He turned to face the southeast toward Baytown, Texas City, and even Pasadena, where he worked at Endeavor Chemical Refinery as an instrumentation technician. Will gasped at the sight of all the burning buildings. Thick black smoke was everywhere.

There were at least thirty refineries in the Houston area. If there hadn't been an evacuation for the hurricane, Will would have been at work. He knew better than anyone how deadly the situation was. No doubt, chemicals such as hydrofluoric acid, isobutane, butadiene, and benzene were being propelled into the air.

If the people in that area hadn't evacuated because of the hurricane, they were being exposed to a deadly cocktail of chemicals. If it had been just an ordinary day without a mandatory hurricane evacuation, Will, Cayden, and thousands of others would have been going about their day at work or school. Will hoped that whatever had happened to cause all this devastation was limited to the Houston area, because if it wasn't and scenes like this played out elsewhere, nowhere would be safe from all the deadly toxins that would pollute the air and ground. Chemicals like hydrogen chloride gas become hydrochloric acid, which can burn, suffocate, and kill. Drinking water sources would be ruined for decades. Chemical poisoning would occur in people coming in direct contact with the contaminated floodwaters.

Normally, with the volume of water present in a flood from a hurricane, the chemicals would be somewhat diluted, and Will wouldn't be as concerned. But from the looks of things, no matter how much rain they got, it wouldn't be enough to dilute all those poisons.

Kim was quiet, as usual. If she had concerns about the chemicals or the hurricane in general, he couldn't tell. If she was indeed a biological chemistry major at the university, she should understand the danger of the polluted water. Those close to the fires would have respiratory problems. If they survived the blast and the chemicals in the air, they would likely still suffer long-term effects from things like benzene, which disrupts how cells work which can cause damage to the immune system, and lead to cancer.

"We need to get out of here. We need to go north and east. The hurricane will send chemical-filled floodwaters this way in less than twenty-four hours," Will said. The sky was so black from the smoke he couldn't see if the first bands of the storm had arrived over the coast yet. The sense of urgency threatened to send him into a panic, but he knew that would lead to mistakes. He couldn't afford to make mistakes. Not this time.

"We need to find a vehicle that runs. We aren't going to make it in time on foot," Will said, speaking out loud to himself more than to Kim. He didn't expect her to answer.

"I have a vehicle. It is old. It should start," Kim said.

"It's over in Sharpstown. That's too far west. The winds will carry the toxic plume that way," Will said.

"It is not in Sharpstown. It is in storage not far from here," Kim said.

Will's head whipped around. "Nearby? How far?"

"A mile, maybe two."

"Let's go," Will said, grabbing her by the arm.

The duffle bag she'd slung over her shoulder slid down her arm, and something hard banged into his knuckles. He didn't have time to speculate what could be inside the bag. They were running out of time. If they didn't make it out before the rains started, they could become trapped in the city until the floodwaters receded. They could die of dehydration by then.

Will and Kim raced back down the twenty flights of stairs, occasionally stopping for Will to catch his breath. By the time they reached the tenth floor, they were both winded. Will worried that Kim was pushing herself too hard. He needed her to be able to walk. He didn't want to have to carry her until they reached her vehicle. They took the rest of the steps slower, but Will was gasping for air by the time they reached the others in the basement.

Isabella stood in the doorway.

"We have to go. Now!" Will said through gasps.

"What's wrong?" Isabella asked, her eyes bouncing between Will and Kim.

"The refineries are on fire," Will said, pushing his way past her and into the room. "Cayden, let's go."

"Which one?" Isabella asked.

Will turned back to face her. She didn't seem to be grasping the seriousness of the situation. If she were, she'd be out the door by now.

"All of them!" he said.

"What? What does that mean?"

"A chemical cocktail is being propelled into the air," Cayden said. He turned toward the door. "And the hurricane will cause it all to come raining down on us in a few hours."

Will was proud that his son could recognize the seriousness of their situation and that he wasn't in a panic. Hopefully, that meant he'd be more compliant and do what he told him when he told him.

"I'm going to poke my head out and see if those asshats have moved on yet."

They didn't have time to be dodging bullets. They needed to move fast. It would be a miracle if they made it out of the city and far enough away as it was. Will tried not to think too far ahead to the snarled streets and how'd they'd maneuver a vehicle through the crowded roads. He needed to focus on one step at a time. First up, get to Kim's storage unit.

"Let me go," Kim said, trying to step past Will.

Will held out his arm. "You stay. I got this."

"You take care of your son," Kim said, pointing to Cayden.

He needed to see for himself if the coast was clear, but doing so would be leaving his son with strangers a second time in as many minutes. If he didn't return, would they be able to get Cayden to safety? He glanced back at Isabella and Fahima. He couldn't take him out there until he knew the shooters were gone. He'd have to risk it.

"I'll go with you," Will said. "Cayden, lock the door behind us. Don't open it for anyone but me, all right?"

"Where are you going?" Cayden said, fear lacing his voice.

"I'm just going to see if we can leave yet. I'll be right back," Will said.

He tightly gripped the broken broom handle Kim had given him in his right hand and pulled on the door with his left. The hot, humid air hit him in the face as he stepped into the passageway. Kim stepped around him and sprinted to the alley. At the corner of the building, she stopped, pressed herself against the wall, and peered around.

Will hurried over and fell in behind her. "See anyone?"

She looked back at him. "No."

A second later, a man jumped out from behind a bus and ran toward Kim. He slammed into her, knocking her off her feet. She and her attacker wrestled for her duffle bag.

"Just let it go," Will yelled as he ran toward them.

Her arms were all twisted up in the straps. The man lifted her off the ground and slammed her back down, trying to break her grasp on the bag. Will raised the broom handle over his head and struck the man across the back. He arched and yelped. Kim released her grip with one hand and struck him in the jaw. As the man rolled off her, Will jabbed the handle into his ribs. Kim rolled away and got to her feet. Will raised the handle and brought it down a third time, but the attacker grabbed it and pushed it back, knocking Will off balance. As Will struggled to keep himself upright, the man scrambled to his feet and ran off.

Kim watched him as he leaned against the low wall then glanced back at Will. When she did, she lost her balance and fell backward.

"Kim," Will yelled as he ran toward her. "Kim, are you okay?"

"I am light-headed," Kim said.

"You've suffered a head injury. Fighting like that could have made it worse. You should have just given him the bag," Will said, taking her arm and helping her to her feet. "Come on. Let's get Cayden and Isabella and get the hell out of here."

Will tapped his foot as Isabella tried to convince Fahima to join them.

"Fahima, it's not safe. You have to come with us. You can't stay here," Isabella said, pleading with the elderly woman.

"I'll stay inside until the storm passes," Fahima said. "I'm too old to be running around out there."

"Please, Fahima. Come with us," Cayden said.

Fahima tousled Cayden's hair and handed him a bottle of water. She placed a hand on Will's shoulder and looked him in the eyes. At first, it made him exceedingly uncomfortable, but her words were so kind and genuine that he relaxed.

"You have done such a great job raising that boy. He is smart, kind, and respectful. You need to trust yourself and trust these ladies. You'll get him to a safe place," Fahima said.

It wasn't that he didn't trust Isabella and Kim. He just didn't know them. They might well be strong, capable women, but it was his son's life at stake. He wasn't about to risk it.

"Thank you, Fahima—for everything," Will said, picking up his trash bag and homemade spear and heading to the door.

Will and the others had done their best to persuade Fahima to join them. Will and Cayden had spelled out the dangers to her the best they could, but in the end, she'd refused, choosing to remain behind in her makeshift home in the mechanical room.

Cayden had seemed so forlorn as they walked away from her. He knew as well as Will did the chances that she'd be injured or killed with the deadly combination of storm and toxic flood. Will placed his hand on his son's shoulder and gave it a gentle squeeze as they stepped back onto the sidewalk. He was pleasantly surprised that Cayden didn't cringe or pull away this time. Maybe something good could come from this horrid situation.

The gunshots had cleared the street of people, making it much easier to walk quickly. They were able to go much faster and make better time. Even though Will was concerned about pushing the women too hard with their injuries, it was a risk he had to take. He'd find a hospital somewhere away from Houston to get them treated, but for now, they had to go as fast as possible before the approaching storm made landfall and dumped toxic floodwaters down on them.

Will wasn't the only one keeping a watchful eye out for shooters. Kim scanned every opening and crosswalk as they made their way west toward where Kim's vehicle was stored. They passed several people who, no doubt, wished they'd heeded the warnings earlier and headed out of the city. Some rolled suitcases, others carried trash bags filled with their belongings. Will thought about all his and Cayden's belongings lost with the Jeep. They were all replaceable.

After so many close calls with flooding, Will no longer packed up all the photographs and mementos every time he was forced to evacuate. He'd had all their photos and videos transferred to the cloud, and mementos, like Cayden's first tooth and a lock of hair, were stored in a locker at his wife's grandmother's place in Little Rock, Arkansas. Melanie had feared losing them.

The possession he was most upset about losing was Cayden's computer. Even though Will had been concerned about the amount of time that Cayden spent on the thing, he knew how much it meant to him. All his stories were stored there. Will had given him an external hard drive to back them up on, but he'd hadn't brought that with him. If their house was spared, he could retrieve his writing. If they ever made it back there.

The group stepped around a shopping cart filled with black trash bags left in the middle of the sidewalk, seemingly without an owner. The doors of cars backed up at the intersection had been left open, likely in the occupants' mad dash to flee the city—or shooters. Will stooped over and peered inside an SUV. It looked older. Not quite as old as his grandfather's Jeep, but at least ten years old. The keys dangled from the ignition. Will moved around the front of the vehicle and past the open door.

"What are you doing?" Isabella asked.

"I'm going to see if this SUV will start," Will said.

He slid into the driver's seat.

"Why? You can take it. That's illegal," Isabella said.

Ignoring her, Will turned the key. Nothing. The lights on the dash didn't come on. The engine didn't even attempt to turn over. Will exited the vehicle, not bothering to close the door.

"Were you really going to steal that car?" Isabella asked.

Will turned his back on her and stepped back onto the sidewalk. Cayden fell in beside him. Kim was already several paces ahead.

Isabella ran to catch up. "You ransacked people's homes and now this."

Will stopped in his tracks and spun on his heel to face her. "Listen here, lady. Look around you. Something has happened. Something big. Do you see the police or an ambulance? Don't you think it's strange that there are all these fires and no fire trucks? No one is coming to save us. If we don't do whatever it takes to get the hell out of this city, we are going to die here." Will reached over and pulled Cayden close to him. "I will do anything I need to do to get my boy out and away from here. If you don't like it." Will pointed behind her. "You can go back and die with Fahima."

Isabella looked like Will had struck her in the face. She stood with her hands at her sides, and her mouth opened wide. Tears welled in her eyes. For a moment, Will regretted being so harsh with her. But Cayden was his priority. He wouldn't let anyone stand in his way. Will turned and walked away, leaving Isabella standing in the middle of the sidewalk. When he glanced back, she had her face buried in her hands, and Cayden had his hand on her shoulder.

"Cayden, let's go."

ELEVEN

Savanah

DAY OF EVENT

Ordinarily, when she came to town, Savanah would have stopped in at St. Joseph's and dropped off a couple of bars of lavender soap with the secretary. As she approached the rectory, the groundskeeper, Sam, was raking grass clippings on the rectory's lawn. The old man had worked for the church for forty years. He knew everyone in town. He threw a hand in the air and started toward her. Savanah wanted to continue on without stopping. She didn't have an hour to stand around and gossip; she needed to get out of town before she was spotted.

"Hi, Sam," Savanah said.

"Did your van break down again?" Sam asked.

She wanted to keep walking, but Sam stepped onto the walk. Savanah looked over her shoulder. Being rude wasn't normally in her nature, but she didn't have time for pleasantries.

"Sort of, yeah. It seems quite a few vehicles are having trouble today. Paul thought it might have something to do with the weather," Savanah said.

Sam looked to the sky. "Really? I hadn't heard anything on the news about any storms or anything. You think they'd say something if there was going to be a significant weather event."

"I know. That's what Paul said."

"You plan on walking all the way home?" Sam asked, leaning on his rake.

"I don't see as I have any other choice. Earl wasn't able to get his tow truck to start either, so I'm on foot," Savanah said.

"You wanna come in and get a cool drink for a minute?" Sam asked.

Savanah looked around. Mayor Thibodeau's henchmen could still be out and about. The sooner she got away from town, the better she'd feel.

Savanah's head pivoted, scanning the cross street for any signs of city-owned vehicles. She made a mental note of each of the doors to the rectory and the side door to the church.

"Maybe next time, Sam. I need to get home to the kids," Savanah said.

"Oh, how are those little darlings?" Sam asked. He tilted his head slightly to one side. "I don't think I saw them at mass last Sunday."

"Keegan was sick. I kept everyone home, in case he was contagious," Savanah lied. Keegan was fine. She just hadn't wanted to come into town. She hadn't wanted to risk running into Wade. He'd stayed a little too long after he'd made the last drop off to her. If her farmhand. hadn't dropped by when he did—Savanah shuddered at the thought.

That past Saturday, she'd seen him driving by her house late at night. He'd slowed down and shined a spotlight down her driveway. No doubt checking to make sure there weren't any cars parked there. She knew it wouldn't be long before he'd pay her a visit. Savanah had considered telling her soon to be ex-husband, Derek, what his best friend had done. Maybe, if Derek said something to Wade, the creep would get the message and stay away but she was afraid to bring it up with him. Afraid he'd see that as a sign that she wanted him back or something. Savanah's jaw clenched. That would be a cold day in hell.

"I hope Keegan is feeling better. Is that why they didn't come with you today?" Sam asked.

This was another reason Savanah was glad she lived away from town. There was no such thing as privacy. No doubt, whatever she told Sam would make the rounds before she crossed the city limits. Even the stock boy down at the Thrifty Mart would know why she'd left her helpless children home alone so she could run all over town. By the end of the tale, she would have got her hair and nails done and stopped in and done the dirty with old man Bergeron over at the bank.

"He's much better, but I didn't want to risk it today. Kendra can handle them for a few hours," Savanah said.

And she could. Savanah wasn't worried about Kendra holding the fort until she got home. She was a great kid and such a good big sister to her three siblings. There was practically nothing on the farm Kendra couldn't do. She'd been right there at Savanah's side as they cared for the animals and took care of the day-to-day farm chores. Kendra had helped Savanah with the online store and social media accounts. She even helped with the books. Savanah was so proud of her oldest child. She didn't have anything to worry about. The kids would be fine. So why did she feel such an urgency to get home to them?

"I better get to walking, Sam. It will be dark by the time I get there as it is, I imagine."

Kendra would have to do all the milking on her own if Savanah didn't make it by dark. That would leave ten-year-old Karson in charge of the two little ones. He was a responsible kid, but her six-year-old daughter, Kylie, could be a handful at times. And then there was the baby, Keegan. Her stomach tightened. As self-sufficient as her kids were, she still hated leaving them alone this long.

"All right, Savanah. You take care. I'll see you at mass on Sunday."

"Yep, we'll be there," Savanah said, turning back to the road.

She turned and walked backward. "Sam, let Michelle know that I couldn't stop today. I'll bring her order with me on Sunday."

Sam waved. "Will do."

Savanah wasn't sure how she would get back into town on Sunday with her van still at the bakery. As she stepped back onto the sidewalk, she thought of who she could call for a ride. Her nearest neighbor went to the Baptist church in the opposite direction. She could saddle up the horses and ride over to her best friend Stephanie's place, but what if she wasn't home from Houston yet?

Savanah thought of her brother, Will. It had been months since she'd seen him. A twinge of guilt pricked her. She was a bad sister. She should have called more. Even if he never talked much when she did. Her heart still broke for poor little Cayden, but he too had been hard to reach. What more could she say to either of them? They both knew she was there when they needed her. She just had to hope that someday they'd be the ones to reach out.

Mrs. Robertson waved from her front porch as Savanah passed by. In her hand, she held yellow roses, Savanah's favorite. She returned the greeting and pointed to the roses lining the walkway.

"They're gorgeous, Mrs. Robertson."

Savanah had loved being from a small town, just not this small town. Not anymore. After her marriage fell apart, she'd thought an awful lot about moving away but she had loved her family's farm and had worked hard to make it her own after her grandfather passed away. She'd hoped that Will might decide to move back and help out, but that had never happened. She'd made it a place where she and her children could not only survive, but thrive. It would all be so perfect, if only it were someplace else—someplace far away from Thibodeau. If she could just put back a little more money, maybe she'd have enough to escape this place and find a new little farm somewhere far away from her troubles in Calcasieu Parish.

As Savanah crossed the next intersection, she saw Wade emerge from a house two doors down. Their eyes locked for a moment. A look of recognition crossed his face. He pointed to her. Savanah's heart dropped into her stomach. She put her head down and quickened up the pace. Maybe he had better things to do today than harass her.

"Savanah," Wade called out.

She drew in a breath and held it. Could this day get any worse? She knew it could. She shuddered, recalling the cold steel of Wade's pistol pressed against the small of her back.

His breath had reeked of cigarettes and alcohol as he whispered in her ear. "I own you. You're mine and ain't nothing you can ever do about it."

If not for her some-time farmhand, Jason, Wade might have shot her that day. She'd thought a lot about the look of pity on Jason's face as Wade backed away, and she'd pulled down the skirt of her dress. He'd immediately assessed the situation right and not fallen for the lover's narrative Wade gave him. Maybe it was the tears streaking her bruised cheek that clued him in.

Savanah had driven straight to the school, unenrolled her children, and went home to pack their bags. She was ready to move to Houston and stay with Will and Melanie, but that was the day she'd received the call from the Harris County Sheriff's Department. Will and Melanie had been in an accident. Melanie had died at the scene and Will was in surgery. She'd left her bags open on the bed and driven straight to Houston. Savanah and the children stayed until after the funeral. When she'd returned home, she'd gone to Cameron Parish and purchased a handgun. The next week, she and her children drove back and went to a gun range.

Cocking her head to one side, Savanah listened for footfalls behind her. She heard Wade call her name. She was out in the open and exposed. Savanah arched her back and pulled on one of the straps to her bag. She may be alone, but she wasn't defenseless. But shooting the mayor's nephew in Calcasieu Parish would be a death sentence for her. It wouldn't matter if it were in self-defense. Thibodeau and his henchmen ran the town, and no one would go against them. No one.

Savanah hurried down the street and turned into the alley that ran behind the houses and parallel to Wade. Three houses down, Savanah ran inside Bobby Johnson's shop building. She stopped just inside the doors. Her chest heaved in and out. Not from physical activity; Savanah was fit. It was the fear that seized hold of her insides.

"Savanah!"

Wade had followed her into the alley. Had he seen her duck into the shop? Savanah opened the door, ready to bolt for the opposite street, but Bobby's boat blocked the way. A thought formed. She wasted no time pulling back the cover and climbing into the boat. She pulled the boat cover down and hid. Would he think to look for her there? She hoped not. As she lay on her side, Savanah eased her pack off and slowly unzipped the pouch where she kept her pistol. She didn't need to check to see if it was loaded. She always kept her weapons loaded. What good was an unloaded gun?

Her aunt had chided her for keeping loaded weapons around her children, but Savanah didn't care. She'd taught all her children from an early age how to safely handle weapons. They knew they weren't toys. Kendra was the only one that knew the combination to the gun safe, and the little ones knew not to touch them. A knot formed in her stomach. She wasn't there to protect them, and it would be several hours before she could get there. Regret flooded her mind. She should have brought them with her. But then they'd be in the middle of this mess. She wouldn't want that either.

Gripping the pistol with both hands, Savanah waited and listened. Wade's voice faded as he moved down the alley and away from her. She slid her pack under the cover and dropped it to the ground before throwing her leg over the boat and climbing out. She didn't even take the time to put her pack back on and tighten the straps. Instead, she slipped one strap over her forearm and took off running back toward the street, staying within the trees for cover. Wade continued to call her name, but he was now looking in the opposite direction.

Checking behind her every few seconds, Savanah ran east, trying to make it out of town before Wade decided to double back. If her head hadn't been turned looking over her shoulder, she would have been able to avoid literally running into Derek.

"Whoa there, Savanah. Where you off to in such a hurry?"

Savanah's eyes widened. She'd just jumped from the frying pan into the fire.

TWELVE

Will

DAY OF EVENT

They were heading west, the opposite direction to which Will wanted to go. With each step, they were getting farther and farther from the lake house. But the promise of a working car compelled him to keep following the woman. Why he even believed her, he didn't know. Desperation? Wishful thinking? There was a confidence about her. Somehow, Will got the impression that she knew much more than she had revealed, which was nothing. Was he stupid for following her? It was something he questioned with every step. The rancid smoke that filled the air was a constant reminder of why he was willing to risk everything and trust that Kim did indeed have an older vehicle in storage a few miles away.

But it had only been a guess that older model vehicles weren't affected by whatever had caused all the others to fail. They could travel all that way only to learn that his guess had been wrong, and they were no better off than when they'd started. Will tried to formulate a backup plan in his mind as they walked. Suppose his assumption was incorrect and no other vehicles ran. In that case, they'd need to find another means of transportation to make travel away from the city faster and beat the storm.

Will couldn't stop thinking about all the bicycles parked on the balconies back where they'd met Fahima. When he spotted one of the city's bicycle ride-share stations, he made a note of it. As they walked past, Will thought about the mechanism that kept them locked in place. It might have somehow been disengaged by the same thing that took out the phones and vehicles. He'd come back and check if Kim's car didn't start. He was attempting to calculate how far they could travel by bicycle when Isabella's yelp startled him. Will quickly turned to see what had caused her to cry out.

Isabella was down on one knee. Cayden was helping her to her feet. Will rushed back to them and took her other arm.

She cried out in pain. "My shoulder!"

"Oh, sorry," Will said, letting go and stepping back.

Cayden steadied Isabella as she got her feet under her and stood.

"What happened?" Will asked.

"I tripped on the uneven surface. I wasn't looking at the sidewalk. I was too busy staring up there," Isabella said, pointing above them.

Black smoke billowed from the windows of a nearby high rise.

"The fire suppression system must not be working," Will said.

"I hope everyone got out," Cayden said. "If not, they'll be trapped up there."

"What's causing all this?" Isabella asked.

"I don't know. None of it makes any sense. It's unlike any storm I've ever heard of before," Will replied.

Will had tried not to focus on the cause of the phenomenon, determined to remain focused instead on how to survive it. If he let his mind wander too far into all the possibilities, he might make some wrong assumptions. Wrong assumptions might lead to mistakes. Deadly mistakes. He couldn't afford that now. His one focus had to be to get his son as far away from Houston as was humanly possible.

He was reminded of Melanie's pleas to move somewhere less

crowded, with a lower crime rate and fewer giant bugs. After Hurricane Rita, she'd been terrified of the monster storms. He'd promised her that after he finished his apprenticeship at the chemical refinery in Pasadena, they'd move north. By that time, he'd have more experience under his belt. He would stand a better chance of getting a high-paying job at someplace like Dow Chemical in Michigan. Melanie had been looking forward to her first winter with snow.

Melanie had wanted more children. She desperately wanted a daughter but they'd agreed to wait until they got settled somewhere before trying to get pregnant. She was a wonderful mother and there were times when Will resented how close she and Cayden were. Sometimes, he felt like an outsider in his own home. Melanie and Cayden had worked on projects and stories together. They'd volunteered at the local library and read books to sick children.

Cayden adored his mother. In those first few months after the accident, there wasn't a day that went by that Will didn't think it should have been him instead of Melanie that died in that wreck. She would have done a much better job of raising him. A boy needs his mother. If only he'd listened to her, maybe everything would have been different for them. She'd still be here, and he and his son wouldn't be running for their lives from a monster hurricane.

The windows of the building where they were standing shattered, sending fragments down around them. Smoke billowed from the gaping hole. Walking downtown wasn't safe. At any moment, something could fall off one of the buildings and crush them.

"We better keep moving. We need to get the hell out of here before all of downtown lights up," Will said.

"How much farther is it?" Isabella asked.

"Not far," Kim replied without slowing. It was the same response she'd given the last three times Isabella had asked.

Will wanted to ask her why she stored her vehicle downtown if she lived in Sharpstown, but he wasn't sure she'd answer him.

He'd found her guarded, but a lot of people were private with their personal information these days. You had to be. But he needed to know if he could trust that she wasn't leading them into some situation that would further endanger his son. He didn't like it, but really, she was his best hope of saving him.

"Cayden, stick close by. Who knows what is around the next corner," Will said.

Cayden stepped in front of them and fell in behind Kim. Isabella had slowed somewhat and appeared to be limping on her right foot.

"Isabella, is your leg all right?" Will asked.

At first, she didn't respond.

"Isabella!" Will said louder.

She glanced back.

"Is your leg all right?" Will repeated.

"My ankle is swelling," Isabella said.

Will's ankle was sore from stomping on the brake so hard back at the gas station. Up until then, he'd ignored it.

"Let me take a look at it," he said.

They stopped, and Will motioned for her to take a seat on the curb. Isabella unzipped her boot and rolled up her right pant leg. Will removed her boot and felt her ankle.

"Is it broken?" Cayden asked.

"I don't think so. It's hard to say. You'd need an x-ray to be sure, but I'd say if it were broken, you wouldn't be walking on it at all. That's just my uneducated guess," Will said.

Isabella tilted her head to the side and nodded toward her foot. "You gonna let go?" Her eye contact made him feel uncomfortable, and he looked away. Cayden was glaring at him.

"The next time we stop, we need to find something and wrap it tight. That should help some," Will said.

"Are we following her or what?" Isabella asked, pointing to Kim. She was nearly at the end of the block now.

Will paused on the "we" part of her question. They weren't a "we." Offering the woman a ride to the hospital didn't obligate him to her. But if she were deferring to his judgment as to whether they should follow Kim, he didn't have an answer for her.

Will reached his arm out to Isabella. She stared blankly at him for a moment before accepting and lacing her arm under his. He gently pulled her to her feet. They drew apart, still staring at one another. Her upturned face waited for him to say something.

"Hold on to me. I don't want you to fall again."

Isabella bit her lower lip. The brisk wind blew a strand of hair across her face. He wanted to reach out and move it for her, but from the corner of his eye, he saw Cayden step past them and continue on.

"Hold up, Cayden. Don't get too far ahead," Will said.

Will's head rotated, scanning the street behind and in front of him. Time was their enemy. Nothing was going to stop that hurricane. He didn't know what was responsible for the cars and phones not working or the fires everywhere across town, but he needed to stay focused on getting Cayden to safety. He had to. With his Jeep carjacked, Kim's vehicle seemed to be their only hope. Until some other opportunity presented itself, he'd have to follow her.

As they hurried to catch up with Kim, Will ran through various scenarios in his mind. He racked his brain, trying to come up with an alternative solution—some other means of transportation to get them out of harm's way. He'd considered staying put and going to higher ground by finding an office or hotel room with an interior space away from the windows. If they chose a hotel, they'd have food. He could at least scrounge food and water, maybe enough to ride out the storm and wait for the floodwaters to recede.

The more he thought about it, the better it sounded. Downtown Houston was far enough away from the coast to not get the full impact of the hurricane-force winds. Most of the buildings there had stood through multiple storms with little more than a few windows breaking. It was the flooding that caused significant issues for the downtown area.

A deafening explosion echoed through the tall buildings, sending Will and Isabella scrambling for cover behind a city bus. Will ran over, grabbed Cayden, and hovered over him, shielding him from any falling debris that might rain down on them from the high-rise buildings above as he led him behind the bus.

Will's head swiveled, searching for the source of the explosion. Thick smoke filled the street, turning the light from day to night in an instant. He heard screaming.

Cayden struggled beneath him. "Kim… she might be hurt. We have to go help her." He finally wriggled free and bolted off.

"Cayden, stop! Get back here!" Will yelled, running after him.

They found Kim hunkered down behind a construction dumpster parked on the street. Flames shot from the openings of the windows and door of a bar. Tiny explosions continued as the bar's liquor ignited.

"We have to move," Will said, taking Kim's arm.

"Cayden, stick close," Will said.

Will rushed into the intersection, "Which way, Kim."

Kim slowly stood, clutching her duffle tight against her chest. She was coughing so hard she couldn't respond. She pointed west. They walked for several minutes to get away from the smoke. Kim was still coughing and struggling to breathe.

"Here," Cayden said, holding out the bottled water Fahima had given him. "Have a seat here and take a drink."

Kim and Isabella sat on the curb outside of the House of Blues, where he'd taken Melanie once for their anniversary. They'd enjoyed voodoo shrimp and listened to her cousin play in the band. Recalling that day made him homesick for Calcasieu Parish. The memories were everywhere. Grief ambushed him. If only he could turn back time—do things differently.

Will glanced at Isabella and Kim. Had he made the right decision? Would he live to regret offering to help them? Would he and Cayden live to regret it?

Will thought about his sister, Savanah, and her four kids. He hoped that everything was still working for them there. If not, he knew they'd be all right. They had the farm to sustain them until the authorities got everything figured out and services back on. His sister was tough and she'd taught her children to be resilient. If anyone could make it through this, his bet would be on them.

THIRTEEN

Will

DAY OF EVENT

After finishing her water, Kim attempted to stand, but she was unsteady. Will reached out a hand to help her to her feet. She nodded slightly and slung the duffle over her back.

"Why are you so willing to help us?" Will asked as they stepped back onto the street. She didn't know them. Isabella had been the one she'd plowed into and injured. He wasn't used to people helping out of the goodness of their hearts. Usually, they wanted something in return. Before they went any farther, he needed to know what she expected from him.

"I need you," Kim said.

That answer stopped Will in his tracks. He was surprised by her honesty.

"You need me, how?" Will asked.

Without slowing, Kim said, "I don't have keys."

Will caught up and walked alongside Kim. "So you think I know how to hotwire a car? Is that it?"

"No. The key is in the vehicle. I do not have a key to the door where the car is stored."

"Okay. You need me to bust down the door," Will said.

"Yes."

"You couldn't figure out a way to get in yourself?"

"No. Not with my injuries," Kim said.

That made perfect sense to Will. Kim was pragmatic. He could work with that. "So, do you aim to ditch us once I get you inside and you get your vehicle?"

Kim glanced over. "No. I will still need you."

Well, that's good. What happens when Kim doesn't need us any longer?

"So we need each other, right? We need a ride out of here, and you need our help to get into your vehicle. Why should I trust that once you don't need us anymore, you won't dump us on the side of the road somewhere?"

Kim stopped and turned. Will looked around to see if there was some threat he needed to address.

"I have a vehicle, but nowhere to go. I need you. You need me. That is how it works," Kim said.

"I can live with that. Cayden and I were heading up to Lake Livingston. We have a house on the lake. It's stocked with food. Enough for a week or so, at least." But he hadn't planned on guests. He ran a mental inventory on what he recalled was in the pantry. It'd be a stretch, but they could catch fish.

"You give us a ride, and you can stay with us up at the lake until you figure something else out. Do we have a deal?"

"We have a deal," Kim said.

"My apartment is southeast of the city," Isabella said, walking up behind them. "How am I getting home?"

Kim said nothing. It wasn't Will's vehicle. He couldn't speak for Kim, but he wasn't too keen to backtrack that far south, anyway. They could get trapped by snarled streets or worse, get carjacked again.

"You can come with us too," Cayden said. "You won't be safe at your apartment. Didn't you say that it flooded last time?"

"Not my floor, but the water was up to the floor below us."

"Come with us," Cayden said.

"But my boyfriend," Isabella said.

They both looked at Kim. She ignored them and continued walking. An uncomfortable silence stretched as they walked down the block. Will was relieved that it appeared Kim shared his concerns about taking Isabella home. If she'd had something Kim needed, she'd be in a better position to get what she wanted, but it didn't look like Kim would be taking her. He'd need to have a conversation with Cayden about volunteering their home without his permission.

With four of them staying at the lake house, resources would be stretched pretty thin, especially if the lights were out there as well. The food in the freezer would spoil. That would be a shame. He had some excellent steaks in there. The beer would be good, but it would get hot pretty fast without refrigeration or air conditioning.

He thought about life without air conditioning. He'd tried it once. It wasn't good. They'd attempted to sleep in a tent in the backyard when there'd been a large family gathering at the lake house. The heat had been relentless, even with the lake breeze blowing. They'd stayed awake all night listening to the bird-sized mosquitos trying to find a way inside their tent. Eventually, they'd given up, and around three in the morning, they'd gone in and slept on the living room floor.

Drinkable water might become an issue, as well. The pantry was stocked with a couple of cases of bottled water, but how long would that last between the four of them. If he hadn't lost their go-bags with the Jeep, they'd have a decent water filter and could get water from the lake but he wouldn't dare drink it without filtering it first. Will recalled seeing a Red Cross go-bag on the back seat of one of the vehicles they'd passed a while back. He'd have to deal with Isabella's sanctimonious rebuke. Still, if they came across another, he'd smash the window and take it.

As Isabella walked along the sidewalk, Kim sidestepped something on the ground next to a vehicle in the street. It wasn't until

Will stepped around a box van that he saw what it had been. Will grabbed Cayden and shielded his eyes as they approached the man lying on the sidewalk outside a piano bar. He was bleeding from his scalp. His white dress shirt was torn, and his shoes were missing. He looked dead.

"What is it?" Cayden asked, trying to catch a peek.

The man moaned, and Will stopped at his feet. The man reached his hand out as if to ward off a deadly blow. Cayden slipped out from under Will's arm and dropped down beside the man.

"Kim. Isabella. Wait up. We need to help this guy," Cayden yelled.

Isabella turned. Her mouth dropped open, and she began walking back their way. Kim never stopped or looked back.

"Is he all right?" Isabella said as she rushed toward them.

"He's bleeding," Cayden said.

"Are you all right, mister," Cayden asked.

As Cayden cradled the man's head in his arms, Will ripped a piece off the man's torn shirt and wiped the blood from his eyes. They were swollen, nearly shut. From the amount of blood on the pavement below him, Will wondered how he was still alive. The man tried to speak, but his words were too slurred to understand. Will didn't smell alcohol on his breath, which meant it likely resulted from his head injury. He didn't want his son witnessing this man's last breath.

"Cayden, catch up to Kim and tell her to wait up."

"But, Dad," Cayden said.

"She's our ride out of here. Go!" Will barked.

"Is he going to make it?" Isabella asked as Cayden ran to catch up with Kim.

Will shrugged. He didn't want to say so out loud, but he doubted that even with immediate medical treatment, the man would live. He had an apparent open skull fracture. Someone had beaten him badly. From the looks of it, they'd robbed him too.

Was a man's life worth the few possessions this man carried with him?

There was nothing they could do for him, but Will knew that Cayden and Isabella would refuse to go on and leave the man there to die. Under normal circumstances, Will would never even consider leaving someone in the street to die alone, but these weren't normal circumstances.

Will slid his arm under the guy's shoulders and sat him up. His head lolled to one side and then flopped back. His left eye opened, but other than that, he made no effort to get up independently.

"Grab the other side," Will said.

"What?"

"I can't carry him all by myself. Slide your arm around his waist. I'm going to lift him to his feet. You hold him steady," Will said.

"You think we should move him? He could have a spinal injury."

"Would you rather I leave him in the street to die alone? That's fine with me. He'll just slow us down, anyway. Wake up, Isabella. No one is coming to save us. No one is coming for this man. He is going to die, and there is nothing we can do about it." Will regretted saying it as soon as it left his lips, but it was too late.

A flush grew behind her cheeks and tears welled in her eyes. But Will didn't have time to sugar coat things. As Isabella turned and walked away, Will gently lowered the man back onto the ground.

"I'm sorry. There is nothing I can do for you."

Will choked back tears. He was torn between self-preservation and keeping his humanity intact. He'd never imagined he'd be at this crossroads, but here he was. He stared ahead at Cayden, who was walking backward behind Kim, watching Isabella approach them. Will knew Cayden wouldn't understand. He was glad of that. He hoped his son never had to make such a decision. It was one that Will was sure would tug at his soul the rest of his life, but he had to do what was best for his son, and carrying a dying man across town on his back wasn't it.

Isabella was uncharacteristically quiet as they continued walking toward Main Street. As they passed hotels, Will made a note of their locations. If things didn't work out with Kim's vehicle, he needed to be quickly en route to a safe place. There were several hotels that could provide emergency shelter. He just hoped they wouldn't have to use them. Will hated the idea of being trapped in one for an extended period without electricity.

As they approached the tracks of the Metrorail system running along Main Street, the smoke became thicker. Someone was curled up on the sidewalk under the awning of a nearby building. Will tugged on the back of Cayden's shirt and led him to the opposite side of the street. He didn't want a repeat of their earlier encounter.

"How much farther?" Will asked. He wished Kim would just tell them where the vehicle was stored so they could stop asking.

"Just up ahead. At the end of the block, we turn left, and the garage is in the middle of the next block," Kim said.

Will's heart sped up. They were close. In a few minutes, they'd be speeding the hell out of there. As they approached Main Street, he was making a mental route in his mind of the best way back to the interstate. He prayed that at least the shoulders of the road would be clear enough to pass. He'd all but determined that with the evacuation traffic that would no doubt be stranded on the interstates leading away from the city, it would be wiser to take the back streets, but he wasn't familiar enough with them so that way would carry the risk of getting hopelessly lost.

Even before they reached the food market near the intersection, Will could see flames shooting from the building's ground floor on the opposite corner. Kim stood in the middle of the street with her hands on top of her head. Will's heart sank. He stared at the smoke billowing from the building.

"Kim?" Cayden said.

"The building is on fire," she said through tears and dropped to her knees.

Will was as stunned at her reaction as he was at the burning building. The look of utter hopelessness on the previously stoic woman's face drove home the seriousness of their situation. There would be no ride away from town. They were all stranded downtown. As desperation crept up from his belly, Will's mind tried to make sense of it all. He knew that they were screwed, but his heart couldn't accept it. He searched all the entrances to the building. Maybe there was another way in. Perhaps the vehicle wasn't affected. There could be a way to get it out before the building collapsed.

Will stepped into the street to go to her, to encourage her not to give up yet.

Isabella approached Kim and placed a hand on her shoulder. "We should go. It's not safe. Debris could fall on us." Isabella reached her hand out to help Kim to her feet.

As Kim was rising, Will caught movement from the corner of his eye. At the same time he registered what he was seeing, Will shoved Cayden behind him and screamed Kim's name.

"Kim! Isabella! Gun!"

Three men stepped into the street, moving quickly toward the women, pistols raised. Will was helpless to do anything about it. Round after round echoed off the buildings. Glass exploded.

Will turned and pushed Cayden behind a concrete pillar. He resisted returning his gaze to the women, fearing the shots had found their target. A second later, Will spotted Isabella edging around the back of the SUV toward the rear passenger door as the vehicle was riddled with bullets. She screamed at the top of her lungs as Kim crawled around the car. Isabella started to stand. She stared back at Will, a look of pure terror on her face.

"Isabella, stay down," Will shouted over the sound of gunfire.

The glass shattered in the building near the women. Seconds later, Kim appeared next to Isabella. Kim reached down and grabbed Isabella's arm, dragging her toward the building's broken window.

Will turned and took Cayden's hand, yanked him to his feet, and they too ran for their lives.

FOURTEEN

Will

DAY OF EVENT

As Will and Cayden ran south along Main Street, the gunfire ceased. Will glanced back to see if the gunmen were pursuing them. They weren't. He saw no one. As Will turned toward his son, Isabella and Kim burst out of a door on the opposite side of the street.

"Go! Go! Go!" Kim yelled as she shoved Isabella forward onto the sidewalk.

"Will," Isabella yelled. "There they are, Kim."

"Run, Isabella," Kim said.

The four of them ran south, finally meeting at the next intersection.

As he ran alongside Kim, Will asked her, "Did they follow you into the building? How did you get away?"

"We escape through an office and out the front door. They didn't see us, " Kim said.

Will repeatedly checked over his shoulder as they ran, expecting any moment for bullets to slam into his back. Who were those men, and why were they shooting at them? He needed answers, but there didn't seem to be anyone to give them. Where the hell are all the cops?

At the next intersection, Will stopped running. He leaned against a truck parked at the curb and placed his hands on his knees. As his chest rose and fell with rapid breaths he vowed that if they survived this, he'd spend more time at the gym.

Isabella dropped down onto the curb and put her head between her knees. Kim and Cayden stood behind her, both were wringing wet with sweat but not appearing as out of breath as Will and Isabella.

"What now?" Isabella asked through wheezes.

Kim shook her head.

Will looked up. His plan to hole up in one of the hotels wasn't going to work either. The last thing they needed was to become trapped in a burning building. Their only option was to head north and attempt to get as far from the bayou as possible. Will glanced down at Isabella's boots. Her ankle was already sore and throbbing now. If he took off his boot, it would likely swell as well. They weren't going to make it far in this shape.

Think, Will. He couldn't let Cayden down now. There had to be somewhere for them to ride out the storm.

"We can go to my place. It survived the last hurricane. I don't have much food, but maybe we can find a store open on the way," Isabella said. "You're all welcome to stay until the storm passes."

Will considered it. That was still miles and miles of walking. They were less likely to get trapped by fire in an apartment but they'd be trapped by the floodwaters. Without a boat, there'd be no way to leave. The waters would be filled with debris, and now deadly chemicals from the refinery explosions. It wasn't optimal. They had to come up with something better.

"I have a friend. He has a place a little south of here," Kim said.

"Where is it?" Will asked.

"I'll take you," Kim said, turning to go.

"Wait, how far is it? Will asked.

"Less than a mile," Kim said.

"Are you sure that is far enough away not to be caught up in the fires? Once the wind picks up, all of downtown could burn." Will said.

"It's across from a park. There aren't any tall buildings around it. There are no buildings next to it either. It is surrounded by vacant lots," Kim said.

"And what makes you think your friend is going to welcome three complete strangers into his home like that?" Will asked.

"I was willing to," Isabella blurted out.

"No offense, but not everyone is as trusting as you are," Will said.

"He will welcome you," Kim said.

Will rubbed his face with both hands. What choice did he have? None that he could see.

"We're following you again, I guess."

As they walked past the tapas restaurant, Will began thinking about how they could get food. It could be a week or more before the floodwaters receded enough to leave the apartment. He couldn't count on his host to feed them all for an extended period. Like it or not, he might have to *borrow* supplies from one of the restaurants they passed. He was glad he'd thought to bring extra trash bags and kept a lookout for anything he could use to possibly pry doors open with. It might not be easy to break into one.

Will pulled on the door handle of the next car they passed. It was locked. He'd need to try one of the vehicles abandoned in the street. He moved over and tried the next one he came to. Bingo! The doors were unlocked. He searched the interior and found nothing. He was leaning over just about to pop the trunk when Isabella appeared at his side. He glanced up at her. She was standing with her hands on her hips, glaring at him.

"What?" he spat. He didn't want to have to explain himself to her again.

"What are you looking for?" she asked.

"Well, if you must know, I am looking for a tire iron, screwdriver, anything that I can use to break into one of these restaurants."

She let her hands fall to her sides, leaned in, and looked into the back seat. "You're going to loot?"

"We're going to be trapped in Kim's friend's apartment for who knows how long. We don't know if he has food and if he does, whether he will be willing to share. By this time tomorrow, it will all be underwater. None of it will be useful for anyone. I can leave an IOU for what we take, but I am not going to let my son go hungry," Will said, straightening.

He towered over her. Isabella stiffened and stepped back.

"What are you guys doing," Cayden asked.

"Looking for tools for breaking into businesses," Isabella yelled back.

"Dad?" Cayden asked.

"Not so loud," Will said.

She turned and made a circle in the middle of the road. "What? There's no one here to hear me."

"Just keep it down, okay. I heard voices back a block or so. We don't know which way they were headed," Will said.

"You can go to jail for looting during a hurricane," Cayden said. He looked so much like his mother as he stood there with his chest out, and his chin tilted up. The last thing Will needed at the moment was a lecture on morality from his thirteen-year-old. They'd have this talk later after they survived this.

"We need food and water to survive. It is all going to be underwater tomorrow," Will said.

"Pop the trunk and then let's get out of here then," Isabella said.

Will blinked several times. Her about-face had taken him off guard. He'd anticipated her resisting him at every turn. He wasn't sure what to make of the change in attitude. Self-preservation?

As Cayden walked back to stand with Kim, Will leaned in and pressed the trunk release button. Nothing happened. No power meant no auto trunk release. Will reached in and felt for the keys. There were none. The owner must have taken them with them.

"See if there are keys in that one," Will said, pointing to a black SUV parked in the middle of the street.

"No keys, but I don't think we'll need them," Isabella said.

She walked around to the back and opened the hatch. An environmentally friendly canvas shopping bag fell to the ground, followed by a soccer ball. The back of the SUV was full to overflowing with stuff. Will rummaged through the contents but found nothing useful. Kim and Cayden walked back and joined them.

"I bet the tire iron is under all that, with the spare tire," Cayden said. "That's where it was in Mom's car."

The image of the last time he'd seen his wife's Volvo SUV caused bile to rise in Will's throat. He felt like he'd been punched in the gut. Typically, Melanie would have driven the Volvo when they took it out on date night, but she'd had more than two glasses of wine and asked him to drive that time. The responsible driver she was, she was concerned she'd get them into an accident. He'd been the sober driver but became distracted by trying to find the game on the radio. He couldn't wait twenty more minutes to find out the damn score.

"Will?" Isabella said. "Are you all right?"

Will swallowed hard and took a deep breath. "I'm fine. Let's get this panel up and find the tire iron."

He glanced at Cayden as he bent and pulled the straps to access the spare tire. Cayden was wiping away a tear as he turned away. Will hadn't seen him cry since the funeral. How could that be? Obviously, his son had been grieving in silence. He'd asked Cayden's counselor how he was doing and she'd said he was processing things in his own way. In their last session, Cayden had taken one of his notebooks. After, the counselor had praised Cayden for his creative writing. He hadn't shared any of his stories with Will in a very long time.

Pushing up the panel, Will revealed the tool kit and jack. He pulled the jack out and held it up to test its weight. It could be useful to smash a window, but maybe a little more wieldy than a tire iron.

"Here, hold on to this," he said, handing Isabella the jack.

Will poked around until he found the tire iron. He walked away from the SUV, leaving the back hatch open. It didn't matter. The vehicle would likely be underwater soon anyway. So would the restaurants. If they were going to scrounge for food, now was the time. There'd be nothing left after the storm.

Of course, they walked three blocks without seeing a single restaurant. When they ran into the first people they'd seen since the gunmen back at the parking garage, Will's first instinct was to turn and go the other way but, unlike the shooters back at the garage, these people had no interest in engaging with them. The three men and two women walked with their heads down, refusing to make eye contact.

Will raised the broom handle he held in his right hand out in front of him and placed a hand in the center of Isabella's back, guiding her to the middle of the street.

"Kim, Cayden, let's cross over," Will said, not loud enough for the other travelers to hear.

They were heading north but didn't seem to be in as big a hurry as the others they'd passed earlier. Maybe they'd traveled a greater distance and were wiped out. The heat could do that to a person pretty quick, especially without water to drink.

Will thought about the homeless man they'd seen with a shopping cart filled with bottled water. That is precisely what they needed—a shopping buggy and water. They could carry so much stuff if they only had a cart. He was sure that Isabella would give him shit if he stole some homeless person's shopping basket, but if he found one abandoned or semi-abandoned, he'd take it. If it were semi-abandoned, as in not physically attached to someone, he'd grab it, but he wouldn't willingly hurt someone for it. He wasn't that desperate yet.

He was reminded of that movie where a blind guy navigates a post-apocalyptic world. The bad guys used a damsel in distress with an overturned shopping cart as a decoy to get the character to stop so they could rob and kill him. Water was an issue for those characters as well. Water, no matter what else he did, Will needed to find bottled water. But where?

FIFTEEN

Will

DAY OF EVENT

After crossing over to avoid other travelers, Will and the others continued south. In the middle of the block, Will spotted a construction truck parked in the angled parking space.

"There." He pointed to the truck. "I bet we'll find something useful in there."

As they approached it, Will noticed a water cooler strapped to the back. As he ran toward it, he prayed that it was full. If it was, it likely held ten or more gallons of water. It would be too cumbersome to carry, but he'd do it anyway, at least until he found a shopping cart or some sort of dolly. Since they didn't have glasses, they'd have to drink directly from the container. It wasn't the most sanitary of methods, but he'd worry about germs later. Staving off dehydration was more critical at this point in the game.

Will removed the bungee strap holding the cooler to the tailgate and shook it.

"Whoo-hoo!" he yelled. "It's almost full."

"Oh, thank God. I am so thirsty," Isabella said, running over to him. She reached for the cooler and then stopped and stepped back. "Here, Cayden. You go first."

Will's heart melted. It was something Melanie would have

done. She always put Cayden first. She would do the same for any child.

"No. Ladies first. Right, Dad?" Cayden said.

Will glanced away. Melanie would be so proud of her son. She'd raised him right. Everyone could see that. He smiled and stared back at Cayden. "That's right, son."

After drinking her fill, Isabella moved to the cab of the truck. "I doubt these workers drank from the cooler's spigot like that. They had to have go-cups somewhere. If not, maybe we can find a takeout cup in one of these other vehicles."

Will silently chuckled. Was this the same woman that a few hours ago had lectured him about taking things that didn't belong to him?

"I'll check this red Ford," Cayden said.

"We should check them all. We should look for food of any kind, water, emergency first-aid kit, tarps, ropes, tape, flashlights, glow sticks would be even better, any type of weapon, like a knife," Will said.

All the toolboxes were locked tight, but Will found a few useful items lying in the bed of the truck. Two flashlights and a piece of rope.

"Hey, Dad. Look at this," Cayden said, holding up a roadside emergency kit. "We can use this, right?"

"Sure. That's a great find," Will said.

Kim took a few sips and headed back across the street.

"Where are you going, Kim?" Will called after her.

"Food truck," she said, pointing to a white box truck parked along the curb.

"Isabella, I'm going with Kim. Let me know if you find anything good," Will said.

Kim rolled up the back door. Cold air hit Will in the face, and then he saw it. He just stood there, speechless at the sight of the food. With the refrigeration unit now inoperable, it would all go to waste within hours. He stepped up into the truck and picked up a case of New York strip steaks. The box still felt cold. They would only be edible for a little longer in the Texas heat. With the electricity out, there'd be no way to refrigerate them. If they found ice and a cooler, they could extend it another twenty-four hours. Will's heart sank. All that food and by this time tomorrow, none of it would be edible.

"These tortillas should still be good," Kim said, practically reading his mind.

"That's true."

Will moved toward the back where he located more fresh beef. He moved a few cases and spotted a stack of frozen burger patties. They might still be usable by the time they reached Kim's friend's house. He picked one up and placed it under his arm, relishing the cold temperature. Although he'd have loved to have relief from the heat, his body temperature would only make it thaw faster.

"What is all this?" Cayden asked from the open door.

"A restaurant food delivery truck," Will said. "It's mostly meat. It won't be good tomorrow."

Cayden pointed to a box on the floor in the back corner. "What is that?"

Will turned and moved a case of Dr. Pepper syrup. He bent and picked up the box Cayden had pointed out. "It's a case of assorted jellies."

"They'll still be good tomorrow, right?" Cayden asked.

Will smiled. "Absolutely. They'll provide sugar for energy."

Among their haul from the restaurant supply truck were various condiments, nuts, and a case of energy drinks.

"How are we going to carry all this?" Cayden asked.

Will pointed to the hand truck in the corner. They stacked the cases onto the hand dolly and wheeled them back to the construction truck. He used the bungee to strap on the water cooler. At this point, he was beaming. They had some food, at least ten gallons of water, and a means to transport them. It wasn't enough to get them through until the floodwaters receded, but it would get them through the storm. In a few days, after the supplies were gone, he'd have to wade into the toxic water to find essential provisions, but he would focus on something finally going their way for a change.

Cayden walked by Will's side as he pushed the dolly down the middle of the street. Kim and Isabella walked several feet behind them. Isabella was still limping and slowing them down. Will tried not to get irritated. It wasn't her fault. It just sucked.

They passed a young couple heading north. The woman pushed a stroller with a case of bottle water strapped to it. The man pulled a rolling suitcase. When they spotted Will and his group, the couple passed over to the opposite side of the street. Will couldn't help but stare at the stroller as they passed by them. He prayed that they'd found it empty and abandoned.

"Dad, how are they going to fix the lights and stuff after the storm if the cars won't start?" Cayden asked.

Will hated that he didn't have an answer for the boy. It had been months and months since he'd asked him anything. He knew that Cayden must be concerned about their situation but for the life of him, he had no clue what their futures held.

"I'm not sure that they can," he finally answered.

Cayden was quiet for a long moment. "Who do you think did this?"

"I don't know that anyone did this. I'm mean, I'm not sure what caused it. I've never heard of anything like this before. It could be atmospheric or some weird phenomena with the hurricane, I just don't have any answers at the moment," Will said.

"That guy back at the gas station thought it was aliens."

Will glanced over at him. "What do you think?"

Cayden screwed up his face and lifted one shoulder. "I think it was the Russians or Chinese." Cayden glanced over his shoulder toward Kim. If she'd heard him, she didn't appear offended.

"Why do you think that?" Will asked, lowering his voice to just above a whisper.

"Because." Cayden moved closer. "We talked about the rising tensions between the U, Russia, and China. I had to do a report on it. I came across something about China's plan to become the world's new superpower by something like 2030. They developed some laser-like weapon that could knock out communication on our aircraft carriers."

"But if they had some kind of weapon that could wipe out electricity, cars, and phones in an instant, wouldn't our government know about it?" Will asked him.

He hated to admit it, but he was clueless about American foreign policy and threats from hostile governments. It had been all he could do to get out of bed every day and haul his sorry ass into work. He'd been going through the motions and barely making it. He hadn't had the emotional bandwidth to add foreign governments' plans for world domination to his list of concerns.

"How do we know they didn't know about them? I mean, we probably have the same capabilities. Look at all those UFO sightings. That is likely our government testing super-secret stuff," Cayden said.

"That could be, but it doesn't prove that some hostile country is to blame for this. It could be the weather, don't you think?" Will asked.

Cayden chewed on his thumbnail. "I guess."

"At this point, I'm not sure it matters much what caused it. We just need to figure out how to get by until they can get it fixed," Will said.

Cayden stared up at him. His dark brown eyes reminded Will so much of Melanie's.

"What if it takes a really long time?" Cayden asked.

Will couldn't bear to think like that. The outcome of such a thing would be disastrous beyond belief. There would be no Red Cross or FEMA bringing in supplies and bottled water to get them by. Charitable organizations wouldn't be coming in to drop off food boxes, and the National Guard wouldn't be handing out MREs. They'd be on their own. He couldn't even imagine what that would look like. They relied on the grocery stores for food and the city for tap water. Just thinking about an extended period without air conditioning made him sick to his stomach.

When Will didn't answer, Cayden let out a long sigh. "We're screwed, aren't we?"

Will racked his brain for something encouraging to tell his son, something that wasn't a lie. He knew he couldn't get by with some sugar-coated recovery message. Cayden was too smart for that. Likely, he'd already thought about the ramifications of an extended period without city services and food deliveries.

"We'll think of something," Will finally said.

"You'll think of something for what?" Isabella said, walking up beside them.

Cayden filled her in on his theory. To Will's surprise, Isabella was quiet, too quiet. She looked like she might be sick.

"What do you think happened, Kim?" Cayden said as Kim caught up to them.

Kim hesitated to answer.

"Don't you have a guess?" Cayden asked.

"I am a person of science and facts. In this situation, I do not have the facts. I can't speculate as to what might have happened."

Isabella pressed her. "You've got no guesses even?"

"I could guess lots of things, but I cannot say I am correct."

"We're not asking you for facts. Just what you think could have happened." Isabella waved her hand in the air. "What could have possibly caused all this?"

Kim tilted her head slightly and stared at the sky. "In addition to the hypotheses Cayden has put forth about weapons of foreign powers, a coronal mass ejection could cause a disruption in all these things. But that scenario is highly unlikely because an ejection would have been detected before it had the opportunity to reach Earth. The scientists would have warned of the possibility of the sun's eruption, possibly days in advance. Especially one of this magnitude."

"Then that leaves an enemy attack as the only cause, doesn't it?" Cayden asked.

Will hoped his son was wrong. An enemy attack would have other ramifications that Will wasn't prepared to even consider.

"But why?" Isabella asked.

"Why what?" Kim asked.

"Why would another country want to take down our electricity, cars, and stuff? What would be in it for them?"

Kim didn't answer.

"To weaken us," Cayden said. His gaze went to Kim. "To become the new world superpower."

SIXTEEN

Savanah

DAY OF EVENT

Although they were technically still married, Savanah hadn't considered Derek to be her husband in four years. Looking into his black eyes, she wondered how she'd ever loved him in the first place.

"Where are my kids?" Derek asked.

He wasn't in uniform. Savanah glanced down the street toward the RV park. He'd come from Sissy's. Not that she cared. Sissy could have him. She didn't want him.

"My children are at my house," Savanah said, defiantly.

"Where's the van?"

"Back at Broussard's. It wouldn't start." She pulled away from him and took a step back. "I need to get home."

"It wouldn't start?" Derek asked.

She tried to step around him, but he put his arm out and blocked her.

"Why didn't you get Earl to give you a jump?"

She didn't have time for this. She was going to be walking in the dark as it was. The kids would worry.

"Paul went to get him, but Earl's wrecker wouldn't start either. It seems that several vehicles are having issues today."

"Um—my car wouldn't start either. Strange."

"If you are finished interrogating me, I need to get home to our children."

Saying it made bile rise in the back of her throat. Derek had never been a father to her children. He'd barely acknowledge their existence. He'd drop in on Christmas with a bundle of presents, acting like Santa Claus, and then not show back up until their birthdays. He'd left the rest of the work to Savanah.

"There you are."

Savanah spun around. Wade was standing there with a Cheshire cat grin.

"Hey, Derek. The mayor said for me to round everyone up and get them to city hall. Something strange is going on with the lights, phones, and cars all going down at once. The mayor said we need to help the police secure the bank and the grocery store," Wade said.

"Has he gotten ahold of the sheriff? He should know something," Derek said.

"Did you miss the part about the phones being down?" Wade asked.

"What about the radio? Derek asked.

"Dead as a doornail."

"Too strange. What's he think caused it?"

"Don't know. All he said was to round everyone up. He doesn't want those Blanchard boys coming into town and getting any ideas," Wade replied.

The Blanchard family were the one group that didn't kowtow to the mayor and his men. Truth be told, Thibodeau was afraid of them. The Blanchard family weren't scared of anyone. You mess with one of them, and you're likely to end up with your throat slashed in your sleep. The Blanchard family ran drugs. They cooked and grew them, but they also used mules to transport them over from Houston. In that way, Thibodeau and the Blanchards were rivals. If Thibodeau weren't a mayor with ties to high-ranking officials within the state of Louisiana, he'd be floating in the bayou by now.

"I'll let you get to it then," Savanah said, stepping past Derek.

"What's in the bag, Savanah?" Wade asked.

She gritted her teeth so hard she thought she might break her crown. Without turning, Savanah said, "Girl stuff. You know, tampons, maxi pads, some menstrual cramp medication, and a change of clothes. It's my time of the month. I'm bleeding."

Derek grabbed her arm. "He asked you what was in the bag. Stop being a bitch and hand it over."

She'd known she'd get a reaction from them but hadn't expected such a visceral response. She hesitated a moment too long, so Derek ripped the bag from her back and threw it to Wade. Savanah's heart stopped as Wade dropped the pack and unzipped it. Her pistol clattered to the ground. Everything after that went in slow motion.

Savanah tilted her head and looked into Wade's eyes. Shock and then anger registered on his face. She stiffened. She did her best not to allow her face to register the fear that had gripped her insides. She'd bought that gun and practiced at the range for months for the sole purpose of unloading a magazine into his skull. She couldn't let that show either.

"What the hell is this?" Wade said, bending to pick up the gun. "You're going to have to come with me. We'll need to go see the chief and have him run this weapon and make sure it's legal and hasn't been used in any crimes."

Savanah felt sick. She racked her brain. Which pistol was this one? If it were the one she'd gotten from Jason, after the incident in the kitchen that day, she couldn't be sure of its history. She'd never even thought to ask him how he'd come by the weapon. Maybe somehow she'd known it might not be legal, with him being related to the Blanchards and all. She couldn't very well tell Wade that she'd gotten the gun from Jason Blanchard. He wasn't here to back her up on it. It could be the one she'd purchased legally. Was she willing to take that chance?

There was no way in hell she was going to let him take her in and lock her up. No freaking way. She'd be trapped for sure. No one could help her. Her children would be left alone to fend for themselves. She couldn't let that happen. Ever.

Savanah looked past Wade, her eyes scanning the RV park. There was too much open ground between her and the nearest motor homes. Her chances of outrunning both Wade and Derek were slim. They were bigger and stronger than her. Her only hope was to out-think them.

When Wade's hand moved to his pistol, she realized she had no choice. Savanah swooped up her pack and took off full speed toward the first row of motor homes. The RV park was located in a popular tourist location. Situated on the edge of town, it was filled with people down on their luck and living in their motor homes out of desperation. She'd lived there herself for a time, right before she and the kids moved in with her grandfather.

The lots were filled with everything from lawn chairs to chicken coops. Savanah headed for the one filled with kid's toys. As a mother of four, she knew how to navigate that terrain. Jumping a two-foot-high fence, Savanah hopped and twisted over toys and around bicycles, toddler slides, and toy trucks. She didn't look back, but she could hear Derek and Wade behind her.

They were breathing hard and cursing her. At the end of the motor home, Savanah turned right and then immediately made a hard left going up the opposite side of the RV. It bought her a few seconds, but they were right back on her heels. A man in his late sixties opened the door to his travel trailer. His small dog ran out, barking furiously. He caught sight of Wade and snatched hold of his pant leg. As Wade kicked and shook his leg, the little dog hung on with all his might.

Taking advantage of the moment, Savanah ran full speed down the street, turning at the last row of motor homes and crossing through another line of RVs. Moments later, she was near the on-ramp of the westbound lanes of Interstate 10.

As she ran south toward the overpass, Savanah tried to come up with a route home that they couldn't follow. She knew they wouldn't track her far. Why would they? The whole town knew where she lived. Anyone from the mayor's office or police department could come to pick her up at any time. She considered that as she passed over the interstate. She'd been compliant and run their illegal drugs and money into Texas, yet they'd continued to harass her. Their aim was to intimidate her and keep her quiet. It had worked.

Savanah had tried to go to Sheriff Beaumont, but she'd thought she'd been followed and backed out. Besides, how could she be sure that he wasn't in on it? Everyone said that no one made a move in Calcasieu Parish that he didn't know about. So maybe he had sanctioned Mayor Thibodeau's illegal operation.

"Savanah. Get your ass back here."

Derek had caught up with her. Savanah didn't stop. Instead, she ran faster, finally reaching the other side of the interstate. She ran across the median, hesitating only a second at the roadway before running to the other side. She glanced back. They were still coming.

"Dammit!" She had nothing but pasture ahead. They could shoot her in the back and leave her for the buzzards. Instead, she chose the side road, not knowing where it led. She could find herself trapped on a dead-end street with nowhere left to run. She clenched her fists and took off in that direction, vowing that she'd always carry a backup gun from then on. She would never allow herself to be in this position again. She couldn't afford to. She was all her kids had in the world.

Scanning the houses as she passed, Savanah looked for somewhere to hide but found nothing. She kept running as the road curved to the left. Sure enough, the road sign said, "no outlet." She needed to cut through one of the yards and make it back toward the main road.

She passed large brick homes on oversized, well-manicured lawns and realized she was in the mayor's neighborhood. He'd been the developer for the subdivision. He'd hoped to attract wealthier citizens to the town, but many of the lots sat empty even after several years.

Derek's and Wade's loud voices sent her into a panic. From the sound of it, they were gaining on her fast. She had to do something, or they'd catch up with her any moment. In seconds, she'd reached the end of the road. The only thing she could do was go back the way she'd come or run down the driveway and around to the back of the house, not knowing if the homeowner was back there or whether they had big dogs that would attack her.

Choosing to risk a dog bite over getting taken in by Wade and Derek, Savanah ran toward the two-story ranch-style home. Lucky for her, the homeowner hadn't trimmed the crepe myrtles lining the driveway. They were tall and bushy and did a reasonably good job of obstructing the view of the right side of the house. Savanah continued around to the rear of the home. Her eyes darted back and forth, looking for somewhere to conceal herself from her pursuers.

When she spotted the boat, she at first dismissed it. It didn't have a cover like Bobby Johnson's had and she knew Derek and Wade would look there. After rejecting the shed, she considered sneaking into the garage through the door in the back. They'd need a warrant to search someone's home, right?

SEVENTEEN

Will

DAY OF EVENT

They walked the next few blocks in silence. Will was afraid that Cayden's bluntness may have offended Kim. He hoped that she hadn't taken Cayden's accusation that the Chinese government was somehow responsible for what had happened as suspicion of her. Will wanted to say something. To somehow smooth things over, but he was frankly afraid he'd just make them worse. She was going to provide them with shelter until the storm passed. If she refused, he and Cayden needed to be looking for somewhere to hunker down now.

"Hey, Will, look, the door to the bar is open," Isabella said, stopping in front of it.

Will and Cayden stopped as well, but Kim just kept on walking. Will looked from the bar to Kim. They needed to stop. The bar might have bottled water or club soda, at least. They would need more than ten gallons between them.

"Hold up, Kim. I need to go in and check it out. We need more water."

He watched Kim stop and turn. Without saying anything, she dropped down to the curb.

"I'll make it quick," he said. Kim still didn't acknowledge him.

"Cayden, stay with Kim," Will said. "Isabella, you want to come to help me carry out whatever we can find in there?"

Isabella nodded and grabbed the crowbar out of the trash bag tied around the dolly's handle. She gripped it tight and held it out in front of her. Will quickly ran over and stepped inside the door to the bar. Inside, he found two large booths flanked the entrance. The space was dark. The only light filtered in from the window along the front of the building. But it would have been dark even with electric lights. The walls were painted a dark charcoal color, and the floor was stained concrete. A bar filled with stools ran along the back wall. That was the direction he headed.

"You want to check the kitchen, Isabella?" He pointed to a door to the right of the bar.

Without a word, Isabella pushed through the door and disappeared. Will set about looking for bottles of water or club soda, moving aside bottles of whiskey and mixers, finally locating a case of ginger ale and a few cans of club soda and stacking them on top of the bar. He was rummaging through the space beneath the cash register when Isabella screamed his name.

"Will! Come quick."

He grabbed a bottle of Jack Daniels by the neck and headed through the door. He stopped in his tracks just inside.

"Whoa there! Let's just take it easy now. We mean you no harm. We were just leaving," Will said, reaching for Isabella's hand. On the floor in the corner of the tiny kitchen were a man and woman in their early twenties. Will fixed his eyes on the gun in the woman's hand.

"You get out," the woman said, jabbing the barrel of the pistol in their direction.

"All right. We're just going to back out of here nice and slow and leave you two alone," Will said.

Isabella pointed to the young man on the floor. "He's bleeding out."

The young woman's gaze fell to the man with his head in her

lap. His eyes were wide. His chest heaved in and out as he gasped for air. The crimson bloom on his shirt indicated he'd been hit in the chest.

"He needs help, but my phone is dead. Can I use yours?"

Isabella stepped forward, but Will blocked her with an outstretched arm. "There's nothing we can do for him," Will whispered.

Will reached for the door. "Our phones are dead too. We'll go try the bar's phone."

"No!" the woman barked. "No. Don't you move."

Will froze. "Just calm down—" He eased the bottle of whiskey to the floor and raised his hands, palms out.

"Don't you tell me to calm down," the young woman interrupted. "Don't you tell me what to do. I'm in charge here. This gun here says I'm in control here, not you."

"Okay. Okay. What do you want?" Will asked.

"I want you to help my brother." Her lips quivered as she looked down at the man. "He's all the family I got left."

Will turned to Isabella. "Go see if you can find a first-aid kit behind the bar."

Isabella nodded and reached for the door. As she did, Will leaned in. "Just run, Isabella. I'll catch up to you."

Isabella shook her head. "No, I can't leave you."

"What are you two talking about? Are you planning something? Are you planning to hurt us?" the woman yelled. She pushed the young man out of her lap and jumped to her feet.

Will threw his hand out in front of him as she sprinted across the floor, closing the distance between them. Will tensed, expecting the gun to go off at any moment.

"We weren't planning anything. I was saying that we should go get our car and take him to the hospital ourselves," Isabella lied.

That only infuriated the woman more. "That's a damn lie. The cars all died. Everyone was stranded on foot. You were planning to rob us and leave us for dead, weren't you?" She wagged the gun in front of Isabella's face, just inches from her nose. Will smelled the strong odor of alcohol on the woman's breath. It appeared that she'd been drinking which made the situation much more dangerous.

Will reacted without thinking, striking out to knock the gun away, but the woman pivoted before he made contact. She twisted and spun, moving back several steps then threw her head back and laughed as she made her way back to the man on the floor.

The woman turned and twitched the barrel of the gun toward the opposite corner of the kitchen. "Take a seat. Put your hands on your knees where I can see them."

Isabella's eyes bounced between them. Will nodded and offered her his hand.

"Aw, how cute? You two make such a lovely couple."

Will didn't bother to correct her.

He sat down beside Isabella and placed his hands on his knees as instructed. His thoughts were about Cayden. Eventually, he'd get concerned when they didn't come out. Will prayed that Kim kept him from coming to check on them. He started thinking about what would become of Cayden if something were to happen to him.

He'd made arrangements with his sister to care for Cayden if he died. He'd made Cayden the beneficiary of his life insurance, with Savanah as the executor. He'd rolled all of the proceeds of Melanie's life insurance into an annuity for Cayden and when he turned twenty-five, he would start receiving a monthly payout from the one-million-dollar policy. But with the way things were, how would Cayden get to Savanah's?

Isabella wiped tears from her cheeks with the backs of her hands and turned her gaze to the woman. "How long are you going to keep us here?"

The woman lifted one shoulder in a half shrug.

"I have to get home. There's a hurricane coming. I have to get home and make sure my cat is all right."

"You have a cat?" the woman asked.

"I do. His name is Otis. He's black and white. It looks like he's wearing a tuxedo. He's such a loveable boy. I'm really worried about him. If the storm breaks the windows, I may never see him again. I just couldn't bear not knowing what happened to him."

"I have a dog—a pit bull. He's only six months old," the woman said. "My brother bought him for me."

She glanced down at the dying man. His skin was pale, and his breaths were ragged. He didn't have much longer. Will feared what the woman might do when he died.

"You can't stay here," Will said. The woman's gaze moved from her brother to Will.

"It's all going to flood, just like last time. This whole bar will be underwater." He let that sink in for a moment. "You need to find somewhere that has a second or even third floor."

She appeared to be thinking it over. "But he can't be moved. I dragged him in here, but he's worse now."

"You don't have much time. Once the hurricane makes landfall, you won't be able to get out."

"What's your name?" Isabella asked, scooting an inch or so closer to the door.

"Rachel."

"Rachel, Will is right. We were stranded here too, and we're looking for somewhere to hole up until the storm passes. I know you love your brother, but he'd want you to live."

Rachel's stared back at Isabella with a blank expression. Will hoped that the alcohol she'd consumed wouldn't impede her judgment so much as to get them all killed. He remained quiet, allowing Isabella to build a rapport with the woman and hopefully convince her to let them go.

"Will has a kid. A boy. He needs to get home and save his son," Isabella said.

"You have a kid?" Rachel asked.

Will nodded.

"How old is he?"

"Thirteen."

She shook her head. "That's a tough age. I remember when Joshua and I were thirteen. It sucked. My parents didn't give a shit about us. All they cared about was this damn bar."

"You own this?" Isabella asked.

"We own it," Rachel said. "We came to board up the place to get it ready for the storm. We were moving some of the perishables into the freezer when a guy came in and decided now was a good time to rob us. Josh went for the gun we kept behind the bar, but the guy was quicker."

"I'm so sorry that happened to you. Please let us help." Isabella glanced over at Will. "We'd love to help you. We can find something and make a litter and move your brother. There's a building down the block that the loading bay door was open. We could help you get him there."

Will wanted to protest. If they moved the man, he could very well die before they reached there. Once they walked outside, Cayden could get hurt. He wasn't willing to take that risk.

"Do you have a back door?" Will asked. "It would be shorter, easier on him."

Will slowly began to rise, keeping his hands out in front of him, palms out, trying not to look threatening.

"There," Rachel said, nodding toward the door in the corner of the room.

She began to get up, and her brother moaned. She froze and stared down at him. He gasped, and his eyes glazed over. Will waited for him to take his next breath. He watched for the rise and fall of his chest but there was none. Long seconds passed as they waited for the man to take a breath. When Rachel grasped what was happening, she wailed. As she clutched her brother to her chest and sobbed into his neck, Will grabbed Isabella's arm and ran. He expected to be shot in the back as he flung open the door, but he wasn't.

"Dad!" Cayden yelled.

Cayden and Kim stood in the middle of the bar. Kim grabbed Cayden's arm and stopped him from advancing.

"Go! Go! Go! Don't stop for anything," Will yelled a second before he heard the shot.

Will looked back. Isabella stopped in the doorway. She turned, and her hand flew up to cover her mouth. "Oh, my God. Oh, my God," she said over and over.

"What happened?" Kim asked.

Will slid his arm around Isabella's shoulders and pulled her toward the exit. "We need to go. There's nothing we can do for her. She made her choice."

"I can't believe she just shot herself like that." Isabella burst into tears.

"Cayden, take Isabella and wait for me outside," Will said.

"But what happened?" Cayden asked as he reached out and took Isabella's hand.

"Just wait outside. I'll tell you in a minute."

Will moved behind the bar and gathered up the items he'd collected. Despite all that had happened, they still needed the drinks he'd found there. That couple certainly wouldn't. He looked around for Kim, but the room was empty. Assuming she'd slipped outside with Cayden and Isabella, Will exited the bar. He found Cayden and Isabella seated on the curb by the dolly. "Where's Kim," he asked.

"Still inside," Cayden said.

Will glanced back as Kim walked through the door. In her hands, she held the woman's pistol and a white rag from the bar. As she approached, she wiped blood from the weapon.

"I could find only one extra magazine," she said.

Isabella stared at her hand. "Why did you take that?"

"Protection," Kim said.

A gust of wind blew a trash can over, causing a loud crash and reminding Will that they needed to find shelter immediately. He was anxious to get to Kim's friend's house and assess this situation. If he found it unsuitable, he still needed time to locate another place for him and Cayden to ride out the storm.

After strapping the soda cases to the dolly with the food from the restaurant supply truck, Will pushed it back into the street. "Cayden, stick close. Things are getting dicey out here."

Kim led the way with Isabella lagging behind Cayden and Will. He could hear her crying softly and sniffling. It was awful what they'd witnessed. He wished he had words that would help her, but he didn't. How does one make sense of such a tragic loss of life? Those two young people had had their whole lives ahead of them. Like with his wife, in an instant, their lives were over. Had there been something he could do to prevent it? He wasn't sure. It happened so fast.

"Dad, you said you'd explain what happened back there," Cayden asked.

Will struggled to think of a way to explain it. He understood death, likely more than most kids his age. Cayden knew that unlike video games where people get killed and then get back up, death is final in real life. What Will struggled with was how to explain violence and suicide. He might understand the young woman's pain at losing her brother, but Will didn't think Cayden should. No one should.

"The bar was robbed," Will said. He thought of leaving it at that, but he knew Cayden wouldn't settle for half-truths. "And a man was shot. His sister..." Will choked, and his voice cracked. "His sister chose not to live life without him."

Will thought about those words and considered why he'd said it that way. He wished he'd been able to talk to the woman, tell her life was worth living—even with the pain. Two years ago, Will wouldn't have been able to say that to her. If he hadn't had Cayden, he might have made the same choice.

"That's sad," Cayden said.

"Yes, it is."

Neither of them spoke as they continued to push on toward Kim's friend's apartment. At each intersection, Will slowed and scanned the area. Twice they'd had to avoid shootings in the streets. They'd been lucky to escape unharmed. Will wanted to make sure they remained that way.

As the hours had ticked by since everything stopped working, it was getting harder and harder to not panic. Not knowing what was happening was torture. If Will stopped to think about it for long, he thought of numerous disastrous scenarios. He had always liked to be proactive and plan things out. He liked having goals and a strategy to achieve them but also had a tendency to over-analyze things. He'd lay in bed for hours going over and over details of their lives, before Melanie had been ripped from them, that is. Since that night, Will had felt like he was drifting; lost in a sea of people. His sole purpose now was raising his son and making his wife proud of the man he would become.

Fortunately, Cayden was an easy child to raise. He never gave him much trouble. He didn't have to get on to him about getting his schoolwork done on time or cleaning his room. Except for the first week or so after the funeral, Cayden had carried on as he had before his mother's death. He got himself up every morning, ate whatever breakfast Will served, and headed off to school. All his teachers called Cayden a model student. Life had gone on, except Will and Cayden rarely spoke. When he'd try to strike up a conversation, Cayden would either ignore him or excuse himself with needing to finish homework.

Glancing over at his son, Will wondered if maybe Cayden was softening some toward him now. He could never expect his forgiveness, but Will hoped they'd be able to build a new relationship.

"Dad, what if whatever is going on here is happening in Calcasieu Parish?" Cayden asked.

Will hadn't given any thought to this phenomenon occurring elsewhere or if it would affect his sister and her kids.

"Well, Tante Savanah lives off-grid. She's prided herself on being self-sustained. She and your cousins have everything they need there on the farm. They'll be okay. You don't have to worry about them," Will said.

"What about food for the animals? She gets that from the feed store."

Will wasn't surprised that Cayden would think about the animals. He loved all animals. Will had considered buying a little place outside of town when they moved up north just so Cayden could have whatever pets he wanted. He knew that whatever animals they got, Cayden would be responsible and take the best possible care of them.

"Remember those two old freezers out in Grandpa's barn? She buys all the animals' food in bulk and has it delivered. I'm sure she's set until all this gets resolved," Will said.

"I hope so. The goats and cows will be all right eating grass, but she feeds the chickens a special diet."

"She does?" Will asked. Other than knowing his sister bought feed in bulk, he'd never paid attention to what she fed her animals.

"Yeah, it's organic. She says it contains lots of omega three."

"They'll be fine for a while on the grass too, I imagine," Will said.

Will's mind drifted to their own struggle for food. He scanned all the buildings they passed for anywhere they might add to their supply. But after what had happened back at the bar, he was leery of going searching again.

When a man and two women appeared in the intersection ahead, Will pulled Cayden close. "Kim, Isabella, people up ahead," he said, moving to put a pickup truck between them and the strangers.

Isabella rushed over and crouched behind the truck. "Do they have guns?" she asked.

Kim stopped behind a mid-sized sedan. The pistol hung at her side. She seemed comfortable with the weapon. Will wondered if she knew how to use it. As far as he knew, guns were illegal for citizens to own in her country. But it was Texas, and someone might have taken her to a gun range while she'd been here. He was concerned. If she wasn't familiar with the weapon, there was a risk she could accidentally shoot one of them.

The strangers passed through the intersection without turning toward them. One was limping pretty badly. Will wondered how far they'd make it on foot.

"The hospital is up ahead. We will probably see more people," Kim said, moving back into the middle of the street.

"We should stop there to see if they have working radios. They might know what happened," Cayden said. "Besides, you two still need to get your injuries treated."

Will knew Cayden was right. They needed to go to the hospital and find someone with answers, but there would be people there. A lot of people, he imagined. So far, they'd had pretty bad luck with people.

"Maybe the Red Cross is there to evacuate people," Isabella said, her eyes brightening.

"Maybe," Cayden said.

"What do you think, Kim?"

"I doubt they have any means of communication or transportation. They will not have the answers you seek."

"But there might be cops there or even FEMA. They'll have some idea, right?" Isabella asked.

Kim hesitated. "If you want to go, I will follow."

Isabella smiled, and she and Cayden crossed the street and turned left at the intersection. Will hoped that Kim was wrong and that they would find answers, but more than answers, they needed help to get out of the city. He wasn't sure what they would face once they escaped the area that would be impacted by the storm, but he was ready to find out.

Will glanced down at Kim's injured arm and thought about all the wounded people he'd seen since the lights went out. If they became exposed to the toxic and bacteria-laden floodwaters, survivable injuries could become infected and deadly. Will added antibiotics to his list of supplies they'd need to be searching for on their way to Kim's friend.

In the best-case scenario, Isabella and Kim would receive treatment and be given a bottle of antibiotics to take with them. Under the circumstances, a prescription would do no one any good. Will tried to recall where the closest pharmacy might be. After the storm passed, they might have to locate one. If he could get to a pharmacy before it was looted out, they could load up on medications that might just save their lives. Too bad none of them were doctors or nurses. He wasn't sure if a chemical biologist like Kim received any medical training, but he doubted it.

"Tell me about this friend of yours, Kim," Will said.

"Betley is a friend from university."

"A student?" Will asked.

"No. A professor," Kim said.

"What does he teach?"

"Biology."

Will wasn't sure if she was purposefully vague, but he needed a little more than she was giving him. He'd need to be more direct with his questions, it seemed.

"Is he a friendly sort? I mean, how's he going to react to you showing up with three strangers? I can't afford to go all that way and be turned back hours before the storm hits."

"He would never turn anyone away," Kim said.

"That's good to hear."

Will stepped around a truck that was blocking both lanes. Kim went to his right and stepped up onto the sidewalk. The cab of the truck momentarily blocked his view of her. When he approached the front of the vehicle, he spotted a man ahead.

"Kim!" Will shouted.

Kim looked back at him. One of the men said something as Kim's head whipped back around. "Run, Will!" Kim yelled as she brought the pistol up, aiming it at the man.

"Cayden!" Will screamed. He watched Isabella grab Cayden by the shoulder and shove him behind an electric transformer.

Will ran as fast as he could to reach them as gunshots rang out behind him. When Cayden poked his head up to see, Will chopped his arm in the air, telling him to stay down. As he ran, Will's legs felt as if they were full of lead. No matter how much he willed them, they would go no faster.

When he dropped down behind the transformer, he covered Cayden and Isabella with his body. When there was a lull in the gunfire, Will glanced up. Kim was standing over the man. He was on his back with his arms at his sides, and her pistol pointed at his face. She said something in her native language and pulled the trigger. Will jumped, startled by the shot. He looked to the nearby parking garage, searching for anyone else, but saw no one.

Kim stepped over the dead man. She held the pistol in both hands and scanned the area before lowering the weapon and walking toward them.

"We need to get to Professor Betley's. Now!" Kim said and walked quickly past them.

"What about the hospital?" Cayden asked.

Will stepped off the curb and took Isabella's hand. "Right now, we need to catch up with Kim."

Isabella was so shaken up by the gun battle Kim had just engaged in that she could barely walk. Cayden held her right hand, and Will had his arm around her shoulder. He was almost pushing her along as they tried to keep up with Kim. He wanted to catch up to her and ask her what the hell had just happened, but he didn't want to let Cayden out of his sight, and there was no way he would leave Isabella.

"Isabella, we need to catch up with Kim," Will finally said.

"Why? Did you see what she did?" Isabella asked. "My God, she shot that man in the face."

"She was defending herself," Will said, unsure why he was trying to justify what she'd done. Truthfully, he wasn't sure what had happened.

"He wasn't shooting at her when he was on the ground. I didn't even see a gun."

"She'd kicked it away," Cayden said.

Will had hoped he hadn't seen any of it, but obviously, he had.

"I want to go home," Isabella whined.

"We can't," Will said, a little harsher than he'd intended.

His patience was shot. He just didn't have time to deal with someone having a meltdown. He needed to find out what was up with Kim and decide where he and Cayden were going.

When they turned the corner at the next intersection, Kim stopped at an entrance to a parking garage and scanned the area. Will took the opportunity to catch up to her, pulling on Isabella's arm and nearly dragging her with him.

"Hurry. Don't fall behind, Cayden," Will said as they ran toward Kim.

EIGHTEEN

Will

DAY OF EVENT

They practically ran for the next two blocks; at least as fast as they could with all their injuries. Will quickly maneuvered the dolly around a manhole in the street and around a box van blocking the road. It felt so wrong running south when they needed to be heading north. Will prayed that he wasn't making a grave mistake. He hoped that Kim was telling the truth and that her friend's place was as she said.

Isabella hung back. Maybe she was still debating whether to follow Kim or maybe her ankle was worse now. Will thought it was likely a bit of both. He and Cayden kept their distance as well, content to keep only close enough to not lose sight of Kim. Will wasn't sure how he felt about what Kim had done. He hadn't seen all of it. It was hard to judge if it was a justifiable shooting. It wasn't like they could hold a gun on the guy and call the cops. But to coldly stand over the man and shoot him in the face like that, Will couldn't have done it.

Kim hadn't shown herself to be any threat to them. But he didn't know her. He was taking a big, big risk following her, but what choice did he have? He could risk it and break into one of the hotels, but they could catch on fire like the other buildings, and they'd be trapped.

As they walked under Interstate 45, Will considered running toward the on-ramp and taking it north. He cursed the guy who'd stolen his Jeep. If he hadn't, Will and Cayden would be safe at the lake house by now. He glanced over to the parking lot under the overpass as he walked. If not for the hurricane evacuation, on a weekday like that, the lot would have been full of cars. Before the city turned it into a parking lot, it would have likely been home to at least a few of the city's homeless population. Will thought of Fahima back in her makeshift home in the mechanical room of that apartment building. They might have been better off remaining there with her, but regrets now would not save them.

There was less smoke at this end of town and it was more comfortable to breathe. That would not be the case near the site of the refinery fires. Will was grateful he at least wasn't dealing with that. He had masks and protective clothing to protect himself and Cayden back home. Some other residents around the refineries did as well. It was something you had to plan for when you lived that close to one.

A lightning strike caused Isabella to yelp. She ran to catch up with Will and Cayden. A light rain was beginning to fall now and Will picked up his pace, trying to keep sight of Kim. He didn't like not knowing where they were going or what to expect when they arrived. Would there be more gunmen at this place? To be safe, he'd drop back and watch from a distance.

"Are you sure that his place will be safe? Midtown flooded in Hurricane Harvey," Will said as they continued to follow Kim.

"His place is on the third floor of a stone building. There are very few windows. It will be safe," Kim said as she turned right and headed west.

Ten minutes later, Kim stopped in front of a tall tan building. The sign on the front said, "Safe Space Self Storage." Will grabbed

Cayden's arm and pulled him behind a car parked along the curb and watched as Kim walked to the door.

"What is she doing?" Isabella asked, squatting beside them.

"I think she's punching in the code," Cayden said.

Isabella flicked her chin toward the door. "Why is she going there?"

"I don't know." Will moved around the rear bumper, trying to get a better look, but trees and shrubs were blocking his view. "Watch that dolly. We can't afford to have it stolen," he told Cayden.

"Will the code work without electricity?" Isabella asked.

"I don't think so," Cayden said.

A second later, Will heard glass break.

"I guess the code didn't work," Cayden said.

"Will, Cayden, Isabella," Kim said, waving them over.

Will rose slightly to look over the hood of the vehicle. He motioned for Cayden and Isabella to stay put and moved along the right side of the car, making sure to keep the sedan between him and Kim.

"What are we doing here, Kim?" Will asked.

"We are here," Kim said, pointing skyward.

"Where? This is a storage facility." A tangled mess of emotions swirled through Will's brain. Frustration, anger, fear, and panic threatened to send him into a rage.

Without a word, Kim slipped inside. Will's face contorted. He wanted to kick himself for trusting her. Why? Why had she played them like that? What could she gain from it?

"Will, are you coming?" Kim asked, poking her head around the door.

"You're not going in there, are you?" Isabella asked.

"Wait here. Let me check it out," Will said, moving toward the street.

"No way. No way I'm waiting out here. I'm coming," Isabella said, looking back down a side street.

Annoyance passed between them as she ran up beside him. He didn't want to take Cayden, but he couldn't leave him outside by himself. Not that Isabella could provide any protection, anyway.

∽

Will pulled the door open, releasing a trickle of glass. Kim stared back at him.

"This is not an apartment building, Kim. What the hell are we doing here?"

"Meeting my friend," Kim said, pointing to the stairs.

"Here?" Isabella said, her voice shrill.

Kim said nothing.

The first floor of the facility contained a small store for purchasing packing supplies as well as smaller storage units. Kim walked past a reception desk and headed for the stairs. She pulled open the door to the stairway and stepped to one side. Will doubted she could see much with the lights out. Kim flicked on a flashlight and scanned with the pistol raised. A second later, Kim climbed the steps and repeated the maneuver at the landing, checking the next flight of stairs.

"Cayden, stay there with the dolly. Hold the door open, so I can see you. I need to check it out up there," Will said.

Isabella remained behind with Cayden as Will slowly went up behind Kim. When they reached the top, Will called down for Cayden and Isabella to follow. Will heard the door shut and what little light had made it to the top of the stairs disappeared.

"It's pitch black. How are we supposed to see?" Isabella called up.

Will flicked on a flashlight and shined it down the stairwell.

"Take the steps one at a time and hold onto the handrail," Will said.

Kim stood to one side and wrenched open the door leading to the third floor. Will tensed, half expecting her to be shot dead in front of him. No shots came. He waited in the doorway as she pressed her back against the wall and slowly moved to her left. Even with the flashlight, it was dark. There'd be no way of really seeing anyone lying in wait.

Will let out a harsh breath. He was starting to turn and leave when he heard a murmured greeting. A male voice. Was this her friend, the professor?

"Will, it is clear," Kim said, and the hallway lit up with light from a lantern. The long corridor was lined with roll-up doors. Intersecting aisles led off to the right and left making a grid pattern. Will couldn't tell how many aisles of storage units there were but from what he could tell from the size of the building, there had to be three or more.

A man stepped through a roll-up doorway, handed Kim the lantern, and then disappeared back into the room. Kim quickly walked back to the stairway. "Hurry, Isabella. Cayden," she called down.

"Why does he live in a storage unit?" Will asked. He had to admit, it wasn't any more strange than anything else that he'd encountered that day, but he had to ask.

"It is inexpensive," Kim said.

NINETEEN

Will

DAY OF EVENT

If not for the roll-up doors, the storage facility corridors would look like the floor of an apartment building. Doors flanked both sides of a narrow hallway. At a T intersection, Will could see the depth of the building. Kim had been correct. This floor contained no windows. Its location on the third floor would protect them from floodwaters. It was strange, but it would work if they had to stay. But Kim had promised a way out of the city. Will was anxious to hear how.

The unit where they found Kim's friend looked nothing like a standard storage unit. It contained no boxes of unused dishes or old books. There was no furniture or exercise equipment. Instead, in the space was a cot, a small table with two chairs, a cooler, and many cases of MREs.

The man took hold of Kim's injured arm. She didn't pull away. "Why are they here?" the man asked.

"They gave me a ride," Kim said.

That was only partially true. Kim hadn't been totally honest with her friend. Why?

"And you brought them here. That's against protocol," the man said.

The middle-aged Caucasian man was dressed in a white shirt, dress slacks, and running shoes. The man ran a hand through his thick black hair and turned his back on Kim. He walked to the small table in the center of the space and stopped then hung his head and shook it.

"This is not good. Not good at all," Betley said.

"If it's a problem, we can go," Will said, backing out of the space. His mind was already at work figuring out how to break the lock on one of the other units with the tools they'd found so far.

"No. It's all right," Kim said.

Kim moved closer to the man and whispered something.

The man turned and looked from Will to Cayden and Isabella. He nodded, then walked to the cooler. He opened it and took out four bottles of water, handing one to each of them.

"Kim said you brought supplies," the man said.

"Yes," Will said. "They're at the bottom of the stairs."

"Well, we better get those moved up here before the storm hits," the man replied.

"I'm James Betley," the man said as Will handed him the six-pack of ginger ale.

"Will Fontenot. That's my son, Cayden."

"Nice to meet you both," Betley said.

"I'm sorry to crash in on you like this. We were trying to get out of town when all the cars just stopped working."

"It's quite all right. I just wasn't prepared for having company. But we'll make do."

After moving the dolly stacked with supplies into the storage unit, Will, Cayden, and Isabella sat on the floor, as Kim and her friend sat at the small table, having a hushed conversation. As Cayden and Isabella talked about her cat, Will's mind drifted to what to do after the storm passed.

How many days could they afford to wait before heading back home? If they even still had a home. There was so much to consider. Without communications, he'd have no idea what condition his neighborhood was in, not to mention his house. They could travel the twenty miles or so only to find that they no longer had a home. And then what?

"My mom was going to let me get a snake for my birthday," Cayden said.

Will faintly recalled Melanie discussing it with him. He'd not been in favor of the idea. Will had planned to take Cayden to Dallas to pick up a boxer puppy, but that trip had had to be postponed due to the evacuation.

"Where is your mom?" Isabella asked.

Will felt the familiar stab of grief. It had been months since anyone had asked about his wife. If Cayden had been asked, he hadn't mentioned it. People who knew tended to shy away from even asking how they were doing anymore.

"She died," Cayden said.

Will expected him to choke up or grow quiet, but he continued. Will felt a mix of sadness and joy. It was good that Cayden could talk about his mother. He wished Cayden would speak about her with him.

"She was killed in a car accident. My mom loved animals too. She grew up on a farm, and she said we might move back there someday."

"I'm so sorry about your mother, Cayden. She sounds like a wonderful person." Isabella reached over and placed a hand on Cayden's shoulder. "I know she would be so tremendously proud of the compassionate young man you are."

Will agreed. He was very impressed that Cayden hadn't

become screwed up and bitter. Other kids who'd lost parents had struggled and become angry with the world.

All the credit would go to his wife for that.

They grew quiet, and Will's thoughts drifted again. It was difficult not to speculate about what had caused this and what it would all mean for them after the storm. Was it possible that whatever had caused the phones and cars to stop working could somehow be resolved quickly after the storm passed? Somehow, he doubted it. The fact that they hadn't seen or heard a single emergency services vehicle told him that they were in a world of trouble.

He needed to consider what he'd do if things weren't restored in a day or two. The lake house was still an option. It would most certainly be spared by the storm. It was far enough away enough all the refineries to not have major ground and surface water contamination. Heading to Lake Livingston was still their best course of action. But what if the restoration of services took weeks or months? Millions of people would likely be without power, and homes damaged or destroyed.

They had some food and water at the lake house. They'd be able to fish, but so would the others evacuating to their second homes there. How long could they all live on fish anyway? He could barely get Cayden to eat lake fish as it was and Will had to agree with him. Lake fish couldn't hold a candle to ocean fish. Being Cajun and from a fishing family, Will had been raised on the sea's bounty. Mostly, they ate what didn't sell at the seafood market his uncle owned.

Will never complained. His grandmother would throw it all into a pot, add seasonings, and he'd eat until he was stuffed. Savanah had been the one to complain. Whoever heard of a Cajun vegetarian anyway? She'd grown out of that phase after high school, but she still would only eat organically raised meats and produce. He pictured Savanah and her four kids working in the barn milking goats and that fat, lazy milk cow of hers by lantern light. Life without electricity wouldn't be much of a change for them. Savanah had lived off the grid for several years. He wasn't sure how she'd adjusted. It had only been a few hours, and Will was going crazy not knowing what was going on in the world.

Will could see that Kim and Betley were having a tense conversation. With their hushed tones, Will couldn't make out what they were discussing. It was none of his concern. But whatever it was must have been quite serious as he could see the vein in Kim's neck bulging. Her body was stiff and her posture defensive.

Betley was leaning in with both arms on the tiny table whereas Kim was sitting erect in her chair, her head down and hands in her lap. Will saw her clench her jaw. Was she getting a dressing down? Did it involve him, Cayden, and Isabella? Will didn't think Kim would react that way in defense of them. She didn't owe them anything.

TWENTY

Betley

DAY TWO

Betley glanced over his shoulder at the three civilians who'd invaded his space. The last thing he wanted was to have four other people to be responsible for. He hadn't prepared for guests.

Ever since joining the task force investigating the Chinese government's theft of corporate and medical research and the overlapping investigation of an increased number of Chinese nationals illegally crossing the US border with Mexico, Betley had known something big was coming. Even though he wasn't read in on the details, which were being kept strictly need-to-know, he'd done some digging, called in a few favors, and put two-and-two together.

When he confided in his partner and shared what he'd surmised, Rodriguez had told him he sounded like one of those prepper conspiracy nuts. Betley scanned the shelves of boxes containing a year's worth of food and supplies. *Who's the nut now?*

"You said you would get me out of this city. Your government would give me a new identity. All I had to do was report Shan Huang's movements and bring you documents of his business meeting with Hui Shi," Kim said.

Betley leaned across the table. "I told you to stay put and not attract attention. They were likely just being paranoid as the last details of the plan fell into place."

"You have contacts. You can call and get us out, right?"

"No, Kim. Your freaking government just sent us all back to the stone age. Even if there are any working means of transportation, they aren't going to waste them on an FBI agent and his Chinese informant."

Betley didn't believe Kim had anything to do with the Communist Party's attack on the United States. He'd been working with her for over a year. She was desperate to get out from under the party's control. Everything she'd brought him so far had been credible and verified. But those in the bureau who didn't know her like he did wouldn't care. She'd just as likely end up in some sort of camp, much like the country had set up for the Japanese during World War II.

"I told you I was being followed. They know something. They were chasing me. They caused me to crash my car into that lady." Kim pointed to the cute brunette.

"Don't you get it? None of that matters now. The CCP succeeded in launching an EMP. I can't know for sure, but it likely covers most of the United States. They aren't going to be able to track you now."

Betley was only guessing. No one could say for sure what electronic equipment would be affected. But from all indications, since the phones were all out, it was likely any global positioning satellite tracking would be inoperable as well.

"What are we going to do now?" Kim asked.

Betley didn't have a clue what to tell her. The bulk of his plan had been to ride out the initial days of the event right there in his storage unit and then head to the coast after everything calmed down. He had a boat there. He'd thought that would give him some flexibility. Now, he wasn't sure it would even run.

"You should go back to your apartment. In a few days, present yourself to the Chinese Consulate. You are a Chinese citizen. They will have a way out for you."

That was another guess on his part. The more likely scenario, they'd put Kim to work on their insurgency. That had to be a reason for the influx of illegal border crossings. When he'd met with friends from the bureau for beers, the talk around the table had been that the influx had to do with the fentanyl and other drugs being brought in from China. Betley wasn't sure. That hadn't made sense to him. He would have thought the Chinese gangs would just have paid off the Mexicans to get the drugs across the border. Why risk having their people cross the border illegally? Now, it all made sense. It had nothing to do with drugs and everything to do with whatever was going on now.

"I cannot go back to my apartment. They will find me there," Kim said.

"What makes you think anyone will care about stolen medical research now, Kim. They aren't going to care. They have something way bigger going on here." Betley waved his hand in the air. Kim flinched like he was going to strike her.

He had been a little rough with her when they'd arrived, but that had been because he was upset that she and three strangers had invaded his bug out location. He was kicking himself for using it to meet with Kim. It had seemed like the perfect place at the time. He would be seen hauling in boxes if anyone was tailing her. He would empty them and give one to Kim to make it appear that she'd come to retrieve something from her own locker. How could he have known he'd be on his way to meet her there when the shit hit the fan?

"I took something," Kim said. "Something that I think has to do with this attack."

"What? What makes you think that?"

"Shi and Huang were talking. When I walked in, they stopped. Huang took this duffle from Shi and shoved it under his desk. He

No Way Out

did not want me to see what was in it. After Shi left, I asked Huang what they had discussed, and he would not say. Later, after Huang was called to the consulate. I went looking for the bag but it was gone. I searched and found it stuffed inside the safe. I had taken it out and was looking inside when businessman Li and his driver came into the house. I didn't have time to put it back and close the safe."

"Kim, dammit. Why would you take such a risk? They could have killed you right there."

"I was scared, so I ran. I called you."

Tears welled in her eyes. That's when he knew. She'd played him. She'd played him like a fiddle, and he'd been too arrogant to notice. His gaze returned to the bag. He'd play along and see where she was going with this little ruse. But was she in for a big surprise? There was no way he was taking her anywhere, especially inside an FBI field office.

"What's in it?" Betley said, grabbing for the bag.

Kim shifted in her seat and, with her foot, pushed the duffle under the table.

"When you keep your end of the deal, I will show you what is in the bag."

He grabbed her arm and stared into her cold black eyes. "You'll show me what is in that bag or you'll never leave this room."

She pretended to be afraid. Betley knew she wasn't. He'd missed all the body language cues before. She'd been good. Very good. If he hadn't been so damn eager to break the case and earn his promotion, he would have seen right through it. He wouldn't have known what she had planned. No one would have guessed that her real role was to wait until this moment to feed the bureau false information.

He wouldn't trust anything she said now, even if they could somehow verify it. He needed to know their plan, and the false information she was so eager to provide might just tell him what she was really up to. Not that there was much at this point anyone could do about it. If there was still a functioning government out there, he wouldn't be able to contact any of them until the hurricane passed. In the meantime, he'd learn all he could about Kim and her scheme.

TWENTY-ONE

Will

DAY TWO

Now that they were off their feet, Will's right ankle was throbbing. He would need to wrap it if he expected to travel far in the next few days. A bum ankle was the last thing he needed when they had so far to go on foot. The ride-share bicycles he'd seen would likely be underwater, making them harder to locate. Pushing them through the floodwaters for miles before they could even ride them wasn't an option. What they needed was a boat.

But where should he go? He had to make a decision based upon the information he currently had. Where he'd really like to be was back in Calcasieu Parish, but that was one hundred and fifty miles away and impossible to reach on foot.

Will drifted off a few times, but he wasn't comfortable sleeping among strangers. Sometime in the night, he heard Isabella ask about the bathroom. Betley had pointed her to a bucket with a toilet seat in the corner. She'd declined. Will imagined that the smell coming from it would be awful by the time the storm was over. He'd suggest they move it out in the corridor in the morning. He didn't feel like conversing with anyone just then. Will felt momentarily guilty for his lack of consideration for Isabella's bladder then quickly dismissed it. This wasn't his storage space.

He awoke with a stiff neck from sleeping, sitting leaning against the wall. The only light came from a lantern on one of the shelves that lined the back wall. Will had no idea what time it was or how long he'd been out. He wished he still wore a watch, but he'd given that up when his cell phone became his constant companion.

As Will listened to Betley and Kim's hushed conversation, something Betley had said when they'd first arrived came back to him. He'd been so taken aback by the fact that the man lived in a storage unit that it had somehow slipped past him, but now, in light of their obviously contentious conversation, it grated in his mind. Against protocol. What had he meant by that? He could see that it would be impolite to bring strangers to someone's home unannounced. Will wouldn't like that either, but against protocol was something different. Whatever it was, Will was sure they were unwelcome.

He stood and walked to the door.

"Where are you going?" Betley asked.

"I thought I'd have a look around, maybe see if I can tell what the storm is doing. It sounds like the wind might be picking up."

He didn't say that he was going to check the rest of the floor and scope out the other units. Maybe he could find one unlocked. He doubted any of the tools he and Isabella had scrounged would be enough to break a padlock. If he found a unit, he and Cayden would move in there until the storm passed. That should ease any tensions between Kim and their host.

Kim stood. "I will go with you."

When she reached under the table to grab her duffle, Betley grabbed her arm. Kim just stared at him for a moment and then walked away. She was likely grateful to have an excuse to break off their conversation. Will would let her know his plan. He looked back at the shelf of equipment. He'd ask Betley if he had some bolt cutters if they couldn't find one unlocked.

"After you," Will said, stepping aside and allowing Kim to go first.

"We will have to go down to the second floor to see out," Kim said as they reached the first hallway. "There are no windows on this floor."

"Is there a way up to the roof?" Will asked. He was concerned about being in the building if the water rose above the second floor.

"There is. You want to check it out first," Kim asked.

"Sure," Will said.

As Kim led Will down the hall to the back corner of the building, he asked, "How long has your friend lived in a self-storage unit?"

"Not long."

"Isn't it against some rule? I mean, there isn't even a bathroom."

"He mainly just works here sometimes."

The whole thing was off. Why would a professor live or work in a storage facility? It was as crazy as everything else that had occurred that day.

They turned down another short hall, and Kim lifted the lantern toward an exit door ahead. The exit sign that would normally be glowing bright red above it was out.

"I think the door should be unlocked. If not, I will see if James has a pry bar or hammer," Kim said.

"I'd like to see if he has a pair of bolt cutters too. I need to break one of these padlocks. I think it would be best if Cayden and I found our own locker to stay in. That should ease some tension between the two of you," Will said.

Kim said nothing.

Will stopped and listened before reaching for the knob and pulling open the door. He heard nothing concerning. The stairway leading to the roof was dark. He could hear the wind howling through a crack in the exit above them.

"Here," Kim said, handing him the lantern.

He took it and illuminated the door then climbed the stairs and pushed. The wind against it made it difficult to open. The sky was getting dark. It was hard to tell what time of day it was. It had to be close to seven o'clock so the sun would be setting. It would be impossible to see the cloud cover. Lightning off in the distance told him that the outer bands of the hurricane had arrived. The light rain was now steady and driven sideways by the wind. As he closed the door, he was relieved to know that they had a way out. When he turned, Kim wasn't there.

"Where is it?" a male voice said in a thick Asian accent.

Will raced down the stairs. Kim was nowhere to be seen. She said something, but Will couldn't make out the words.

"Kim," Will said.

There was a faint light at the end of the hall. Will followed it. When he reached the intersection, the light had disappeared. He stopped and listened, hearing nothing.

"Kim," he called again.

No reply.

Will turned and walked back to Betley's unit. He was seated at the table reading something, but Kim wasn't there.

"Did Kim come back here?" Will asked him.

"No," Betley said, looking up from the papers in front of him.

He straightened them and shoved them back into Kim's duffle. As he did, Will glanced inside. He was shocked to see bundles of cash. He couldn't make out their denomination, but it was a lot of money even if they were all ones. What was Kim doing walking around with that much cash? Betley hurried to zip it and shoved it back under the table.

"We were checking out the door to the roof, and she just disappeared on me. I thought I heard her talking to you."

Betley pushed back his chair and stood. "I'll go check on her."

Will handed him the flashlight and watched him walk down the hall. A second later, gunshots reverberated through the space. Will ran to Cayden and Isabella.

"Get up. We have to go."

"What is it?" Isabella asked.

"Gunshots," Will said, pulling Cayden to his feet.

"Where's Kim?" Isabella asked.

"I don't know. Hurry, we need to get out of here."

"But what about Kim?" Isabella asked.

"I don't know, Isabella. You are welcome to stay here and wait for her, but I'm getting Cayden away now," Will said, approaching the door.

He stopped in the doorway and peered down the hall. It was dark. He cupped the smaller of the two flashlights in the palm of his hand to partially illuminate the space hopefully without giving up their location.

He reached and took Cayden's hand. "Stay close to the walls." And the two stepped into the corridor.

Will made his way back to where the hall connected to another and turned left, away from where he'd seen the light earlier. As they hugged the wall, Will stopped at each door, checking the lock. When they came to a unit that didn't have one, Will stopped. Isabella plowed into Cayden, knocking him into Will. She yelped.

"Shh! We are trying not to get shot here," Will spat.

He turned and felt for the handle. He tugged, and the roll-up door inched up.

"Yes!" he said, pulling it all the way open.

"Get inside." Will tapped Cayden on the shoulder.

"It's dark in there," Isabella said.

"It's dark out here," Will replied, giving her a little shove.

He rolled down the door and hugged the wall, straining to hear if anyone had followed them then flicked off the light and continued to listen.

"What are we going to do now?" Isabella asked.

"Wait," Will said.

"Wait for what?"

"I don't know, Isabella. All I know is that something very strange is going on here, and I don't want my son caught in the middle of it."

No one spoke for a moment. Will pressed his ear against the door and listened. He heard nothing. There were no voices and no more gunfire.

"You didn't have to take her head off like that, you know," Cayden whispered.

"Well, I'm sorry. I'm a little stressed after having shots fired near us for the third time today. Things are a little intense at the moment."

"It sounds like you're making excuses," Cayden said.

Will bit down on his bottom lip. He knew he'd been short with Isabella, but he just couldn't take her questioning. He inhaled deeply and let it out then turned and put his back to the door. Isabella was right. The storage locker was pitch black. He couldn't see his hand in front of his face.

"I'm sorry that I snapped at you. Please forgive me," Will said, trying to sound sincere. He knew that if he didn't, Cayden would likely call him out on that as well.

"I accept your apology," Isabella said.

"Um—Dad, shouldn't we have brought the dolly? We don't have anything to drink now, and I'm really thirsty."

"Shit!" Will said, turning back to the door. "Stay here. Don't open this door until I get back."

Will listened for a moment before slowly rolling the door up enough to slip out into the hall. He gently rolled it down and hurried back to Betley's unit. He had just grabbed the handle of the dolly and started down the hall when he heard voices. Will froze in the middle of the corridor.

"I am telling you, the duffle is gone. They must have taken it. Find them. Now!"

Will wasn't sure who "them" was, but he wasn't sticking around to find out. He raced back to the empty unit.

"It's me," he whispered as he rolled up the door.

"Yay!" Cayden said.

"Shh. They'll hear you. Get inside," Will said.

After shoving the dolly into the unit, Will slowly lowered the door. Every cell in his body was on high alert. When he heard the sound of a door being quickly rolled up, Will jumped.

"What are they doing?" Isabella asked.

"They're looking for someone," Will said.

"Who is? Kim and Betley?"

"I don't know. Maybe. I couldn't tell for sure."

"Who are they looking for?" Cayden asked.

"Whoever stole Kim's duffle," Will said.

"What? When did that happen?" Cayden said. "Betley had it right before he went looking for Kim."

"Um... Will. I have a confession to make," Isabella said.

Will felt his blood pressure rising. "Tell me you did not take Kim's duffle."

"I didn't want it to get stolen. There was no one there to guard it, and I know it is very important to Kim."

"Why don't we just take it back to her and explain. She won't be mad," Cayden said.

Cayden pulled the door up, and light from a flashlight's beam flooded the space.

TWENTY-TWO

Savanah

DAY TWO

As Savanah hid behind sports equipment in the garage, the homeowners had decided to have a barbecue and invite all the neighbors. The laughter had died down sometime just before sunrise. There'd been no indication that Derek and Wade were still lurking outside, but Savanah waited until the sun came up to poke her head out of the garage. Beer bottles and cigarette butts littered the ground around a fire ring in the backyard, but the partygoers had all gone home.

As late as they'd stayed up, she wasn't too concerned about being spotted by the homeowners. Her plan was to run back up the drive, follow the road back out to the highway, and race home. By now, her kids would be worried sick that she hadn't come home all night.

She started around the side of the house and stopped in her tracks when she heard voices. She didn't even wait to see if it was Derek and Wade. Savanah bolted around to the back of the house and was headed back to the garage door, but the sun glinting off the boat caught her eye. Pivoting back to the canal, Savanah ran toward the boat. Beside it, upside down in the tall grass lining the canal, was a kayak. She didn't even think twice before upturning the vessel and shoving it into the water. She ran back, grabbed the oar, and jumped into the kayak. She used the boat oar to push herself away for the shore and paddled down the canal as if her life depended on it.

At the first bridge over the canal, Savanah abandoned the kayak. She needed to go east, and the channel only took her farther south toward the Intercoastal Water Way. Twenty minutes later, after passing over the highway without any sign of Derek or Wade, Savanah felt confident that she wasn't being followed. But she wasn't relieved. They knew where she lived and they'd show up there sooner or later. She'd only delayed her troubles with them.

With the cars not working and Thibodeau wanting them to secure things in town, maybe she had a day or two before she'd have to deal with them. Perhaps by then, they would have forgotten about her—and the gun. It was wishful thinking, she knew.

As she walked, Savanah thought more about using the time to get her children and leave Calcasieu Parish. If they found a boat, they could be in Cameron Parish in an hour or so. But then what? She didn't have anywhere to stay there. She did have a little money saved up, but not enough to get reestablished somewhere else.

Her thoughts kept going to her brother. She knew that if she told Will what had been going on, he'd help her. She regretted keeping it from him all these years. At first, she'd been too ashamed. She'd feared he'd want her to turn them in, to testify against them in court, and knew she could never return to Louisiana if she did that. You can be a lot of things down in the bayou, but being a snitch could get you killed.

She was walking with her head down, struggling to come up with a solution when she heard the sound of an engine approaching. She stepped to the side of the two-lane road and listened. Of course, her immediate thought was that Derek and Wade were coming for her. When the two all-terrain vehicles rounded the corner and came into view, Savanah was relieved to see two teenaged boys. They accelerated toward her looking as though they were going to hit her. She stepped back off the roadway, and the ATVs came to a stop in front of her.

The shorter of the two removed his helmet. His long hair stuck up for a moment before falling across his face. He swiped it from his eyes and flashed a disarming smile. "Hey, you're Kendra Fontenot's mom, aren't you?"

Savanah didn't know the kid. She figured he must have known her daughter from before when she'd attended public school. "I am. I'm surprised to see those things still run," she said, pointing to the four-wheeled all-terrain vehicles.

"Yeah, they're the only thing running, I think. My dad's Tesla wouldn't start," one of the kids said.

She stepped back onto the roadway. "You boys, be careful," she pointed to his helmet. "Even wearing a helmet, you could get seriously hurt driving as fast as you two were."

The second, taller kid gave her the dismissive teen look.

"Okay. Have a nice day," Savanah said, turning to continue home.

"Hey, lady. What's in the pack?" the taller kid asked.

She cringed a little. It was none of the boy's business what was in her bag. It was rude for him to even ask. She thought about giving him the same answer she'd given Wade, but that hadn't ended well. She needed to get rid of these kids. They sounded bored and may be looking for trouble. She was suddenly very aware that she was alone and without her pistol. She slowly moved her right hand to her belt and looped her thumb inside the pocket, trying to make the movement look as natural as possible. She needed to be ready to shove her hand inside and retrieve her knife. Even though they were kids, they were both bigger than her, and the two of them might be able to restrain her.

"Just some junk from my car. Some books, toys for my kids. I didn't know how long it would be before I could get my van running again. I didn't want to leave personal items inside," Savanah said.

"Can we have a look?" the older boy asked.

Savanah thought maybe it was time for the mom voice. It was worth a try.

"Absolutely not. That's rude. Didn't your parents teach you to use your manners? You boys need to get on home."

The kid laughed and turned off the engine. When he threw his leg over the machine, Savanah's heart dropped. She shoved her hand into her pocket and pulled her knife. She flicked it open, squared her stance, and held it out in front of her. The boy's eyes bored into her. She did not want to hurt the kid. She didn't want that on her conscience, but she had four kids relying on her to make it home. She wasn't going to let this snot-nose brat keep her from reaching her kids.

"You best get back on those things and get the hell out of here. My father-in-law is the mayor. You mess with me, and there will be hell to pay," Savanah said.

She'd hoped that might convince him to back down. It didn't.

He snorted. "That old man ain't gonna do shit to us. His kid ain't even with you anymore."

The boy kept coming. Savanah took two steps back. She wanted to turn and run, but they had the ATVs. They could run her down with ease.

"What the hell are you boys doing?" a familiar voice yelled behind her. Savanah wanted to burst into tears.

"We ain't doing nothing. We were just talking to the lady," the boy said.

His brother was already shoving his helmet back down over his head. As Savanah turned to face Jason, the older boy ran back to his ATV. Jason hurried toward her, and she heard the kid's engine rev to life. A second later, the two raced past Savanah and Jason.

"You okay?"

"I'm fine. They were just trying to scare me, I think," Savanah said.

"They're those rich kids from the gated community. They've been tearing up and down the road harassing people all day," Jason said.

"Nothing better to do. That kind of boredom might get them in deep trouble. They'll mess with the wrong person, sooner or later," Savanah said.

"Did your van die too?"

"Yep. Is it happening out here as well?"

"Yeah. I was just going to head into town and see what people have heard," Jason said.

"As far as I know, they're clueless. Thibodeau hasn't heard anything from the state or Calcasieu Parish."

"You want a ride home?" Jason asked.

"Your truck is running?" Savanah asked.

"My old Ford is. I had to change out a couple of parts, then she started right up."

"That would be awesome. I'd love a ride. I'm worried about the kids," Savanah said.

They cut through yards to reach Jason's house. He rented a room above a garage in exchange for manual labor. He was thirty-eight years old and starting over from scratch after breaking ties with his family. He'd done a stint in jail in Texas which had been his wake-up call. His family's connections didn't reach everywhere. Sooner or later, he'd end up in prison or dead. That was the fate he had to look forward to if he continued in the family's drug business. Savanah was proud of him for making a clean break. Starting over with nothing and no real work history was difficult. He'd struggled, but hadn't given up and returned to his old way of life.

No Way Out

Jason held the pickup's passenger door open for her. She threw her pack in the back and climbed in. As they started to pull out of the driveway, a bright red truck with half a dozen people in the bed screeched to a stop in front of them.

"Where you guys tearing off to?" Jason said, poking his head out of the driver's side window.

"We're trying to run down those rich kids that live down at that gated subdivision. They've been robbing people blind. Now, with the lights off and the home alarms not working, they think they can just waltz in and take what they want," the man in the passenger seat said.

"You think it's those two kids I ran into?" Savanah said.

"No, I don't think so. I saw four of them running like a bat out of hell past here a couple of hours ago. They had their back rack loaded down with stuff. One of them hit a pothole in the road and lost a bag of groceries. There were half a dozen steaks and some chicken breasts in there."

"Last I saw them, they were heading east, back toward their gated community."

"Well, we're about to go pay their mommies and daddies a little visit," the man said. He made a chopping motion with his hand, and the truck sped off.

"I don't know if that is going to end well. Those boys look pissed off," Savanah said.

"You should be careful, Savanah. Things are liable to get crazy before they get back to normal."

"Speaking of that," Savanah said as Jason pulled out of the driveway, "what do you think is going on with everything not working? And why have just some of the vehicles stopped working?"

"I have no earthly idea. All I know is this ain't good."

TWENTY-THREE

Will

DAY TWO

Before his eyes could even adjust to the flash light's beam, Will knew they were in trouble. He stepped in front of Cayden and held the broom handle out in front of him. He'd be no match for a gun, but it was all he had.

Three men stood behind Kim.

"Get the bag," one of the men said.

An Asian man in a white wife-beater shirt and gold chains stood in the doorway, a black jacket draped over his shoulder. In his hand, he held a pistol.

"I'm sorry. I wasn't trying to steal it. You were gone, and there was no one there to watch it. I didn't want to leave it unattended," Isabella said.

Kim took the duffle from Isabella, opened it, and examined its contents. Her head whipped up, and Kim stared Isabella down. She took a step closer.

"Where is it?" Kim asked through gritted teeth.

"Where is what?" Isabella asked, wide eyed.

Will slowly took a step back toward the door.

"Do not play dumb. I want it now. These men are not patient people," Kim said.

"Really, Kim. I don't know what you're talking about. I didn't take anything," Isabella was near tears now.

"I want it back now," Kim said as she grabbed Isabella by the hair.

"She said she didn't take it," Cayden said, trying to step out from behind Will.

"Quiet, Cayden," Will said.

Will took a step toward them, but the man thrust a pistol in his face.

"I swear. I didn't take anything out of the bag," Isabella said as Kim dragged her toward the corridor.

Cayden picked up a canned energy drink and threw it at Kim, hitting her in the back and causing her to release her grip on Isabella. Isabella broke free and bolted down the hall disappearing into the blackness. Kim and the men sprinted after her, leaving Will and Cayden behind.

"Dad!" Cayden yelled. "Do something."

As much as he wanted to help Isabella, he was helpless against a man with a gun. If he had attempted to stop them, he could have gotten Cayden killed. If only Isabella hadn't taken the duffle.

"There's nothing we can do right now, Cayden. I'm sorry."

"No, you're not. You don't like her, so you won't help her."

His accusation stung.

"The man has a gun. What do you want me to do, hit him with my stick?" Will asked.

Will spun around and felt for the handle of the dolly. "Take hold of my belt."

"Why?"

"Just do it, Cayden."

He felt Cayden's fingers tug on his belt loop.

"Okay. We have to go before they come back."

"Come back?" Cayden asked.

"Yeah, when they search Isabella and don't find what they're looking for, they're coming after us."

Will and Cayden pulled the dolly down the hall back to the junction. A light came from Betley's unit. Will couldn't see anyone. His gut clenched. As much as Isabella got on his nerves, he didn't want anything to happen to her. The image of Kim staring down at the man in the street as she pulled the trigger, ending his life, made Will shudder. If only he had a real weapon. If only he'd had his pistol on his hip instead of locked away in the glove box of the Jeep. He knew better. He'd just gotten too complacent. He hoped to God that it didn't cost Isabella her life.

"We have to do something, Dad. We can't let them kill, Isabella. Please, Dad. Do something."

Will headed toward the stairs. He decided to leave the dolly and take only what they could carry. Kim and the others were bound to hear the cart thumping down the stairs. There was no way they were going to let them walk away. Not without finding whatever it was they believed had been stolen from Kim's duffle bag.

As Will pulled back the door to the stairs, he chastised himself for not trusting his instincts about Kim. He'd known something was off about the woman. Why had he allowed her anywhere near his son? He didn't know what kind of mess she'd gotten herself wrapped up in, and frankly, he couldn't care less. All he cared about in the world was getting Cayden away from there as fast as possible.

"You aren't going to help her?" Cayden said, standing defiantly at the top of the stairs.

Will picked up the emergency car kit.

"Grab a box of those energy drinks."

"No! We have to do something. I'm going to do something if you don't."

Will reached out and grabbed Cayden's arm. "And just what the hell are you going to do besides stop a bullet. Think, Cayden. Think. We are no help to anyone dead. Now, help me get this stuff downstairs, and then I'll tell you about my plan."

No Way Out

~

On the second floor, Will found a similarly configured layout of storage units. There were no windows. Will hoped it was high enough from the ground to not flood. He located the back stairs to the roof and let out a sigh of relief. At least they wouldn't be trapped.

"Check all the doors on that side," Will said, pulling on each of the roll-up doors along the corridor. In the back corner, he finally located an unlocked unit.

After putting his armload of food on the floor, Will slowly lowered the door. He placed the flashlight on the stack of food and turned to Cayden.

"Okay. You are going to stay here and guard our stash." Will opened the automotive emergency kit and pulled out the flare gun.

"What are you going to do?"

"I'm going to find Isabella."

Cayden pointed at the flare gun. "What are you going to do with that?"

"It will do some damage at close range. It might buy us time to get away."

"That sounds dangerous," Cayden said.

"I might just use it as a diversion."

"And you think they're going to fall for that?"

"I sure hope so, it's all I got."

"Good luck," Cayden said as Will rolled up the door.

"I'm going to leave one of the flashlights here for you, but you should leave it off until I get back. It might shine under the door and make it easier for them to find you," Will said. Cayden moved toward him. "I love you, son. I'm proud of you, you know."

Cayden nodded. As Will rolled the door closed, Cayden called to him, "Dad."

Will stopped.

"Be careful." Cayden sounded scared.

"I will," Will said. "Don't…"

Cayden interrupted him. "I know. Don't open the door to anyone but you."

Will climbed the stairs slowly, trying not to make any noise. He stopped at the door and listened, but heard nothing then pushed back the door and looked for light. He saw none. He listened again. Will thought he heard crying, but it was faint, maybe muffled. But the wind had picked up outside, and it could have been that.

He flicked on the light only long enough to scan the corridor then turned it off and moved along the wall to the first intersecting hall. He stopped and listened. He heard sniffling. It had to be Isabella. But where was she? The sound echoed in the space, and it was hard to tell which direction it was coming from. He was afraid to call out to her for fear that Kim and the man with the gun would hear him.

Will traversed the hall and pressed himself against one of the doors. He flicked on the light and swept it down the corridor to his right. He saw nothing. Will turned it back off and stepped into the hall. When he did, he felt a hand grab his arm and yank him back. Another hand wrapped around his head and covered his mouth.

Betley released him and shone a tiny pin light on the badge he held in his hand.

"Don't make a sound. They'll hear you. I'm an FBI agent and I need your help."

TWENTY-FOUR

Savanah

DAY TWO

Savanah hit the door full speed and didn't stop until she reached the gun safe in the back of her closet.

"Mom, what's going on?" Kendra asked.

Savanah spun around, grabbing Kendra in an embrace and hugging her tight.

"Mom? You're scaring me."

Savanah released her daughter and returned her attention to the gun safe. She punched in the code and pulled on the handle. As she reached in and grabbed her purple camo print AR-15 and two thirty-round magazines, Keegan and Kylie entered the bedroom.

Savanah tossed the weapon and ammo onto her queen-sized bed and turned to her children.

"Where's Karson?"

"The pigs got out again. We rounded them up and put them in one of the stalls in the barn. He's trying to fix the fence where they dug under," Kendra said.

"Kylie, run and get your brother. Tell him to come right now," Savanah said as she picked up the rifle and loaded the magazine.

"Mom, are you going to tell us what's going on? Where have

you been all night? We were just about to come looking for you," Kendra said.

Savanah lifted the strap of the rifle's sling over her head and reached for her daughter. "I'm sorry I worried you. I don't mean to scare you, but we need to talk about that later. Right now, we need to get ready?"

"Ready for what?" Kendra asked, her eyes wide with fear.

Savanah turned, reached into the safe, and held a rifle out to Kendra. "To defend the farm."

"From what? Mom, please stop treating me like a kid and tell me what the hell is going on."

Savanah stopped what she was doing and stared at her daughter. She knew she should chastise her for cursing at her, but she suddenly looked so grown up standing there with her fists at her sides.

"Sit down. You too, Keegan."

Keegan crawled onto Savanah's bed, sat cross-legged, and placed his elbows on his knees. He didn't look the least bit worried. He was her carefree child. Nothing ever seemed to bother him, unlike Kylie. Savanah took a seat next to her daughter and pulled Keegan into her lap. A second later, she heard the screen door slam, and Karson and Kylie bounded into the room.

"What's wrong," were the first words out of Karson's mouth. "Kylie said you grabbed your rifle."

It had been wishful thinking that she'd been able to hide her fear from her children all this time. Even though she'd tried to make all the gun practice and bug out drills seem normal and fun, they hadn't bought it. How much did they know? How much did they suspect?

"Something strange has happened. The lights are out all over town, and phones and cars aren't working. I'm not sure what's caused it, but people are freaking out. They're panicking, and fear makes people stupid—and dangerous."

"What did you see out there?" Karson asked.

"Where were you, Mommy? Karson had to tuck us in last night, and then you weren't here this morning to cook us breakfast," Kylie asked.

Savanah smiled at Karson. She knew she could count on him and Kendra to take care of the little ones. She reached over and slid a loose strand of long brown hair behind Kylie's ear.

"My car wouldn't start. I had to walk home," she said.

"Oh. Karson wouldn't let me help him milk Sophie. I told him that you always let me milk Sophie after dinner," Kylie said.

Kylie was her dramatic child. Savanah patted Kylie's leg. "You can milk Sophie in a little while. Right now, though, we have things to talk about. Do you want to go color or do a puzzle while I have a little chat with your sister and brother?"

A huge grin spread across her face. "Are they in trouble?"

Savanah lowered her chin and narrowed her gaze. "Kylie, what have I said about that?"

"It is none of my beeswax," Kylie said, slipping down from the bed. Her princess slippers tapped on the floor as she walked toward the door.

"You want to go play too, Keegan?" Savanah asked.

He nodded. She lifted him from her lap and placed him on the floor. As he padded off to the living room, Savanah returned to the safe, removed a box of empty rifle magazines, and an ammo can full of rifle rounds.

"I have no idea what catastrophes have happened out there, but I know we need to be ready to defend our home. With the electricity off and no communication, people are scared. Jason thinks we might see trouble from that new subdivision down the road."

"Why?" Karson asked. "Why would they bother with us and our stuff? They have their big houses and fancy cars."

"Mom said cars don't work, stupid," Kendra said.

"Kendra," Savanah scolded.

"Remember that run-in Jason had with those boys in that truck after they thought they'd go mudding in our pasture?"

Karson nodded.

"But if the cars don't work," Karson glared at Kendra. "They can't tear up our fields."

"Jason said he saw them out on quads this morning. One of them had a boatload of groceries strapped to the back rack."

"So. They went shopping," Kendra said. "What's the big deal about them going to buy groceries."

"I doubt seriously that they bought them. At least not from the grocery store. It's closed. The police posted guards out in front to keep people from looting like they did during the hurricanes two years ago."

"So, we should be worried they might come here looking to steal stuff from us?" Karson asked.

"Them or someone like them, from what Jason says," Savanah said.

"Jason says," Kendra said, rolling her eyes.

"What? You have a problem with Jason now?" Savanah asked.

"No. Not really. It's just—"

"I don't have time for this right now. We'll have this conversation later. Right now, we need to get all the animals brought up and secured inside the barn. After that, we're going to start boarding up the windows."

Karson's eyes grew wide. "The windows? Why? Is the hurricane coming here?"

Her children were terrified of hurricanes after the double hit they'd taken with Hurricanes Laura and Delta.

"No. Not that I know of. It'll make it easier to defend the house. It won't be as easy for someone to break in," Savanah said. She reached out and tousled his hair. He was still so young, just a little boy really. This was too much to put on a ten-year-old.

"We live alone here. It's just us. We can't expect anyone to get here in time if we get into trouble," Savanah said.

"I'll go put the hogs back in the barn," Karson said, slinging his rifle over his back.

"I'll get the goats," Kendra said.

"Very good, guys. I'll get the cows, and we'll move the chickens together."

"Are you going to move their pens in the barn? I don't think they'll all fit," Kendra asked.

"The chicken tractors won't. But it'll make it easier to move them in and out if we move their pens all up next to the barn," Savanah said.

Karson stopped in the doorway. "Mom, how are we going to stop someone from breaking in the barn?"

"I'll have to sleep out there, Karson."

"In the barn?" Kendra asked.

"Not in the barn. In the outdoor kitchen."

Since she spent so much of her time making soap and herbal remedies, she'd hired Jason to build her an outdoor kitchen. It was more like a screened-in pavilion with a dirt floor and plywood that hinged down when it rained.

"After we get all the animals squared away, we'll need to move the stuff in the pantry into the secret room."

The door to the room was hidden behind one of the shelves in the pantry. The shelves there held their long-term storage food items. It was also where they'd hidden when the hurricanes ripped through and the mayor wouldn't allow her to evacuate with the rest of the area's residents. They'd survived. The old house stood proud and only lost a few shingles but the old oak in the front yard had been blown over and barely missed their home. Savanah had been sad to see it fall. There had been so many memories under its canopy.

"Okay. You two get started, I'm right behind you," Savanah said, pushing her tired body off the bed. She was barely thirty-one years old, but today, she felt ancient.

Savanah glanced out the big front room windows as Jason

exited his truck and made his way up the walk. *Why had he come back?*

"What are you doing here?" Kendra said from the door.

"I came to help."

TWENTY-FIVE

Will

DAY TWO

"What the hell is going on here?" Will whispered. "What has Kim pulled us into?"

"I don't have time to explain everything to you right now. I need to get this out of here." Agent Betley held up a tiny flash drive and a folder of papers.

"What's on it? Will asked pointing to the storage device.

"I believe it contains names and locations."

"I'd love to help you, but those assholes have guns. I have a kid."

"None of us are getting out of here alive if we don't take them out first," Betley said as he reached behind his back and produced a pistol. Will stiffened and stepped back.

Betley handed it to Will. "Here, now you have a gun too. There's one in the chamber."

Will wasted no time dropping the magazine on the pistol and counting the rounds. It wasn't the Dan Wesson 1911 that he carried, but he liked the 9mm Glock 19 too.

"What's the plan?" Will asked.

Betley pulled him toward a storage unit and pointed at a wall of shelves. "We take those sons of bitches out."

Will stepped inside, and Betley slowly rolled down the door. He shone the light on an open black case containing a Holt M4 Carbine rifle.

"First, you need to tell me what you are doing with storage units filled with food and weapons," Will said.

"Just being prepared," Betley said.

"For what? War?" Will asked, eyeing all the boxes of ammunition.

"Yes," Betley said.

Will stared at him, unblinking. "Really?"

"I've been concerned about something like this happening."

Will leaned back against the wall to steady himself. Had Cayden's suspicions been right? Was a foreign government to blame for all the technology not working?

"So, it was an attack of some kind?" Will asked.

"I'm afraid so," Betley said as he picked up an M4 rifle and slung the strap over his head.

"My God." Will felt like the breath had been sucked out of his lungs.

Fear yanked hold of his insides. He thought he might puke. What did that mean for the country?

"What's going to happen now? Invasion?"

"Maybe. Maybe not," Betley said.

Will thought of the attack on Pearl Harbor and the bombing of an oilfield near Santa Barbara, California, during World War II. Both attacks led to widespread panic and talk of invasion by enemy forces, but that had never happened.

"With what they've done to us, they won't need to invade to control us. They've brought the most powerful country in the world to its knees. In a few weeks, when all the food runs out, and people are starving, they will have us right where they want us. People will do anything for a bite of bread at that point," Betley continued.

Will shook his head. It was too much to take in. His mind

wanted to reject it. But how else could he explain what was happening? Aliens?

"How do we stop them?"

"We can't. They've already done it. All we can do now is survive and live to fight another day," Betley said.

"I can't accept that. You're telling me there is nothing that our government can do?"

"Right now, our government is crippled by the lack of communication and transportation. If it can't move and communicate, it cannot direct resources where they're needed. They will try and may even succeed on a limited basis and where supplies have been pre-positioned."

Betley picked up a pair of night-vision goggles and stared at them for a moment before discarding them back in the box.

"Can't we use those?"

"No. They were destroyed by the EMP," Betley said.

"The what?" Will asked.

"An electromagnetic pulse. A nuclear explosion high in the atmosphere. It produced two hundred volts per meter EMP. It would destroy anything electronic; computers, phones, the power grid," Betley said.

"Destroy? As in never working again?" Will was unable to wrap his mind around the prospect of all this being permanent. He'd imagined some sort of large-scale jamming device, not total destruction.

"Yes, destroyed. A high-altitude nuke detonated above the center of the United States would cause an EMP field that would cover the US, most of Canada, and Mexico, knocking out the Texas electric grid and both the east and west power grids. The Canadian and Mexican grids will have collapsed as well. Anything electronic, including components required for most modern vehicles to run, will be inoperable."

Will leaned against the wall and ran his hand over his close-cropped hair, trying to comprehend the ramifications of such a thing. He knew how long it had taken to recover after the destruction caused by hurricanes. Sometimes, it could take weeks, even months, to get power restored. It took almost eleven months to restore power to the people of Puerto Rico after Hurricane Maria. The cleanup and rebuilding of all the buildings and homes ripped apart or flooded could take years. But this, how long would it take to replace everything destroyed by an EMP?

"And you believe that's what happened? An EMP wiped out everything?"

"I believe so, yes," Betley said.

Will felt sick. The fact that there may be no recovering from this heinous attack was unfathomable. It made the threat caused by the incoming hurricane pale in comparison, even though it was an imminent danger.

"Does this mean that the power will be off indefinitely?" Will asked.

"For a very long time. The enormous transformers designed to carry hundreds of thousands of volts were melted by the EMP."

"If you knew this was going to happen, why didn't you tell someone? Why didn't you stop them?" Will asked through clenched teeth.

"Our government has known of the threat for many years. They even formed an EMP Commission to assess it. As with most things, it moved too slowly. While the commission conducted research, Russia, China, Iran, and North Korea created weapons capable of delivering an E1 EMP field of two hundred thousand volts per meter capable of devastating even EMP resistant infrastructures and communications. Even hardened United States military systems are vulnerable to such a threat," Betley said.

"How do you know this?"

"We learned that something big was coming. There has been a huge influx of Chinese nationals being moved across our border with Mexico. We were trying to find out why. I think we now have the answer."

"Ground forces?" Will asked.

He felt his insides twist and crouched with his back against the wall, resting his elbows on his knees. He rubbed the barrel of the pistol across his forehead as he envisioned what a ground invasion from the Chinese Communist Party's million-man army would be like with the US Military's technology devastated. Without them, what hope would the population have?

"Not enough personnel for a military attack, no. We'd notice that amount of movement," Betley said.

"Who then?" Will asked.

"Technicians and engineers."

"Why? That doesn't make any sense. They knock out our power grid and wipe out our communications and transportation and then, what, rebuild them after?" Will asked.

None of this made sense. Sure, tensions had been high between the two countries of late. The trade war was taking a toll on the Chinese economy. The United States had imposed tariffs and made efforts to bring manufacturing jobs back to the country, especially medical supplies and medications following the deadly pandemic China had unleashed upon the world. Lately, the news had been that there were increased tensions over China's takeover of the South China Sea and skirmishes with the US Navy. But this was over the top. He'd never really thought anyone would attack them like this.

"It makes perfect sense. The CCP wants to be the world's only superpower. An EMP neutralizes the government and military capabilities of the United States, leaving it powerless to stop them from exerting global power," Betley said.

"I can't believe this. I can't accept this. This cannot be happening," Will said as he shoved the pistol in the back waistband of his jeans.

A gust of wind blew something into one of the windows downstairs, reminding Will of the ticking clock. It was only a matter of hours before they'd be trapped inside with Kim and her crazy countrymen. Will wanted to take the time to analyze everything he'd just learned, to form a long-range plan that would ensure their survival past escaping the hurricane. They needed somehow to stop whatever the enemy was planning following their EMP attack.

"You said you thought the thumb drive contained names. Are you saying they are the names of the technicians and engineers?" Will asked.

"Not just them, but the network, including allied officials in our government," Betley said.

"Allied officials? Are you claiming that someone in our government is involved in this?" Will's head was about to explode. He shut his eyes and fought back a boiling rage. He wanted to believe that Betley was lying—about everything—but somehow, in his gut, he knew what Betley was saying had a ring of truth.

"It's only a guess on my part. Without being able to see what is on it, I can't be sure. But if those guys want it badly enough to be out here in the middle of a hurricane to get it back, I'd say there's something of great significance on it. Since there's no way for me to boot up a computer to check it out, I need to get to Kim and force her to tell me. I'll know what to do with it after that."

Will thought of Cayden. He'd been through hell with losing his mother, and now this. As much as Will wanted to go play hero and be a part of saving the world, his obligation was to his son. Being involved with Betley put Cayden at risk. Very dangerous people wanted what was on that thumb drive. They no doubt would be willing to do anything to get it, including killing a child.

"I can't risk Cayden's safety to help you find out what is on that thing."

"I understand. I'm not asking you to help me capture Kim. I can handle that on my own." Betley grabbed a bullet-proof vest from one of the shelves and slid it over his head.

"But wait, you said you suspected something like this. Wouldn't our government have prepared? Would they have done something to at least protect government vehicles and communications?" Will asked.

"Of course. They've been doing that for decades. They formed congressional commissions, task forces, assigned personnel to study and implement preparedness and mitigation plans. But we've hardened our infrastructure and equipment for a fifty volts per meter EMP blast, not two hundred volts and not multiple attacks."

Will balled his hands into fists. Rage mingled with fear. "I don't know what to do."

"Right now. We need to survive this. Kim messed up, and she brought the Chinese mafia down on us. She took something that they desperately want back. She thought she was so smart, and she could leverage it with the FBI for a new identity and citizenship papers."

"I thought she was working with the Chinese," Will said.

"She is. Kim was involved in the Chinese government's theft of United States technological secrets. She's stolen millions of dollars in trade secrets for the Communist Party," Betley said.

"Why is the mafia after her then?"

"The Chinese mafia works for the Communist Party. They are the enforcers when they can't, or choose not to, use their military or law enforcement. Over here, they can't very well go after people with their own forces so they utilize organized crime elements to do their bidding."

"This freaking sucks. I cannot believe I got my son involved in this mess," Will said. He ran a hand across his forehead and scratched his scalp. "So, what do we do now?"

"First, we find your friend before they do. If they locate her and don't find what they're looking for, they'll kill her," Betley said, handing Will two spare magazines for the pistol.

"Shit!" Will said

Betley gently rolled the door open, scanning the hallway as he did, before stepping out into the corridor. "Let's find your girlfriend."

"She's not my girlfriend. We just met today," Will said.

"Um," Betley said. A huge smile spread across his face. "You won't mind if I ask her out then."

Reluctantly, Will followed Betley back up to the third floor. As they crept along the wall toward the end of the long hallway, Will thought about how odd it was that the guy could joke at a time like this. He'd known people that became comedians when they were nervous. Will hoped this FBI agent wasn't one of those people. He wasn't in the mood for levity.

Betley stopped and pulled on the handles to each of the units. "You try the ones on that side. She has to be here somewhere."

Will found an unlocked door at the end of the corridor. "Here's one."

Betley rushed over. "Call her name," he whispered. "She'll recognize your voice."

Will whispered her name and waited, listening for her reply. None came. What he did hear was the wind howling through cracks in the door downstairs as well as any other opening in the building. He dreaded being trapped in the storage facility and hunted by the Chinese mafia while the world outside was being ripped apart by the storm.

He'd lost his roof in Hurricane Rita. It was terrifying to listen hour after hour to the hundred-and-twenty-mile an hour winds rip apart his home. He'd thought he was a tough guy. He'd chosen to stay and ride out the storm. He'd invited a friend over and they'd partied as Rita made her way toward the coast. At twenty years old, he'd thought he was invincible right up until the moment his roof disintegrated above him. He'd been shielding Melanie with his own body for hours, listening to her cry, and curse at him for not evacuating. They'd survived, but their home was destroyed.

"I don't think she's in there," Will said.

"Let's keep looking. We'll try the next row," Betley said, moving toward the next corridor.

Again, they tried every door. Nothing.

"What if she made it outside already?" Will asked.

"I guess that's possible. Let's finish checking the next row."

At the next unlocked unit, Will eased up the door partway. He thought he heard a sound coming from inside, but he couldn't be sure with all the noise from the storm. "Betley," Will whispered. "I might have something."

Betley stood to one side with his flashlight and pistol raised. Will yanked up the door. It made too much noise. He cringed and looked over his shoulder. When he glanced back around, Isabella's frightened eyes greeted him. She was crouched in one corner with her hands up, guarding her face. Betley lowered the flashlight.

"It's me, Isabella. It's Will."

Isabella launched herself in the air and flew into his arms.

"Oh, thank God. I was so scared. Let's get out of here before she finds me," Isabella said through tears.

"We can't leave just yet," Will said.

"Why? We have to go. They have guns. They'll shoot me." Isabella was trembling so much Will had to hold her up.

"The storm is coming in. The winds have picked up. It's too dangerous to travel out there now," Will said, taking her hand. He wondered which was more dangerous, the Chinese mafia or the storm. He needed to get to the roof and check it out. He hated not having his phone or weather radio to check the radar and get updates from the National Hurricane Center. They could have minutes or hours. There was no way of knowing. The storm could send in outer bands for hours before the eye made landfall.

"What are we going to do?" Isabella turned to Betley. She gasped at the sight of the weapon at his side.

"He's with the FBI," Will said.

"What?" Isabella asked, her shock evident in her tone.

"He's an FBI agent."

Isabella tilted her head to the side. "I don't understand."

"We don't have time for this," Betley said, turning in the opposite direction.

"I'm going to take you down to the second floor. You can stay there with Cayden."

"Where are you going?" Isabella asked.

"I have to help Betley find Kim," Will said, leading her toward the stairs.

"And then what? It's too dangerous. Why can't Betley just call for backup?" Isabella asked.

When they reached the stairs, Will pushed open the door.

"The phones aren't working, remember?"

Isabella stepped into the stairway and turned. "But doesn't he have some official radio or anything to call for help?"

"I guess not."

"Cayden is in unit two-four-one," Will said as he started to close the door.

"What if you get killed?" Isabella asked.

Will stopped and stared back at her. It was something he'd thought an awful lot about. Not just since all this began, but ever since he'd lost his wife. It changed how he went about things. He took fewer chances. He avoided the interstates and most of the highways, not just because Houston drivers were notoriously bad drivers, but also because of the increased road rage cases lately. He avoided areas of town that might have higher crime rates. He got his yearly check-ups. He exercised and changed his diet. He did whatever he could not to leave his son an orphan.

He thought of Savanah and her children. If Betley was right and this thing extended across the country, then his sister and her four children would be affected. She's prepared, Will told himself. She'll make it.

"I won't get killed," Will said. He wanted to say to look after his son if he didn't come back, but he couldn't think like that.

"Let's go, Will," Betley called.

Isabella started down the stairs.

"Isabella, wait." Will ran down to meet her. "Here," he said, holding out the pistol Betley had given him.

Isabella took it and racked the slide. Will's mouth fell open.

"What? I'm from Oklahoma. I know how to shoot a gun."

He reached into his back pocket and retrieved the spare magazine, handing it to her. He wanted to say something, but words weren't his thing.

"Be safe, Will. Don't play the hero," Isabella said.

"I won't," Will replied.

She didn't have to worry about him playing a hero. He was far from it. But he would do whatever it took to protect his son. Will fought thinking about the future and the struggles they'd undoubtedly face in the days to come. He couldn't even allow himself to think about what life would look like without modern technology —or worse—under communist rule.

Will turned to face the FBI agent. "What now, Betley?"

Something crashed below them and echoed up the stairs. Will stepped into the corridor of the second floor. Isabella's flashlight illuminated Cayden's face. He hadn't followed Will's order to remain inside.

Again Will heard banging and cocked his head to listen.

"It's coming from the first floor," Betley said. "It's probably from the storm."

"I don't think so. That sounds like someone slamming down the roll-up doors to the units. They're searching for us down there."

"Smart. They're working their way up. Someone is guarding the exits. If they don't find us down there, they know we are trapped up here," Betley said.

"We *are* trapped up here then," Will said.

Betley racked the slide on his pistol. "Not for long."

TWENTY-SIX

Will

DAY TWO

"Damn, Betley. Were you preparing to take on the communists all by yourself?" Will asked as he stared down at the footlocker filled with ammunition.

Betley handed Will an AR-15 and four magazines of 5.56 NATO ammunition. Betley slung the strap of his Colt M4 Carbine rifle over his head and placed four extra thirty-round magazines into pouches on each side of his tactical vest. He grabbed a vest off a shelf and thrust it into Will's hands.

"Put this on," he said."

Will strapped the bullet-proof vest on and looked down at the extension covering his groin. He looked up and smiled.

"You gotta protect the family jewels," Betley said.

Betley stuffed more magazines into a pouch on his belt and slid a Springfield .45 caliber pistol into a holster on his thigh harness. He handed Will a tactical knife and an extra flashlight. He picked up a scope and then set it back down.

"That not work either?" Will asked.

"Fried, like everything else. My Faraday box didn't work. I was afraid of that. A super-EMP is just too strong," Betley said.

"If you have to come back here, the medical supplies are in this corner," Betley said, pointing to a tub labeled "medical supplies." He attached a medical pack to his belt and handed one to Will. It connects to the plate over your groin."

Will felt like he was preparing to go to war. Everything in him wanted to back out, to go and protect his kid. But he didn't. He wasn't sure why. He had no special skills to qualify him for this mission. He wasn't even sure why he trusted this guy. He could be some batshit crazy lunatic and not a federal agent at all. He could have got that badge on the internet along with all the weapons in that unit.

He almost had himself talked out of following the guy when he heard voices somewhere in the building. He stiffened and listened. Betley stopped too.

"Let's step out into the hall and get ready," Betley said, easing open the door.

Qualified or not, it looked like there was no backing out now. But Will's mind still wanted to remind him how absolutely crazy what he was about to do really was.

As if he'd read Will's mind, Betley patted Will on the shoulder. "Just follow my lead. You'll do fine."

Betley slipped around the corner and pressed his back against the wall. Will listened for a moment but heard nothing.

"You yank open the door to the stairs, and I'll clear it," Betley said.

Will pictured Betley opening his rifle on full auto and bodies tumbling down the stairs as he gripped the handle. He pulled hard and pressed his back against the wall as Betley jumped into the doorway.

"Clear," Betley whispered.

Will let out an audible sigh of relief and poked his head around the door to see for himself. The light from Betley's rifle illuminated the space, confirming it was clear of bad guys with guns.

Betley flicked off the light, and they waited in the dark, listening for movement in the stairway below them. Will heard only the howl of the wind. Betley briefly flicked on his light and then shut it off again.

"We're going to have to go down blacked out. I don't want them to see our light and know we're coming."

"Really?"

"Just hold onto the railing and go slow," Betley whispered. "I'll go first. Try to tread lightly and not make much noise."

"Okay," Will said.

He'd try, but he was sure that they'd be able to hear his heart beating all the way down on the first floor. *This is crazy. I'm no soldier or law enforcement officer.* He puffed out a breath and stepped down onto the first tread. *Surely they'd see the mafia guys' lights before they were fired upon, right?*

Will heard one of the unit's doors being opened and then closed, and then someone said something. A thought struck him. He hoped he never had to learn to speak Chinese.

When they passed the door leading to the second floor, Will realized that he and Betley were the only ones standing between Kim, her mafia enforcers, and his son. Whatever he did, he could not let those people get past him.

He heard his grandfather's voice in his head. "A man takes care of his family. If that means pulling the trigger, you want to be the last man standing."

He didn't want to be the last man standing. He needed Betley to make it too. He knew what was going on. Will knew he hadn't divulged all he knew about what was happening with the lights going out, but Will needed to learn all he could. It might make the difference between surviving this thing and not.

As they drew closer to the door to the first floor, the sounds grew louder. Will was struck by how the absence of light amplified his hearing. He could hear Betley breathing and the swish of his clothing as he moved though his footsteps were barely audible.

He'd done this before, Will was sure of it. He hoped he'd never have to do it again himself.

Just a few years ago, the old Will would have eaten this shit up. He'd been an adrenaline junkie and loved living on the edge. Even for a few years after Cayden was born, he'd street-raced his Ford Mustang and off-road raced his motorcycle. After breaking his leg crashing his bike, Melanie had been the one that had convinced him that he needed to stop taking such risks. She hadn't nagged him or anything like that, or even tried to guilt-trip him into stopping. No. In true Melanie fashion, she'd visited their life insurance agent and increased his policy to one million dollars. She said if she were going to be a widow in her twenties, she would be a wealthy widow. Will had told her that the policy wouldn't pay out if he died from crashing his bike. She'd flashed him her sweet and innocent smile and said, "This one will. You're just paying an extremely high premium." They'd kept that policy for several years after he'd quit until she was sure that he wasn't going to start back up again.

"We're at the door," Betley whispered.

Will listened but heard no sounds on the other side.

"Stand here," Betley said, reaching out a hand and patting Will on the shoulder. "You're going to open the door slowly at first. I'm going to check for lights and sound. Be ready. If I see anything, I'll have you yank it open. Make sure you stand back out of the doorway if the firing starts."

Will felt around for the handle. After locating it, he stood back and slowly pushed it down.

"Okay, slowly pull it open," Betley said.

The self-closing hinges squeezed slightly, and Will stiffened, expecting bullets at any moment. Light trickled in, and Betley moved toward the door. Every cell in Will's body was on high alert. His heart drummed so loud in his ears that he wasn't sure he would hear Betley's instructions.

"Pull it open just a little more," Betley said.

More light came in and now Will could make out Betley's form in the doorway. The door was open about a foot, and Betley burst through the opening.

"The light is from the windows on this floor. It's going to get dark outside soon. We'll lose that light," Betley said. "I don't see anyone. Let's move to the end of this hall."

Betley motioned for Will to stand on the opposite corner. Will wanted to protest. He pictured himself being cut off from Betley and, worse yet, his way up to Cayden on the second floor. He thought of Melanie. Any minute he could be there with her. He was just about to ask Betley to trade places when he heard Kim's voice echoing down the corridor.

"She is not here," Kim said.

Will shuddered at the thought of what they might have done to Isabella if they'd found her. Old gangster movies came to mind, and images of broken fingers and other means of torture. Will heard the door slam and then a sound as if someone hit or kicked it. They were pissed. It was only a matter of seconds before they'd be coming down the hall where he and Betley were waiting.

Will's stomach flip-flopped as panic rose in his throat. He wasn't even sure how many of them there were. He rehearsed what he'd do if he had to take one of them on in hand-to-hand combat. He'd wrestled some in high school, but that had been what, twenty years or so ago. He hadn't even been in a bar fight since college. He hoped he still knew how. What he really prayed was that wouldn't come to that.

A thought struck him. What if he had to kill Kim? Could he do that? Could he pull the trigger on a woman? God, he hoped it didn't come to that. It would screw him up for a long, long time.

"Get ready," Betley whispered. "Keep your eyes on me. When I tell you to fire, you unload the damn thing."

A lump had formed in his throat and he couldn't get words out. Will nodded that he understood. But really, he didn't. He was in way over his head. As the voices grew louder, Will went through the steps in his mind of how to aim and fire the rifle. It had been at least two years since he'd even held one. He hoped it was like riding a bike, and it would all come back to him. He had the feeling he was about to get in a lot of target practice.

One of the men yelled something in Chinese, and then Will heard footfalls on the concrete floor. As they grew fainter, Will realized they were moving away from them, not closer.

"He said he heard something outside," Betley said.

Will leaned around the corner and peeked. "It's just the wind," he said.

Betley nodded and went about checking the gear on his belt. Will got the sense that he too was nervous. Who wouldn't be? He imagined even seasoned veterans would be a little anxious about being in this type of situation with no backup and no calling in reinforcements.

"Maybe we should use this advantage to take off. We could get my son and Isabella and go. I saw several places that we could hole up in down the street. They might not follow in the storm," Will said.

"They'll follow. Besides, I'm not leaving all my stuff. That's how I survive this shit," Betley said.

Will felt anger rising. Was he only worried about himself?

"You intend on staying in here until things return to normal?" Will asked.

"You don't get it. Things are never returning to normal. Without food and the weapons to protect it, you won't survive. How far do you think we'll get without water? There won't be drinkable water for fifty miles after the flooding starts."

Great, he was trapped with a pessimist.

"I think I should go. I need to protect my son," Will said, starting toward the stairs.

Betley cleared his throat. "My weapons and ammo," he said, pointing to the rifle.

As Will held out the weapon to Betley, he thought about what he'd said. He'd seen firsthand what panic over the lack of food could cause. He'd been there when the relief trucks rolled in days after people had been stranded in the aftermath of Hurricane Rita and the devastation without electricity, clean water, or food. It was crazy. People stormed the trucks, and there were fistfights over the last cases of bottled water. This time, it would be a thousand times worse, and from what Betley said, there would be no aid trucks coming.

He didn't have food to protect, not here. If they somehow made it up to the lake house, he had a couple of weeks' worth. And then what? Would he be one of the ones that people like Betley would be fighting to protect their food from? What was he willing to do? What was he willing to do to make sure his son lived? The answer was simple. Anything.

"I'll stay—on one condition," Will said, clutching the rifle to his chest. "Well, two."

Betley tilted his head to one side. "What is it?" He sounded almost impatient.

"I want some of your food—enough to get my boy and me up to Lake Livingston," Will said.

Betley said, "I can do that. What else?"

"I get to keep the weapons and gear."

Betley didn't look happy about it, but in the end, he agreed. Will had never dreamed that he'd be willing to risk his life for some MREs and a few weapons, but there he was. He didn't think he and Cayden stood a chance in hell of reaching the lake house without those things and, without the weapons, they didn't stand a chance of keeping the food they had there or getting more. He didn't want to think about what he'd be forced to do to feed his son after that ran out. He just had to pray that Betley was wrong, that the government would come through and restore services soon.

Betley led Will toward the intersection of the next corridor. As they rounded the corner, Will caught a flash of light. "Stop," he whispered as he grabbed Betley's arm, pulling him back. "Someone's coming."

TWENTY-SEVEN

Will

DAY TWO

Will and Betley stood two feet back from the corridor and listened for the footsteps to grow closer. Will did his best to slow his breathing. He focused on his core; inhaled and slowly exhaled.

Betley gestured for Will to use his pistol. Will allowed the rifle to dangle on its two-point sling and unholstered his firearm.

"Three-round bursts. Aim for the neck above the vest or below it," Betley whispered.

Will had never practiced anything but making body shots, and he'd never tried to hit a moving target while someone was shooting at him. He gripped the pistol so tight his knuckles were white.

Seconds ticked by as they waited. Will's eyes never left Betley. Then he heard it. The swishing of clothing as the man approached. Betley heard it too. He leaned slightly and adjusted his stance, turning his back to Will. He gripped his pistol in both hands and held it close to his chest. Betley was ready. Will was not.

"Make sure your weapon is off safety," Betley whispered.

Will flicked the pistol to the firing position and mimicked Betley's stance as best he could. A flashlight's beam swept the hallway and then stopped. What were they waiting for? Did they somehow know he and Betley were waiting there to ambush them?

No Way Out

They were better trained than Will thought mere gang members would be. He wondered if Betley had been wrong about their affiliation. Maybe they were part of some elite team—but it didn't matter what they were. All that mattered was that they lose, and he and Betley win.

A moment later, the light's beam moved again. Slowly, the men advanced on their position until a man's hand came into view. Black gloves held a pistol. That is all Will saw before Betley took one step to his left and fired. The sound was deafening in the space. Will wanted to cover his ears, but when the man fell back and began returning fire, Betley yelled for Will to cover him.

Will moved up behind him as Betley fired around the corner and stepped into the corridor. When Will moved in beside him, he saw someone disappear around the next corner. He pivoted around to where Betley was standing. The black-clad man was on his back, his eyes wide. The man tried to sit up. He reached for a weapon a few feet to his right. Betley seated a boot on the man's chest and pointed his pistol at the man's face. The man's mouth formed an O. Betley squeezed the trigger, and the deep throaty handgun fired, nailing the man in the throat.

Will caught movement to his right and spun. He fired, and the man ducked back behind the wall. Betley ran down the hall in a crouch. Will followed, watching both corners, expecting to be fired upon at any second. When they reached the end of the hall, Betley stopped for a second and swept his pistol to his left and then back to his right before stepping into the corridor. Will was blind at that moment. He had no idea if anyone was around that corner. He had to totally rely on Betley. Since he didn't immediately begin firing, Will assumed the hall was clear, and the person had slipped away.

Will cursed the maze they were in. The crisscrossing corridors left so many places for a gunman to hide and evade them. But at least they had the enemy on the run. A moment before, they were the prey being pursued. Somehow, this seemed riskier to Will.

Betley moved quickly to the next intersection. He stopped,

pressed his back against the wall, and reloaded. Although Will had only fired a few shots, he too dropped his magazine and replaced it with a fresh one. He stuck the mostly full mag into the back left pocket of his jeans. It reminded him of having a can of wintergreen Skoal chewing tobacco back there. He hadn't chewed tobacco in thirteen years. It was strange to think about it now. His mind wanted to grasp hold of something besides what he was currently doing.

Betley shifted his weight, spun, and like a flash, he lashed out and smashed his pistol into a man's face. He jumped into the corridor and swept the barrel of his gun from left to right.

"Watch him," Betley said and ran down the hall.

Will stepped into the corridor, his pistol trained on the unconscious man. He was awkwardly leaned against the wall with legs splayed before him. Will was torn between keeping his eyes on the man and seeing where Betley had gone. He checked the hall to his left, sweeping his flashlight back and forth.

Will stepped back to scan the hall that they'd just come down. The man moaned and then moved. Will brought his pistol around and shone his light on the man's hands. No weapon. That didn't mean the man wasn't a threat. He could have a hidden gun or knife. He could be an expert in martial arts or just a good wrestler.

The man's eyes opened. Unlike his compatriot, he was not surprised. Nor did he look concerned. He looked pissed. He glanced to his left. Will's eyes followed his gaze to the man's pistol several paces away. The man lunged forward and got to his knees. He was going for the gun. Will yelled for him to stop. He didn't want to shoot him. There'd been a reason Betley hadn't shot the man himself. He'd said to watch him, not kill him. He'd wanted him alive.

The man scrambled on his hands and knees toward the weapon. Will ran toward him and kicked him as hard as he could in the ribs. The man sat back on his butt and pivoted toward Will, preparing for another kick. Instead, Will clocked him on the jaw with the butt of the pistol. His eyes rolled back, and he slumped over.

A moment later, Betley reappeared. He grabbed the man by the back of his shirt and began dragging him.

"Keep a watch that way," Betley said, hiking a thumb over his back. "I want to ask this gentleman a few questions."

Will's eyes bounced between Betley and the man and the end of the hall. He didn't like standing around out in the open like that. Especially not knowing how many of them there were. Betley smacked the guy on the face several times and said something in Mandarin.

The man stiffened and then relaxed. His mouth formed into something more aggressive than a smirk. Betley stared him down.

"I will tell you nothing, G-man," the man spat, his accent thick.

"Maybe not. What does it matter now anyway? What's done is done. But one thing is for sure," Betley paused.

"What?" the man asked.

"You are as stuck here in this mess as we are."

"You are wrong. You know nothing. We won. We own you," the man said, his eyes blazing with triumph.

Betley regarded the man with amusement.

"You don't own me," Betley said, punching every word.

The man coughed out a laugh, and Betley reached down and punched him. The man rolled his head with the punch. He laughed.

"Soon, you will know everything. Or maybe not. You might not live that long," the man said.

Betley rubbed his knuckles. "Maybe not, but it won't be by your hands."

Sneaking quick glances down, Will looked at the man's hands. They were balled into fists, ready to strike. His body was rigid. His words may have been cocky, but his body portrayed fear.

A bullet whizzed by Will's head and struck the man in the temple. Betley turned in a crouch and fired.

"Go, Will! Go!" Betley yelled over the sound of the gunfire.

Will fired down the hall as he quickly moved back around the corner. Betley was retreating as well. A second shooter joined the first and rounds peppered the wall opposite them.

"Get to the stairs," Betley said as he reloaded his pistol. "I'll hold them off."

"No. We go together," Will said.

Will turned and scanned the hall behind them. Betley remained facing toward the shooters as they crept back toward the stairs. Will yanked open the door and checked the steps.

"Stairway's clear," he said, moving through the doorway.

"Stop at the door," Betley said as Will climbed the stairs to the second floor.

Will prayed that there were no shooters up there. If there were, he prayed that he reached Cayden and Isabella before they did.

Betley ascended the stairs and tapped Will on the shoulder. "Let me."

Will did as instructed, even though everything in him wanted to burst through the door and run to his son.

Betley moved past him on the landing and through the door. "The hall is clear."

Will and Betley raced to unit two hundred and forty-one.

"It's Dad, Cayden. Isabella, we're coming in. Don't shoot," Will said.

"Dad," Cayden said, rushing into his arms.

Will melted. Relief washed over him. Cayden was safe for the moment. Will looked up, and Isabella was seated in the corner of the unit with the gun pointed in their direction.

Betley rushed over and placed his hand on the barrel, pushing it toward the floor. "Whoa there, it's okay. We're on your team."

Isabella burst into tears. Betley glanced back at Will and then tentatively placed a hand on Isabella's shoulder.

"We need to go," Will said. "I need to get my son the hell out of here."

"What about the food and weapons?" Betley said.

"The hell with them. We don't even know how many of those asshats there are. There could be an army of them for all we know."

"An army?" Isabella asked, breaking down again.

"Let's just hold on a minute and let me do some reconnaissance. I'll see if we can make it up to the weapons at least."

"It's Texas. We can find more weapons. We need to get out of here before the storm traps us here for hours," Will said.

Isabella stood. Her arms dangled limply at her sides. She looked as if she was about to have a meltdown. He didn't have time to deal with that.

"Cayden, stuff as many bags of nuts as you can into your pockets. I'll grab the club soda," Will said, pivoting toward the stash of supplies.

"What makes you think they won't mow us down as we try to flee?" Betley asked.

Isabella's eyes grew wide. Fresh tears streamed down her cheeks. Cayden looked from Will to Betley. He was doing a very good job of scaring them. Not Will. He was more afraid of staying and being killed by Kim and her comrades while the storm blew in.

"I think it's a chance we have to take. We only have a very short window in which to escape this hellhole."

"How many men do you think are waiting down there?" Betley asked.

Will stopped what he was doing and straightened. He'd heard several voices, including Kim's. At least some of them had gone off in search of the noise outside. Then there were the two they'd killed. He had to admit that he had no idea. He didn't know which door they'd gone out and whether they completed their search and returned.

Certainly, they'd heard the gunshots. They would have rushed back and started searching for them on the first floor. Will stepped back into the hallway and listened. It was quiet, too quiet. They could be moving up the stairway now.

"We need something to block off the stairway," Will said.

"What? I thought we were going?" Isabella asked.

Will spun around, scanning the space. There had to be some way to block the door.

"Betley's right. I hate it, but we can't run until we know they aren't down there just waiting for us to go down those stairs."

"Who are these people? Why is Kim doing this?" Isabella asked.

"She isn't a student," Will said.

"Then who is she?"

"A spy?" Cayden said.

Isabella cocked her head to one side. "A spy?"

"She works for the Chinese Communist Party," Betley said.

"What? Really? What does she think I stole?" Isabella asked.

Betley reached into his front pants pocket and held out a pink flash drive. "This."

"Shit. You took it," Isabella said. "What's on it?"

"I won't know until I'm able to load it onto a computer," Betley said.

"What do you think is on it?" Cayden asked.

"Names likely. Names and locations," Betley said, stuffing it back into his pocket.

"What names and locations? Other spies?" Cayden asked.

"Sort of. We received intelligence that Chinese nationals had been using Mexican coyotes to get them into the United States. Langley thought it might be for the movement of drugs, namely fentanyl. The case was given to the Drug Enforcement Agency, but we had agents on the task force. One of those agents was a friend of mine. He wasn't convinced it was drugs. The guys never surfaced in any of the known drug corridors. Many came here to Houston. They tracked one to a restaurant in Sharpstown. His path crossed Kim's. I asked her about him and she lied."

"You think they caused the grid to go down and cars to stop?" Cayden asked.

"No. Not them. They are just the second string."

"Second string," Isabella asked.

"What comes after," Betley said.

"Invasion?" Cayden asked.

Betley didn't answer.

"Is there going to be an invasion? Are there enemy troops heading for us now?" Isabella asked. Will glanced down at her balled fists. She no longer looked frightened. She looked pissed.

TWENTY-EIGHT

Will

DAY TWO

Betley never had a chance to answer Isabella's question about an invasion. The heavy boom of something hitting the windows sounded downstairs, startling them. It was followed by a gust of wind that howled through the structure. The storm was intensifying. It was likely only hours before the eye moved onshore, trapping them inside the storage facility for at least eight to twelve hours as the ferociously powerful storm chewed through the area with winds in excess of one hundred miles per hour. At least, that was if the storm had stayed on course and made landfall west of Galveston. Without a radio, there was no way of knowing where the storm's eye was heading or if it had weakened from its predicted category five status. That scared the hell out of Will.

Melanie had been pregnant with Cayden when Ike had moved through Houston and blown out windows in the JP Chase Morgan building downtown. They'd fled to Little Rock, Arkansas, to stay with her aunt. If they had had relatives farther north, Will had been sure Melanie would have insisted they go there.

Will and Betley stepped outside the unit. Cayden started to follow. "Wait here. I'm going to see if I can find something to block the door to the stairs," Will said.

Cayden's shoulders slumped, but he obeyed.

Will and Betley walked back toward the stairs and stopped. The gale whistling through the cracks in the door sounded like something out of a horror movie. He half expected a ghost to appear at any second.

"What we really should do is make our way up to my weapons," Betley said.

"But we don't know if any of them are up there. They could be anywhere right now," Will said.

"Including right here on the second floor. This might not be the only unlocked unit," Betley said.

He had a point. Will hadn't checked every single door. But they would have heard the shooting and come to help their compatriots, right? Will hated the idea of taking Cayden into the stairway without knowing what they might face but they did stand a better chance surrounded by all Betley's weapons. Besides, his stomach was starting to growl, and Betley had food up there on the third floor.

"Okay, let's move upstairs," Will said.

"Are you sure?" Isabella asked. "This doesn't seem like a good idea to me."

"I told you. Our best shot is to make it back up to Betley's unit and load up on weapons. We can hole up back in his unit with all the food until after the storm passes," Will said.

"And then what?" Isabella asked.

"And then we figure something out," Will said, being purposefully evasive. He didn't want to scare Cayden with the truth that they might have to shoot their way out of there. It looked like Kim wasn't going to stop until she got what she wanted, and Betley wasn't about to let her have it.

Sweat beaded on his brow as they abandoned the scavenged food supplies, and all four headed for the stairs. Betley took the lead, followed by Isabella and then Cayden. Will brought up the rear, making sure to watch for anyone coming up behind them.

At the stairs, Will moved ahead and grabbed the door handle. Betley put up one finger, then two, and finally the third. Will tugged the door open, and Betley rushed into the doorway, pistol raised.

"Clear," he whispered, and he ascended the steps.

Isabella hesitated in the doorway.

"It's okay," Cayden said. "My dad has your back."

Will was taken aback by the vote of confidence from his son. Isabella moved up the stairs; Cayden followed her. They both climbed and waited behind Betley at the top, just outside the third-floor door. Before closing the door and trapping them in the stairwell, Will took a step back and scanned the corridor. He listened but only heard the sound of the wind. The stairwell was too narrow for Will to pass everyone. Betley was forced to open the door and clear the hall without immediate backup.

Betley eased open the door only wide enough to shine the light through. Will stiffened. If anyone had been on the other side, they would have immediately noticed it. Isabella gripped her pistol out in front of her with the barrel pointed at the floor.

Betley glanced back, nodded to Will, and then shoved the door open. He bounded through the doorway, scanning his pistol back and forth from left to right.

"It's clear. Hurry. Stay on me. Don't lag behind," Betley said as he quickly moved toward his unit.

As Will stepped out of the stairwell, he saw a light reflect off one of the metal roll-up doors at the far end of the hall. Betley must have seen it too. He stopped, turned, and made a gesture for them to stop. He put one finger to his lips. Will hurried up beside him.

"This is not good, Betley. We are sitting ducks out here," Will whispered.

"I think they were moving to our left. We'll go right down the aisle and then cut back left at the next."

Will grabbed Cayden and motioned for Isabella to stay close.

They stopped at the corner while Betley assessed the corridor. He flicked off his light, and Isabella gasped. Betley raised his pistol and scanned to their left.

"See anything?" Will asked.

"It's clear," Betley said. "Isabella, grab hold of my belt loop. We're going to move blacked out," Betley said.

"Cayden, hold my hand," Isabella whispered.

Will turned and walked backward as they made their way to the next aisle. He bumped into Cayden when Will stopped abruptly.

"What is it?" Will asked.

"The light is moving away. They're down at the end near my food cache."

"Can you tell how many of them there are?" Will asked.

"No way to know. I only saw the one light though," Betley replied. "Let's hurry and get to the weapons."

Betley stopped outside the last unit at the end of the corridor. Will pressed himself against the wall and watched their backs as Betley used a key to remove the lock. Will heard the door slowly being rolled up.

"Slide under," Betley said.

Will glanced down as Cayden and Isabella dropped to their hands and knees and disappeared inside.

"Go ahead. I'll cover you," Betley said as he put the lock back.

Will gave one last quick scan before letting his rifle dangle and crawling under the door. A second later, Will heard the door close, and he flicked on his flashlight. Betley wasn't there. He reached down and pulled on the door, but it didn't move.

"Betley, what the hell are you doing?" Will asked just above a whisper.

"Get your kid and the girl outfitted with vests. I need to find out where everyone is, and then I'll be right back," Betley said.

"But what if you don't come back?" Will asked.

He received no reply. Betley had already slipped away.

They were trapped. Will scanned the room. He needed something to use as a pry bar.

"Did he really just lock us in here?" Cayden asked.

"He sure as shit did," Will said.

Will rummaged through box after box and found nothing useful to pry up the door. He searched again and, this time looked for something that he could use to cut a hole in the metal door. There was nothing.

Will picked up a bullet-proof vest and handed one to Isabella. "Put this on."

He expected questions or some kind of commentary, but he received none.

He looked through the box but found nothing small enough for Cayden so slid a vest over his son's head, pulling the Velcro as tight as he could. He tugged on it but it was still too loose and hung lower than it should. Will rummaged through another box and located a body armor neck guard, wrapped it around Cayden's neck, and secured the Velcro tightly.

"I can't breathe with all this stuff on," Cayden said.

"Here, put this helmet on," Will said, successfully ignoring his son's complaining.

"Can I have one of those too?" Isabella asked.

It was unbearably hot in all that gear. Even though the storm had brought the temperature down outside, it was still like a sauna inside the closed-up unit. Will was continually wiping sweat from his face. He handed Cayden and Isabella bottles of water and downed one himself. He shone his light and counted the remaining bottles. Two cases. That should be enough for the three of them. He'd need a minimum of six bottles in this heat a day, maybe ten. He turned to Isabella. She looked like she weighed no more than a hundred pounds soaking wet. She'd need a minimum of three to four. And then Cayden would need about that many. They had enough for two or three days.

Will stood and walked to a shelf containing a stack of meals ready to eat. There were only five MREs. He picked one up. "Veggie burger in barbecue sauce? Yuck!"

"I'm not eating that one," Cayden said. He pointed to Isabella. "You can have it."

"What? Do I look like a vegetarian?" Isabella laughed.

Actually, she did. She didn't look like she had an ounce of fat on her though she wasn't as thin as his sister. Will tried to recall if Savanah was a vegetarian this month. He couldn't remember.

"You can have the chicken fajita," Will said, handing it to Cayden.

"Wait," Isabella said. "I love chicken fajitas." She lunged at him and began tickling him. Even though her bony fingers couldn't reach far under the vest, Cayden laughed like Will hadn't seen him do in two years.

Will turned his back on them and sucked in a breath. He was glad his son could laugh. He deserved to be a kid and have fun. Melanie would be happy. The thought of her pricked his heart.

Will heard a noise outside and spun around, motioning for them to be quiet. He flicked off the flashlight and listened. Someone was right outside the door. He pulled the rifle up and gestured for Cayden and Isabella to get behind him. Isabella stood, gripped the pistol he'd given her earlier in both hands, and adjusted her stance. She looked fierce in her black tactical vest.

"It's me. Don't shoot," Betley said through the door.

Will and Isabella both let out audible sighs of relief as Will opened the door and Betley's face came into view.

"You scared the hell out of me," Isabella said, slapping him on the shoulder.

He held out a chocolate bar and smiled broadly. "Sorry. Forgive me?" He winked at Will.

The way Isabella snatched up the candy bar, it was evident that he'd scored huge points with her.

He reached into his vest and produced another. "Here, kid."

"No, thanks," Cayden said.

Betley blinked a few times and then shrugged.

"He doesn't like chocolate, but I do," Will said, snatching the bar from Betley's grasp. "What did you find out there besides chocolate?"

"Kim and another man are holed up by the stairs to the roof. The rest of the floor is clear," Betley said.

Will nodded. He was trying to figure out if that was good or bad. He was sure that he and Betley could take Kim and the other man but if they engaged them, Cayden and Isabella would be vulnerable to attack from the other men, and they had no idea where or how many of them there were.

"I say we lie low here for a few hours, get some chow. Oh, I see you've started without me," Betley said.

"Sorry. We were starving," Cayden said.

"I haven't eaten yet. I was just about to wrestle Cayden for the chicken fajita," Isabella said, reaching out and trying to snatch it from him.

"I've got some canned spam," Betley said, walking over to the shelves.

"Ugh. No thanks. I think I'd rather eat the veggie burger."

"It's good. You should try it," Betley said. "I should tell you about the time when my partner and I were on a stakeout watching this counterfeit ring. We sat on that warehouse for days waiting for someone to show up, and my partner must have had beans every day for lunch. I'm telling you..."

Isabella was enthralled with the G-man's story. Will tuned him out. He was exhausted. The last two days had wrung him out. His mind kept trying to make sense of it all, to somehow wrap his brain around the loss of technology and electricity, along with being trapped in a storage facility with a Chinese double agent and her mafia enforcers. It was the stuff of fiction. He couldn't think himself out of this situation and that had every nerve in his body on edge.

Will glanced over at Cayden. He looked so small in his oversized vest. He too was all caught up listening to the agent's stories. Will fought off the woulda coulda shouldas and tried to think about what he could do to keep his son safe. Where could they go to weather this until the government could get a handle on things? Will couldn't think about the possibility that they wouldn't be able to put together some recovery plan. If they could just hunker down somewhere safe and feed themselves for a while, they might make it. But where?

"Betley?" It was Kim's voice coming through the door.

Will jumped to his feet and grabbed his rifle. To his surprise, so did Isabella.

"Betley? It's Kim. Let me in."

"What the f—reak," Will said, almost letting the curse word slip.

Betley moved to the door. "What do you want, Kim?"

"I'm alone. Let me in," Kim said.

Betley shifted his position and Will thought for a moment that he was considering it.

"You betrayed me. You led them to my door," Betley said.

"I did not betray you, Betley. I told you when I called you that they knew, and they were following me. You said to come here, remember?"

Betley said nothing.

He bent to open the door, but Isabella jumped on his back. "No. She's lying, she's with them. She was going to hurt me. We can't trust her."

Betley reached back and placed his hand on Isabella's arm. "It's okay. I won't let her hurt you. Just stay behind me."

"I don't like this, Betley. We have no way of knowing if she's lying," Will said.

As Isabella slid off his back, Betley turned to Will. "You're right. We don't know if she's lying. But I need her. She has valuable intel that I need—that our country needs. I need to secure and interrogate her, if at all possible."

"And the information she may have is worth risking Isabella's and my son's lives to get?"

Will could think of nothing that the woman could tell them that would be worth losing his son for.

"You stand there," Betley said, pointing to the wall by the door. "I'll stand here. As I roll up the door, you will have a view to our left and I will have the right. If you see anyone other than Kim, shoot."

Will still did not like Betley's plan. Not one bit, but he was set on doing it, and the only way to stop him was to shoot him. Will wasn't ready to kill a federal agent.

"Okay, Kim. If you are armed, put it on the ground and kick it away," Betley called through the door.

Will heard a thud and then the weapon skidding away.

"All right, now place your hands on top of your head and turn around. And, Kim, no sudden moves when I open this door or I will drop you where you stand. Got it?"

"Yes," Kim replied.

"Let me know when you are in position," Betley said.

He nodded to Will. "You ready?"

"No, wait," Will said and ran toward Cayden. "Get behind those shelves." He stuffed his son between the shelf and the wall and then dumped the box of body armor on the floor. Isabella ran back and helped him cram them into the space around his son.

"Thank you," Will whispered.

She placed her hand gently on his shoulder. "I'll stand back here. She'll have to go through me."

"Let's go, Will," Betley said.

Will hurried back and positioned himself with his back against the wall. He raised his pistol and gave a quick nod. "Ready."

Betley yanked up the door in one quick motion. Will covered him as the door rolled up, revealing Kim with her back to them. Will scanned the corridor for signs of her compatriots. He saw no one.

"Right's clear," Betley called.

"Left's clear," Will said.

"Cover her," Betley said, moving into the hall.

He scanned right and left. "How many are out there?" he asked, looking past her.

"I'm not sure. How many of them have you killed?"

"How many were there before that?" Betley said, growing impatient.

Will got the impression the man had never been all that patient anyway.

"Eight. I believe. I only saw eight," Kim said.

"You took out one," Betley said.

"Two. I took out two. One before they captured me." She glanced past Will toward Isabella.

Will followed her gaze. Isabella remained in her position guarding Cayden, never taking her eyes off Kim. She was not going to let her guard down with the woman, that was clear.

"So that leaves…"

Before Betley could get the words out of his mouth, a shot rang out, sending everyone scrambling to locate the shooter. A black-clad figure raced down the parallel aisle to Will's left.

"There," Will yelled.

Betley pivoted and fired, but the figure was gone. "Cover right," he yelled, taking chase after the man.

Another man popped out to Will's right, and he fired. Kim dove inside the unit as the first man opened up on Betley. Will watched the man on his right drop. Will ran, making sure there were no others behind him on the next row.

The firing continued in Betley's direction. But he'd disappeared. Will peered around the corner and saw no one. He lifted his pistol and shone his flashlight. It was clear. Just as he turned to go back to make sure the shooter was dead, a round struck him in the chest. He dropped to one knee as the gunman spun his pistol toward the inside of the open unit where his son hid.

"No!" Will screamed. Two shots rang out. The gunman returned fire as he dropped to the floor. Finally, Will managed to get his feet under him, and he ran back toward his son. Will's legs couldn't move fast enough. He stopped at the entrance to the unit and stared down at Kim. She was on her knees with a pistol held out in front of her. A crimson stain bloomed across an area in the middle of her chest.

"Take care of son," she said softly. Kim looked down at her wound. "Get him out of city."

Will rushed to her. "What's going to happen? Tell me. Are we going to be invaded?"

Kim looked up. Their eyes locked. She opened her mouth to speak, but nothing came out.

"Kim," Will said. He shook her. "Kim, please tell me."

She slumped forward, her head falling to the floor. Will placed two fingers against her neck. She was gone.

He saw movement behind her and then a hand on his shoulder. "She saved us, Dad. Kim saved us."

TWENTY-NINE

Will

DAY TWO

Gunshots rang out—lots of them. They echoed through the corridors, making it impossible for Will to determine their direction.

"Stay here," Will said, stepping outside the unit.

He scanned the hall to his left and then right. Clear. He listened. The shots were coming from the direction Betley had gone. Will crept to the corner and peered around. Nothing. Brass bullet casings littered the floor, practically leaving a breadcrumb trail for him to follow. He kept his eyes focused ahead as he inched closer to the end of the hall. The next row over, bullets pierced the metal doors. Will heard shouts, not in English. More than two, possibly four. Bile rose in his throat as he continued toward the battle.

Betley stood with his back pressed against the wall. He was reloading as rounds slammed into the steel doors across from him. The enemy was located to Will's left, but out of sight.

"How many?" Will asked.

"At least six. I'm low on ammo. Give me yours," he said, pointing to Will's belt.

Will handed him two spare magazines and fell in behind him.

Betley nodded behind Will. "Go back and make sure they don't flank us."

Will ran to the end and checked the aisle. He traversed the hall and stationed himself at the corner with a full view of the next row of units. It also put him between the shooters and his son. He felt his ammo belt and counted the magazines. He cursed under his breath. He only had two spares.

He was kicking himself for not grabbing more before going to search for Betley when the firing began again. Will's eyes darted from the opposite row to Betley. He was blindly firing three-round bursts around the corner. Will didn't understand why he would waste ammo like that. There would be no way for him to hit anyone firing like that. He hoped Betley knew what he was doing.

The unit across from Betley looked like swiss cheese with the number of bullet holes in the door. The enemy seemed to have an endless supply of ammo. In a lull in the firing, Betley stepped out and fired. This time, he unloaded on them in full auto mode. In seconds, he ducked back behind the wall and reached for a fresh magazine—his last one. Thirty rounds left. Betley looked at Will. He didn't look confident about their circumstances. Will felt the urge to run back to Cayden and Isabella. He needed to get his son out of there before Betley ran out.

The gunmen sent a quick three-round burst into the wall Betley was hiding behind. The round passed easily through the steel door three feet from Betley's right hand. He dropped to the floor in a crouch. Will froze, waiting to see if the man had been shot. He stood, pivoted, and stepping into the corridor, he unloaded his weapon on the men. They returned fire, sending Betley scrambling back to cover.

"I'm out," Betley mouthed.

Will's heart sank.

"Get them out," Betley said, pointing toward where Cayden and Isabella were hiding.

"Let me run and get more ammo," Will said.

No Way Out

"No. There's too many of them. You have to go. Pitch me your ammo. I'll hold them off as long as I can," Betley said.

Will stepped closer and slid two magazines down the slick concrete floor to Betley. "I can bring back more ammo," he repeated.

"It won't matter," Betley said as he loaded his rifle. "No! Go! Get your son out of the city." He stepped out, shooting a three-round burst. The gunmen returned fire. Miraculously, they missed. Betley was reloading as Will spun and took off to get Cayden.

Cayden and Isabella were full of questions when he reached Betley's arms unit. Will didn't have time to explain.

"Bring me those rifle magazines," Will said, holding open a large black duffle bag.

Cayden and Isabella carried over a box of empty rifle magazines. Will dumped them into the duffle. "Now the boxes of ammunition." Will dumped the dozens of thirty-round boxes of 5.56 NATO rounds into the bag.

He hoisted the bag up and slung the rifle over his shoulder. He turned, and Isabella was standing behind him, slinging the strap of an AR-15 over her head.

"Do you know how—?"

She dropped the magazine, felt the rounds, reinstalled the mag, released the bolt, dropped the magazine again, and inspected the rounds.

"Hand me that tactical belt, Cayden," Isabella said as she slapped the mag back into the rifle.

Will stepped out and checked the corridor as Isabella loaded rifle magazines into her belt.

"Let's go. Be as quiet as possible."

"Let's go deliver some love," Isabella said.

"What?" Will said.

"Let's go take the fuckers out."

Will blinked several times. More and more it was like he was in an unending episode of the *Twilight Zone*.

"We're getting out of here," Will said.

"Without Betley? What about the flash drive?" Isabella said.

Will had forgotten all about that. But that wasn't his priority.

"Where is he?" Isabella asked, stepping in the opposite direction of the stairs.

"He's pinned down three rows over."

"Okay," she said, running off in that direction.

"Dad," Cayden said.

"I am not putting you in the middle of a gunfight," Will said.

"But, Dad—"

"But nothing." Will shoved Cayden behind him. "Stay behind me. We're heading for the stairs."

A barrage of gunfire sounded. Isabella had joined the fight.

Will and Cayden crept down the hall and turned toward the stairs. Will checked from his left to his right before stepping out to traverse the hall. They'd made it halfway when he caught movement to his right. He spun, pulling Cayden with him, putting himself between Cayden and the people advancing.

"Go! Go! Go!" Betley yelled as he ran toward them.

Isabella was running alongside him. Will flung open the door to the stairs. He shoved Cayden through it and turned. Isabella had stopped and was returning fire at several men running toward them. Their returning bullets scattered across the floor narrowly missing her.

"Isabella, hurry," Will said.

Betley and Will fired as Isabella sprinted to the stairs.

"Go, I'll cover you," Betley said.

Will stepped onto the landing. When Betley pivoted to move into the doorway, Will spotted blood running down his left arm. He'd been struck.

"I'll cover it. You've been shot," Will said.

"It's just shrapnel. Go. Get your son out. I'll be right behind you," Betley said.

Betley pulled a flash-bang grenade from the quick release pouch on his vest and tossed it down the hall. Even over the sound of sporadic gunfire, Will could hear the grenade skidding across the concrete floor. As Betley stepped back to close the door, the grenade went off and lit up the hall. The door barely muffled the high-pitched burst of sound.

Will turned and raced down the stairs. Isabella was holding the door open and Cayden was standing on the sidewalk outside. The wind was driving the rain sideways across the parking lot. Trees were whipping back and forth.

Grabbing hold of Cayden's shirt, Will took off across the parking lot, Isabella running behind him. Will glanced back. He couldn't see Betley.

"Where's Betley?"

"He's coming," Isabella said, seconds before yellow smoke billowed from the front of the building.

Betley rounded the corner, chopping the air with his hand. "Run! Run!"

THIRTY

Will

DAY TWO

Despite the pain she must have felt due to her injuries, Isabella sprinted through the intersection, heading south away from the storage facility. Cayden and Will were close on her heels. Betley halted near the stop sign and popped a few rounds through what had been the door to the building.

"Where? Where do we go?" Isabella yelled over the sound of the wind.

Will could barely see. The rain was stinging his eyes. He knew this was only the beginning. They were likely only hours away from the eye of the hurricane making landfall. They needed to find somewhere before it became impossible to travel on foot.

"There," Will said, pointing down the block at a multi-story building.

By the time they reached it, the men that were chasing them had gained on them. Betley stopped behind a mid-sized sedan and returned fire. Will ducked behind a medium-sized tree and fired in their direction, but he knew there'd be no way to be accurate. He couldn't even see them in his sights. All he could do was aim down the street, shoot, and hope it kept them pinned down long enough for Isabella and Cayden to get inside.

"The door is locked," Cayden yelled.

Isabella was beating on the glass with her hand. If anyone was inside, they weren't coming to open it.

"Stand back," Betley yelled. "Cover me, Will."

Will shifted and fired continuous rounds at their pursuers.

After Isabella and Cayden backed a safe distance from the doors, Betley rose from his crouch, fired at the glass, and returned to his firing position behind the sedan.

Isabella kicked the remaining glass out of the door and unlocked it. "We're in," she shouted.

"Betley, you go first," Will yelled. Betley was injured. It would take him longer to get to the door where he would be hidden from the shooter's view.

Will fired as Betley ran from the sedan, ducked behind a tree, and then sprinted to the door. Will was now out there alone. He had at least fifteen feet to cover, all of them exposed. He wiped the rain from his eyes and focused on the door. Fifteen feet. With his stride, he could make it in probably fifteen seconds. He unloaded his magazine on the enemy's position and ran toward the door. Rounds peppered the side of the building to the right of the door.

Chunks of concrete flew up and struck him in the arms and legs. He didn't stop. He couldn't stop. He leaped up the three steps and flung himself through the opened door, dropped to the floor, and slid on his stomach through the tiny pieces of glass. Betley and Isabella both descended on him, yanked him to his feet, and the four of them bounded up the stairs to their left.

Offices flanked both sides of the hall. The wind whistled through the building from the broken door downstairs. At the end of the corridor was another set of stairs that likely led to the third floor. That would be the safest place to ride out the storm. If they could somehow barricade themselves in and keep the bad guys out, they might just survive the night.

Light bounced off the walls and ceiling as the gunmen pursued them up the stairs. They were in the building. There wasn't time to barricade themselves in now. Betley fired as one of the men's heads appeared at the top of the stairs. Bullets ripped right through the thin drywall. Even if they barricaded themselves in, all the gunmen had to do was fire through the walls.

"This is no good," Will yelled.

"I'll hold them. See if you can find a back way out," Betley said, continuing to send rounds in the enemy's direction. Will dropped the duffle loaded with ammo, grabbed four spare magazines, and slid them down the hall in Betley's direction. They came up short. Betley had to take his eyes off the shooters to retrieve them. Will cursed. "I'll get them, Betley," he yelled. "Isabella, find a back way out."

Will fired as he ran toward the ammo on the floor. Without taking his eyes off the men crouched on the stairs, Will kicked one of the mags toward Betley, dropped down, and slid across the floor, scooping up two of the magazines before crashing into the wall beside Betley. He dropped them and began firing.

He took a quick glance back to see if Isabella and Cayden were still there. They weren't. He patted Betley on the shoulder. "Let's pull back. Isabella and Cayden took the stairs."

Before they reached the second set of stairs, the shooters were pouring into the corridor behind them. Will yanked open the door and shoved Betley through it. He lunged just as a round struck the glass in the door—Isabella and Cayden were nowhere to be seen.

Will slammed the door closed, and he and Betley raced up the stairs. Betley made it to the next level, and the door flung open and Isabella popped into view.

"Will, get down," she yelled, seconds before raising her rifle and firing. The sound was deafening in the confined space. She yelled something else, but he couldn't hear her over the ringing in his ears. Isabella stepped back, and Betley flew through the door. As Will climbed the steps, he expected to receive a bullet in the back at any moment.

When he reached the top, Betley slammed the door while

Isabella and Cayden pushed two desks in front of it, end to end, wedging them between the door and the opposite wall. There'd be no way the shooters could open the door. Even if they broke out the glass, they would not be able to push the desks aside to get in. They'd done it. They'd barricaded themselves off from the gunmen, but at what cost? Now they were trapped up there on the third floor, without food or water.

As the men tried to shoot their way through the door, Will and the others moved down the hall, looking for a safe place away from the windows. Isabella checked one side while Cayden opened doors on the opposite side. Betley and Will trained their rifles on the door to the stairs.

"We should check to make sure there's not any other way onto this floor," Betley said, opening and then closing the door nearest to him.

"There's a door down here that might lead to another stairwell," Isabella said.

"I'll check it out. You got this one?" Will said.

Betley nodded.

"Cayden, come with me," Will said as he walked past him.

There was indeed a back staircase leading down to the ground floor. As Will stared at the door exiting out the side of the building, an idea formed. If they slipped out without the shooters knowing, they had a chance of getting away. It would mean being back out in the storm and in search of a new place to hunker down, but it beat being trapped like they were. It was worth a try.

"Watch the stairs. Run if you see anyone," Will told Cayden as he headed back to fill Betley and Isabella in on his plan.

"I don't know. This looks safe to me. We can drag more chairs into the hall and barricade that door as well. If we stay in the hall with the doors closed, we should be safe from the storm," Isabella said.

"What do you think, Betley?"

Betley turned toward him. Blood soaked his left shirt sleeve and trailed down his arm. It had dripped down his dress slacks onto his shoes. He was losing a lot of blood. He needed medical attention, that was clear.

"We need to take care of that wound," Will said, pointing to his arm.

Betley glanced down and lifted his right shoulder in a half shrug. "It'll keep. Right now, we need to get the hell out of here before they discover those back stairs."

Isabella looked pissed but followed Will and Betley back to where he'd left Cayden. Will descended the stairs first, followed by Cayden, Isabella, and then Betley. Will stood guard at the bottom of the stairs while everyone else filed out the side door. They'd made it. They'd got out without being detected.

Betley pointed down the street to what looked like a three-story home. The windows were boarded up. Will did not want to get trapped in a house, but it did look like their best option. All the other buildings were single story. Not suitable for the amount of flooding Will expected to see.

"Go. I'll cover you," Will said.

Betley and Isabella took off in that direction. Cayden looked back at Will seeming torn.

Will gestured toward Betley and Isabella. "Go with them."

As they disappeared around the side of the house, Will checked the exit one last time. No one was following them. Had it really been that easy to lose them? He sprinted across the street and hopped the four-foot wrought-iron fence that surrounded the yard. When he reached the front, a sign attached to the brick facade beside a paneled front door told him that the structure was a law office—a criminal defense attorney. That made Will's skin crawl.

He hurried up the landscaped walkway to the columned front portico. The sidelights flanking the door had been covered with ugly three-quarter inch plywood. It would do very little to keep floodwater out, but it might save the ornate glass that likely was under it.

Betley pressed his back against the door and kicked. To Will's surprise, the lock gave way and the door flew open. Isabella and Cayden rushed inside as Will and Betley watched for the gunmen.

"We need to find more plywood and secure this door," Betley said as he motioned for Will to enter.

"They might hear hammering, don't you think?" Will asked.

"You're right. Let's get inside before we drown out here," Betley said, wiping rain from his eyes.

"Keep your voices low. Try not to make any noise," Betley said as they entered. "Will, I'm going to need your help to clear the building before we get settled in."

"Clear the building?" Will asked.

"We need to make sure there isn't anyone still inside. We don't want surprises popping out of the woodwork," Betley said.

"What do we do?" Will asked.

"Leave everything here, except your pistol and ammo. The rifle is no good in close quarters like this," Betley said, placing his M4 on the ornately carved reception desk.

Will handed Isabella his rifle and the duffle of ammunition.

"What are me and Isabella doing?" Cayden asked.

"You're guarding that door. You stand here." Betley placed his hands on Cayden's shoulders and moved him to the corner of the front room. "You now have a view of anyone attempting to enter from the other room."

"And I'm guarding the door?" Isabella asked.

"Yes, exactly. Stand here." Betley placed his hands around her tiny waist and guided her to the space along the wall that would give her a view of the walkway and adjacent intersection outside. "You'll see anyone before they reach the house."

"Okay, Will, follow me. We'll start down here."

Standing at the door, the reception desk lay ten feet ahead. Beyond that and to the left was a short hallway. Will couldn't see where it led. To the right of the desk was a set of French-style doors. The glass was covered with curtains, blocking the view into the room beyond. Will wasn't at all comfortable letting Cayden out of his sight but Betley was right; they needed to be sure no one else occupied the building.

Betley moved to the right of the door, parallel to the wall. His pistol was raised but held close to his chest. He motioned for Will to fall in behind him.

"The door opens toward the inside of the room. See the hinges?" Betley asked.

"Yeah."

"I am going to move through the door and away from the hinges. If the door opened out, I'd move toward the door hinges. Okay, make sense?"

Will nodded.

"You stand behind me, ready to follow. Don't point your weapon at my back. You must maintain muzzle discipline. You can't get all sloppy and shoot me in the spine."

"I won't," Will said.

"Your AOR will be the right corners of the room," Betley said.

"AOR?" Will asked.

"Area of responsibility."

"Right," Will said.

"Are you familiar with the term interlocking field of fire?" Betley asked.

"Um—not really."

Betley sighed.

"We're going to breach the room. If I go right, you go left or vice versa. The corners are the points of domination. You want to move quickly through the doorway and into the room. Move toward your corner. After your first corner is cleared, turn your body and scan to the back corner. When that corner is cleared, scan to the center of the room. Don't stop until you've cleared to the center of the back wall. Stop at the center of the room. Do not swing your weapon in my direction."

Will was trying to picture the movements. He'd seen it hundreds of times on television and in movies. He'd even done it in video games, but that was fiction. This was real life with real bullets. He glanced at Cayden and then Isabella. He couldn't afford to screw this up.

"I think I've got it," he said.

"Okay. Let's go," Betley said as he reached for the knob.

Betley shoved the door open and was in the room in seconds. He moved to the left of the door, which meant Will had to go around the opened door. He'd be blind to what might be behind it. As Will rushed through the door, he could tell the space was a conference room from its long table and shelves lined with books. No one lurked behind the door. Will moved to the corner, turned to face the back wall, and scanned along the shelves. He took three steps forward to examine the space on the opposite side of the conference table. He saw no one hiding there.

"It's clear. Let's move back into the reception area. We need to clear that hallway and beyond next. There have to be stairs to the second and third floors back there somewhere," Betley said.

They cleared the hall, a small bathroom, a kitchen and break room area, and a copy room before approaching the stairs.

The staircase was walled on both sides and at least five feet wide. The treads were oak. Betley shone his flashlight at the top of the stairs revealing a hallway above that went from left to right. If anyone was up there, they'd see the light and know that they were coming, but Will didn't want to take the stairs in the dark.

Betley stepped onto the bottom tread and stopped. He slowly climbed two more steps before motioning for Will to move to the opposite side and follow him up the stairs. With his index and middle fingers, he motioned for Will to watch the left side of the opening at the top of the stairs. Will held his pistol in both hands and pointed at the floor as they climbed.

One of the treads squeaked under their weight and Will froze. Betley didn't. He kept moving, quickly rounding the corner at the top and moving into the corridor. Will rushed to catch up and moved to the left. Two rooms lay on the left. There were two closed doors and a small window at the end of the hall. He wasn't sure what to do at that point.

"Will, stack up behind me," Betley whispered.

They cleared the rooms to the right of the stairs. Both were large offices with oversized desks and expensive leather furniture. One was neat and orderly—the other messy with files and books stacked on the desk and floor. Client boxes lined one wall.

They moved to the rooms on the left. Will stood behind Betley as he turned the knob and rushed into the room. He heard screaming before he rounded the door jamb.

"Show me your hands! Show me your damn hands!" Betley yelled.

Will jabbed his gun in the direction of a young man and woman seated on a sofa along the wall to his right. Fear showed on their faces. Their hands were raised. Will trained his weapon on them as he scanned the rest of the room with his eyes. Two more young men sat in the leather armchairs that flanked a large oak desk.

"Keep them up," Betley said. "You two, get over there with your friends on the sofa."

Will stepped back as the two frightened men slowly rose, walked backward toward the sofa, and took a seat.

"Who the hell are you people," a pudgy kid in athletic shorts and a ballcap said.

"FBI," Betley said, producing his badge.

"We didn't break in, man. The door was unlocked. I had an appointment," a skinny pockmark-faced kid said

"Shut up. I don't give a shit. Who else is here with you?" Betley asked.

"Nobody, man. It's just us. We're waiting for my lawyer. I told you—"

"I said, I don't care why you were here. Is there anyone else in the building? Have you seen anyone besides yourselves?"

"No!" the girl said.

"Can we go now?" a second guy asked.

"Not yet," Betley said. "Watch them. I need to clear that last room. Betley backed toward the door.

"Ain't nothing in there but boxes. We checked already," the skinny kid said.

"Watch him," Betley motioned toward the scrawny lad.

Will's eyes darted from the pudgy kid to the skinny one, and then to the broad-shouldered boy and the girl. They looked harmless, except for the guy at the end who couldn't seem to sit still.

Betley returned. "It's clear."

"Can we go now, officer?" the girl asked.

The boy at the end of the sofa shifted over and over in his seat. His twitchy movements made Will nervous. He was on something, that was for sure.

"Will, grab me that lamp," Betley said.

Will backed toward the desk. He knocked his knee on the armchair as he turned to get the table lamp from the desk. Ignoring the pain, Will grabbed the lamp and held it out to Betley.

"Cut the off the cord," Betley said.

Will removed the knife from his tactical belt and cut the lamp's cord.

"What are you going to do with that?" the skinny kid asked.

"I'm going to tie your ass up, and then I'm going to put a gag in your mouth so you'll shut the hell up like I told you to," Betley said.

He nodded toward the floor. "On your faces."

As the young people moved to lie on the floor, Will gathered cords from all the lamps in the room and tied the four young people's hands and feet. Betley made the mouthy guy remove his shirt first so he could use it as a gag. The other three remained silent.

"Now what?" Will asked.

"We find the steps to the attic," Betley said, backing out of the room.

THIRTY-ONE

Will

DAY TWO

The pull-down attic steps led to an enormous open space. Four eyebrow windows, one on each wall, let some light into the room. The area was filled with boxes stacked nearly to the ceiling. All the boxes had a name and a number, likely a client name and number.

"This is our last resort. We'll leave the steps down, in case the lower levels flood quickly," Betley said.

Back downstairs, Cayden and Isabella were relieved when they returned. Will saw Isabella's shoulders relax, and Cayden stopped chewing his thumbnail.

"We need to secure that door next," Betley said.

With a little ingenuity, they managed to cover the door with a bookcase and wedge enough furniture in front of it to keep anyone from easily making entry. Now the only way out was the small window at the end of the hall upstairs or the back door that led to a porte cochére. They left that door unimpeded but locked for a quick exit if needed. Betley pulled a leather office chair in and plopped down in it with a clear view of the door.

Cayden took a seat behind the receptionist's desk. He searched the drawers, locating a box of cookies and two breakfast bars.

"Hey, Isabella, want some cookies?" he asked, pushing himself away from the desk.

As he stood, the office chair flew back and bumped into the wall. A panel behind the desk opened.

"What's that?" Isabella asked, pointing to the crack in the floor-to-ceiling bookcase.

Cayden stuck his head into the opening. "Cool. It's a secret room under the stairs."

Isabella rushed over to check it out. "It is cool. How'd you open it?"

"I didn't. All I did was bump it with the chair."

Isabella pushed the bookcase back into place and then pressed around until she found the latch to open it again.

"Good to know. It could be a place to hide. You know, if they find us," Cayden said.

"Yeah," Isabella answered.

"Not really. You could be trapped in there and drowned if this place floods," Will said.

Cayden nodded. "True."

"What time do you think it is?" Cayden asked.

"I don't know. Maybe six or seven o'clock," Will said.

"I'm hungry."

"Me too, buddy. We should look in the kitchen and see if there's anything to eat," Will said.

While Isabella went to use the bathroom, Will and Cayden left to find food. In the kitchen, they found peanuts, crackers, condiments, and someone's leftover Chinese takeout. It wasn't much. There were a couple of cases of bottled water and enough alcohol to supply a party bus through all of Mardi Gras.

Will gathered up the nuts and bottled water and headed for the conference room to try out the large leather sofa flanking the wall by the door. He could recline and watch the front door while he ate.

"We all need to get some sleep. It's going to be a long night, and none of us will sleep once the eye of that hurricane makes landfall."

"What about the kids upstairs?" Cayden asked.

Will stuffed peanuts into his mouth and washed them down with the water. "What about them?" he asked.

"I bet they'd like something to eat. We should at least take them some water. It's hot and stuffy in here. I bet it's even hotter up there," Cayden said.

It was hotter up there. Not as hot as the attic, but without air conditioning, it was likely around eighty-five or ninety upstairs. Will hoped they didn't end up having to sleep up there. He recalled the window. Maybe they could crack it open just a little and let a breeze in. It was on the north side of the building, but with the wind blowing like it was, rain would come in. It might be worth it.

"I'll talk to Betley about it later. Right now, I'd like to rest a bit. It's been a long, long day," Will said.

Cayden went off to join Isabella in the reception area. Will could hear them whispering, but tuned them out. His mind was on what Betley had said about the power grid not coming back on. He was mapping various routes away from Houston when he heard the thump upstairs.

He sat up and listened. Had the kids gotten themselves untied? When he heard the second thump followed by a loud bang, he jumped to his feet. In that instant, all hell broke loose. Betley was upstairs. He was screaming, but Will couldn't make out what he was saying over the sound of rifle fire.

Will raced to Cayden and Isabella. He could see the light coming from the stairwell. They needed to make it to the back door, but he was unsure what was going on up there. All he knew was he needed to get Cayden out of the line of fire.

Isabella ran toward the secret room. Will grabbed Cayden and shoved him under the stairs.

"If it starts to flood, get to high ground," Will said as he started to close the door. Cayden rushed over to him and threw his arms around his waist. "Come back, okay, Dad?"

Will kissed his son on the top of his head and turned to leave. He pivoted to face Isabella. "You get to higher ground," Will repeated as he closed the door.

Will stopped and scanned the stairwell. It was dark. The only light came from upstairs in the direction of the office where they'd tied up the college kids. He slowly ascended the steps to the second floor then stopped before going through the doorway. He pressed his back against the wall on the left and peered down the hall to his right. It was clear. He switched sides and looked down the hall to his left. He saw nothing. He burst into the hall and immediately, something crashed into his face. He cursed as he fell backward, hitting his head on the wall.

He felt hands pulling him from behind. They dragged him into the room where the college kids were bound on the floor. Will frantically tried to get away, but one of the intruders poked a pistol in his face. He tried to speak, but that earned him a boot to the ribs. He coughed and wheezed, trying to catch his breath. Will rolled onto his back and tried to sit up, reaching for the knife on his belt. The man stomped on him, twisting and grinding his boot against Will's hand.

He writhed in pain and rolled onto his left side. When Will opened his eyes, he could see Betley on the floor near the desk. One of the men from the storage facility held a knife against Betley's throat.

"Where is the drive?" the man in black asked in a thick Asian accent.

"I don't know what you're talking about," Will said. "I don't have a drive."

"You may not have the thumb drive, but you know where it is. Now hand it over."

"I don't know where any thumb drive is. I don't—" the boot of a second man landed in the middle of Will's chest. If not for the body armor, he might have broken his breastbone with the blow. As it was, it knocked the wind out of him—again.

Isabella screamed. Will sat up and fought to get to his feet. The man landed a knee to his chin, whipping his neck back. His head bounced off the hardwood floor. Will was dazed, but through the haze, he heard Cayden yell his name. His world was spinning. He couldn't move. He couldn't get to his son.

One of the men yanked the girl to her feet and threw her back onto the sofa. He shoved a pistol in her face. "Where is the flash drive?" he demanded.

"I don't know. We aren't with those people. We were here for an appointment with—" The attacker struck her in the jaw with the butt of the gun. She fell back, screaming. The man spun around and grabbed the skinny kid, hauled him to his feet, and tossed him onto the sofa beside the girl. He stuck the barrel of the pistol in the boy's mouth. "You will tell me where it is," the attacker said.

"I'm telling you I—"

He pulled the trigger. Will struggled to get up, but the man above him placed his boot on Will's head. When the man turned to grab another of the college kids, the girl flew off the sofa and landed on his back. He flailed and spun around, trying to throw her off, but she had two fists full of the man's hair. She locked her legs around one of his thighs and held on.

THIRTY-TWO

Will

DAY TWO

As the attacker struggled to shake off the girl, Will caught a glimpse of Betley passing the door. Betley's movement also attracted Will's attacker's attention. He shifted his weight as he turned to look. Will grabbed the man's ankle with both hands and pushed up with all his might, knocking the attacker off balance. He fell back, hitting his head on the corner of the desk. He was dazed but still conscious.

Will jumped to his feet and scrambled for his gun on the floor. He scooped up the weapon, spun around, and quickly backed out the door. He aimed at the man with the girl on his back, but the way they were facing, Will couldn't get a shot off without hitting her. The third kid was on his knees. Both his hands and feet were still tied, so there was little he could do. He bounced on top of the man Will had flung off and sat on him.

Will heard something and turned to his right. Betley was at the end of the hall. He had one of the attackers pinned against the wall. Betley was asking him something in Chinese. The man head-butted Betley, and he stumbled back.

Will took aim at Betley's attacker and was about to squeeze the trigger when felt a blow to his back. He dropped to one knee. The pistol skidded away. As he reached toward the weapon, an arm wrapped around his neck. Will rose to one knee, trying to throw him off. The man's grip tightened and Will twisted under his arm as he stood. He landed a solid blow to the man's rib cage and his attacker doubled over, releasing his grip on Will. Taking two steps back, Will tried to catch his breath. The man spun around, landing a foot to Will's knee. He cried out as his knee buckled. As Will dropped to the floor, the man landed an uppercut to his chin. Will's head whipped back, hitting the wall. His hands fell to his side. He felt the knife attached to his belt and quickly unsnapped it. When the man came in to grab him again, Will jammed the knife into the man's groin.

Isabella screamed as she emerged from the stairs. Gunshots came from the office where the college kids were still fighting with the third attacker. A second later, the third attacker appeared in the hallway. Isabella raised her rifle and fired. The attacker dropped. The man on the floor at her feet groaned and rolled from side to side, holding his bleeding groin. She fired again, and he stopped moving. Betley's attacker let out a primeval scream and charged him, knocking him to the floor as they wrestled for control of Betley's knife. Will got to his feet, grabbed his pistol from the floor by the stairs, and ran toward them. He aimed but couldn't get a clear shot. The man had the knife and was repeatedly stabbing Betley in the leg. He leaned back to swing the blade at Betley's chest, and Will fired, hitting him in the arm. Will fired again, finally striking him in the side of the head. He fell to one knee, still clasping the knife. Betley grabbed it and rammed it into the man's throat just below his Adam's apple. The man slumped, and Betley lowered him to the floor. The three attackers were down. Betley was injured. Will was bleeding from blows to his head and face. His knee hurt like hell.

Isabella ran to the office where the college kids were. She cried out. Will ran to her.

"They killed them. They had nothing to do with this, and they just killed them."

"Where's Cayden?" Will asked.

"Still under the stairs. I told him to stay put and gave him my pistol," Isabella said. "I hope that was okay. I didn't know what else to do. He was going to come to save you."

Will didn't respond. He turned and ran down the stairs, pounded on the door to the secret room. "Cayden, it's me. It's your dad."

A second later, the door opened, and Cayden flew into his arms. Will hugged his son and cried like a baby. He'd almost left his son an orphan. The thought of what would have become of him if he'd died upstairs overwhelmed him.

Will grabbed him by both arms and held Cayden out in front of him. "Are you okay?"

"I'm fine," Cayden said. "But you don't look so great." Cayden touched the split in Will's lip.

"You should see the other guy," Will said.

"Did you get them all?"

"Isabella got one. I got two," Will said, wearing an ear to ear grin.

"Is it over?"

"I think so," Will said, bring Cayden back into an embrace.

"What about Betley?"

"He's banged up, but I think he'll make it."

"And the college kids?"

Will hesitated. The death of cold-blooded killers was one thing, but explaining the senseless death of four innocent kids was difficult. How could his son understand and process that kind of violence when he himself couldn't?

"Can I get a hand?" Isabella called from the stairs.

Will didn't want to leave his son down there alone, but dead bodies littered the floor upstairs.

"Will, he's bleeding really bad," Isabella yelled.

"Go, Dad. I'll be all right," Cayden said.

"Shut the door," Will said as he headed for the stairs.

"Betley needs a doctor," Isabella said.

Will pointed to the broken window. "I don't think we can make it in this storm."

The wind howled, and the rain blew in through the broken glass.

"I'll make it. Help me up," Betley said.

"I thought I saw a shower in that corner office. See if there are towels or something we can use to put pressure on his wounds to control the bleeding," Will said.

As Isabella ran to gather towels, Will moved Betley to the office where the college kids' bodies were. Will helped him climb over the girl and placed him on the sofa. He put pillows under his feet and inspected Betley's wounds. He was pale, his skin clammy, and he was going into shock.

Will pressed the palm of his hand down hard on the largest gash in Betley's leg. He cried out and bit down on his hand. Isabella returned with an armload of towels.

"Here," Will said. "You press here." He pointed to the wound to Betley's right groin.

Betley smiled.

"Cayden," Will yelled. "Cayden, grab some bottles of water and bring them up here."

Will hated to have his son see the carnage up there, but Betley needed fluids, and he couldn't release the pressure he was applying to go get them. He knew that, unfortunately, there would likely be lots of bodies floating outside after the storm passed. Hundreds of thousands of people were on the road evacuating when the EMP stuck stranding them in the city. The ones that had not fled on foot to higher ground would likely be injured or killed in the storm. There was no way to shield Cayden from that sight.

Will heard Cayden run up the stairs. "Don't look at them, son. Just bring me the water," Will said.

"Eyes right here, Cayden," Isabella said as Cayden entered the room.

For some odd reason, that triggered the memory of watching movies with his wife and son. When a particularly steamy scene would come on the screen, Melanie would instruct Cayden to look at her until the scene passed. What would Melanie think about the situation he'd put their son in? Would she have made different decisions? He had no doubt that Melanie would have been all for taking the injured women to the hospital. After the carjacking, she may have done things differently. But he would never know. He'd made the decisions he'd made, and here they were. Second-guessing now wouldn't change any of it.

"Open the water and help him take a drink, Cayden," Will said.

As the storm intensified outside, Betley's bleeding lessened. He'd lost a lot of blood, but a closer inspection revealed that the wounds weren't near major arteries.

When the water began to rise on the floor below, Will knew it was time to move.

"I think we should move upstairs to the attic. The floodwater could rise quickly, and we need time to get Betley up there," he said.

"I'm not sure he can make it up those narrow attic steps," Isabella said.

"I can make it. You go first, and Will can get behind me and catch me if I slip," Betley said.

Cayden helped Will carry all the bottled water up to the attic. And then Isabella and Will helped Betley to the attic steps. Isabella turned, climbing the steps backward, holding on to Betley's hands while Will supported him from behind.

They left the stairs down until the storm had intensified so much that wind whipped through the attic.

Will stood at the small window overlooking the parking lot. It was difficult to see anything at all in the dark. The winds howled and whistled. Loose items were tossed around and banged against buildings. It went on and on, hour after hour.

Cayden was seated in the middle of the room. He and Isabella had stacked boxes together, making a U-shaped sofa like structure. Betley lay on one end. Cayden and Isabella lay on the other. Will paced, unable to rest, every bump causing his blood pressure to rise. They were far enough away from the coast that it was unlikely they'd see roofs ripped off or buildings completely destroyed but his body remembered what it felt like. He dreaded what they'd find after the storm passed. How many lives would be lost due to the EMP stranding people on the freeways?

THIRTY-THREE

Will

DAY THREE

Will lowered the steps to the attic and leaned over to get a look at the floor below him. He glanced back to Cayden and Isabella, who were huddled behind him. Betley looked on from his spot on their makeshift sofa.

"It's dry. Stay here. I'm going to check the stairs and main floor," Will said, descending the steps. Some light was shining through the window at the end of the hall. The sky still looked gray, and there was a light rain, but the storm had passed. The worst of the danger was over; he hoped. After the craziness of the last two days, he didn't know what to expect. All he knew was that they had survived thus far. Now, they needed to figure out what to do next.

He quickly moved to the stairs leading to the first floor. The water rose to the third step. If they left now, they could wade through the waist-deep water and make their way to dry land. If not, who knew how high the water could rise. Without communications or a way to find out what the weather was doing, he had no idea how much more rain would fall and how flooded the bayou would become.

It wouldn't be an easy trek, not with Betley's injuries. Will doubted he could be much help to the man. He could barely move himself. His sides and abdomen were black and blue and he was sure he'd suffered broken ribs at the very least. His knee was swollen and sore, but he could walk. He hoped he didn't have any permanent damage. Isabella, despite the injury to her ankle and the burn on her arm, was the least injured, except for Cayden. Will was grateful. So grateful nothing had happened to his son.

"How's it look down there," Isabella called to him.

"About four feet of water downstairs. I'm going to mark the wall and see if it rises," he said.

They needed to leave right away. He knew that, but Betley was in no shape. They were all exhausted after two nights of no sleep and the harrowing battle they'd been through. He wanted to give everyone just a little more time before they attempted to make their way through the floodwaters.

Will went into the office, found a sharpie pen, descended the steps, and put a line just above the wall's high-water mark. He'd come back and check in an hour. If the water was above the line, they might need to move sooner.

He moved to the window and glanced out. The trash cans their attackers had used to climb onto the roof of the port cochére had been blown away. They couldn't go out that way. Betley wouldn't survive a jump from that height. They'd have to wade through the water and go out the back door.

Will returned to the attic and waited. Cayden and Isabella huddled on their makeshift sofa. The cushions taken from the offices below added to the look. Will scooted over near Betley. "We're going to have to wade through waist-high water. You gonna be able to walk?"

"Yeah. Don't you worry about me," Betley said, adjusting his position.

"What are you thinking? Head north toward Humble or northwest toward The Woodlands?" Betley asked.

"I don't know. We'd have to cross the bayou no matter which

way we go. The rain seems to be moving from west to east. That means we haven't seen the worst of the flooding. It's only going to get deeper," Will said.

"What then?" Betley said.

"I thought we'd head to Eastex Freeway and take it north as far as we can," Will said.

Betley tried to get up, but Will placed his hand on his shoulder. "Not yet. I placed a mark at the high-water mark downstairs. I want to see how quickly the water is rising."

"That's smart," Betley said. "Well, I'll be ready when it's time."

"Good to hear," Will said.

He moved to the window, looking east. All he could see was the parking lot to the side of the building. Trees were toppled, and debris floated in the water. They would risk being injured by the floating debris as well as all manner of sickness and disease from chemicals and bacteria in the water. Will wondered if they'd be able to see the refineries from the freeway. He'd like to see if the chemical fires were still burning, spewing toxic chemicals into the air. There wasn't any way to put them out and he wasn't sure whether the hurricane would extinguish them. Usually, it was during or after the storm that the fires started. He had no frame of reference to know the other way around.

"What's that sound?" Cayden asked. They all stiffened, listening.

Betley tilted his head.

"I don't know. It sounds sort of like a generator maybe," Will said. The sound of generators was common following a hurricane. Even in category one storms, power sometimes went out. Nearly everyone kept a generator to power up their refrigerators and charge their phones, running them only a few hours a day to conserve fuel.

"I don't know. That doesn't sound like a generator to me,"

Betley said. "In fact, that sounds more like a vehicle—or several vehicles."

"Do you think?" Will said, getting to his feet.

"I think it's possible."

"What?" Isabella asked.

"The National Guard," Cayden said, standing and joining Will at the window.

"I'm going down to see if I can hear more clearly from that broken window over the port cochére.

"I'm coming," Isabella said. She ran up to Will and Cayden, then pivoted back to face Betley. "You'll be all right for a moment?"

"Of course. I'm fine. I keep telling you people, I'm a lot tougher than I look. You don't need to worry about me."

Will leaned out the window on the second floor, craning his neck to listen.

"That's definitely a vehicle. I think Betley is right. It could be the Guard. Those Humvees can go through a lot of shit and still run."

"Should we go check it out?" Isabella said.

"Of course. That could be our ride the hell out of this stinking town," Will said.

"Let's go then," Isabella said, walking toward the stairs.

"We need to get Betley—and the rifles," Will said.

"You think it's a good idea to carry the rifles to meet the National Guard? What if they think we're hostiles?" Isabella said.

"I'm not going anywhere without a weapon ever again," Will said.

"Okay, but if you get shot dead by our own side, remember I warned you."

"We can put them down after we confirm that it's our troops and not the enemy's," Cayden said.

That kid was so smart. Will hadn't thought that the Chinese could already have brought their military vehicles inland. It was something they needed to be cautious about. It would suck to go running up only to find themselves as prisoners of war or shot.

Will helped Betley down the attic steps. Before descending the stairs to the first floor, he glanced over at the high-water mark. It had risen one inch in the last hour. It wasn't bad, but it showed that it was rising. They'd picked a good time to move to higher ground. Will prayed that the sound they heard was vehicles and that they were friendlies.

"That water looked nasty," Isabella said.

It did. Papers and trash floated it in. That would be nothing compared to what they are about to wade into.

"It smells awful too," Cayden said.

"Oh, my God. If it's up over the toilet," Isabella said, shuddering.

"At least the door is shut," Cayden said.

"What about the crack under the door," Isabella said.

"Just don't touch anything you don't have to," Will said.

Isabella looked at her feet. "I really liked these shoes."

"We'll need to look for clean clothes and shoes as soon as we get out of the floodwaters," Will said.

"Let's hope that's the Guard we hear. They might be able to take us to a shelter with showers," Betley said.

"Seriously?" Isabella's eyes lit up at the prospect.

"It's possible."

"Let's go then. I've never felt so dirty in all my life. I'd kill for a shower and clean clothes," she said, stepping into the stairwell.

Wading through the knee-high water was made more difficult by having a hundred-and-eighty-pound man leaning against him. Betley tried, but it was slow going.

They saw the first victim of the storm as they approached the freeway. Bodies were lodged against the bridge supports. Isabella turned away. Cayden did not. Will studied his son. He saw compassion on his face. It was a tragedy beyond measure. The impact it would have on them all, Will could not know, but seeing how his son had handled himself thus far, Will was hopeful that somehow, someway, they'd make it through okay.

THIRTY-FOUR

Savanah

DAY THREE

With the windows covered with heavy plywood, it felt more like they were preparing for a hurricane than defending her home from marauders. So far, there'd been no sign of Derek, Wade, or anyone from the mayor's office. Jason's brother had sent word that his family was going to move on the town. The Vincent police department was going to be busy repelling the Blanchards from taking over the city. Although Savanah was grateful that Mayor Thibodeau and his henchmen would be too tied up to bother her, she was concerned for the small town's residents. Folks like Paul Broussard, Sam, Peggy from the flower shop, and many others were good people. They didn't deserve to be caught in the middle of a drug war between their mayor and a rival gang.

Jason had stayed on to help Savanah guard the house and barn. The rich kids from the gated community had raided several farms nearby. Raymond Johnson had fought back. His wife was now a widow and he left three small children behind. Savanah was scared. She wasn't sure the farm was worth dying for and had almost given up and taken off after she'd heard. Jason had been the one to convince her to stay.

Kendra had made him a nice bunk out in the barn. She'd

always liked Jason, at least that was what Savanah had thought. She couldn't understand her attitude toward him now. Kendra almost acted like she thought there was something romantic going on between Savanah and Jason. She would set her straight about that when they sat down for dinner. In the meantime, they had work to do. Moving all the animals to the barn to protect them from thieves meant she had to feed them the hay she'd put up for winter. Not only did that cut into her winter feed rations, but it created a lot of extra work.

"Mom!" Keegan yelled from the front door to the house.

Savanah dried her hands and poked her head into the living room. "What's wrong?"

"Jason said to come quick. Karson heard those boys coming down the road."

Savanah ran out the door. She stopped at the bottom of the steps to their wrap-around porch and listened. She didn't hear anything for a moment. As she walked around to the side of the house and approached the barn she heard engines start up.

"Mom, they're at the Richardsons," Karson said.

"Did you see them? Maybe the Richardsons got their utility vehicles running."

"No. I saw the ATVs. Three of them."

"Shit," Savanah cursed under her breath.

"I think you should get the children inside. I'll lock the animals in the barn and stand guard. If they decide to pull down the driveway, I'll give them a Fontenot Herbal Farm welcome," Jason said, holding up his shotgun.

"Rock salt?" Savanah asked.

Jason scrunched up his face. "Is that the message you want to send?"

"I sure don't want to shoot kids," Savanah said.

"Mom, they killed Mr. Johnson," Kendra said.

Savanah furrowed her brow. This was her fourteen-year-old daughter advocating shooting and possibly killing someone.

Savanah was shocked and speechless. She blamed herself. Had she failed to provide the type of home where her children felt safe? That was the only explanation she had for her daughter's attitude. She must be terrified and believe that her mother couldn't protect her.

A flash of red caught her attention, and the ATV riders came into view. In seconds, they'd cut the lock on the gate at the end of the drive. It all happened so fast, and then they were there, in her driveway, at the home where her children were. Their intentions were obvious. They wouldn't have cut the lock if they were there for a friendly visit.

"Kendra, get Kylie and Keegan inside. Karson, get my rifle," Savanah said as she drew her pistol from its holster on her hip. "And extra magazines."

The intruders turned back at the sound of the first shot. Savanah had aimed for the motor of the front ATV, but missed and hit the back tire. The rider in the rear reached for the rifle strapped to the back. Jason took aim. Savanah screamed at the same time he squeezed the trigger and watched in horror as the kid's head flung back and then forward. The quad continued down the driveway for another twenty-five feet before the kid slumped off. The vehicle came to rest in the ditch.

Savanah covered her mouth with her hand and willed the kid to get up. His companions never even looked back. They tore through the gate and sped away, leaving the friend lying in her driveway, bleeding from a wound to his head.

"Kendra, get the medkit," Savanah yelled as she holstered her pistol.

"No, Savanah. Wait. Let me secure his weapon," Jason said. He sprinted down the drive—Savanah on his heels.

"Is he?" Kendra said as she held out the medical kit to her mother.

Jason placed two fingers on the side of the kid's neck. Savanah didn't need Jason to tell her. There was no doubt in her mind that

No Way Out

the boy was dead. The growing crimson stain in the gravel was all she needed to tell her that his wound was not survivable.

Jason shook his head. "He's gone."

Kendra took three steps back and covered her mouth. "Oh my God, Mom. What are we going to do?"

Savanah didn't have an answer for her. Usually, when one shot an intruder, you would use a phone and call 911. The police would arrive in their patrol cars, and an ambulance would come for the body. Under the circumstances, none of that was going to occur.

Savanah ran a hand down the length of her braids. As much as she hated to, she would have to see if she could borrow Willow's horse and ride into town to report this to the police. There just wasn't any way around it. The shooting was justified. The kid had broken onto her property and pulled a gun. But with the bad blood between Jason's family and the mayor, there would be no way he would get fair treatment. They'd lock him up.

Savanah turned to face Jason. He looked like he was going to be sick. If they reported this shooting to the police and they came to arrest Jason, that could start a war. Would he even go? Would her children be caught in the crossfire?

"I don't know, Kendra. I just don't know what to do," Savanah said.

"You think those guys will go to the police?" Kendra asked, practically reading her mind.

Savanah considered it. They had broken the law. They were responsible for terrorizing the countryside and allegedly killing Ray Johnson. Would they go to the police?

"Jason, do you think the tractor will start?" Savanah asked.

"Should. If the ATVs run, that old tractor of your papaw's should," Jason said. "What are you thinking?"

"I think we need to fill in the hole out where we pulled that tree stump."

"What about the boy's quad?"

Savanah looked around. She pointed. "Sink it in the pond."

Everyone was silent as they ate dinner by lantern light that night; Savanah wanted to conserve the batteries on her solar power system. It had been cloudy since the storm had rolled in. There was no way of knowing where the hurricane had ultimately landed, but southwest Louisiana was getting a significant amount of rain from it. After three days of little sunshine, the batteries for her solar electric system were lower than she'd like.

Kendra picked at her red beans and rice. Savanah looked around the table. No one was eating much. Not even the boudin. It was usually a family favorite. Savanah had heated the pork and rice sausage over the grill as she boiled water for everyone to wash up after burying the body at the back of the property.

"I better get back out there and keep watch," Jason said, pushing himself away from the table.

"Can I come?" Karson asked.

"No!" Savanah said abruptly.

All she wanted to do was keep her children safe. She wasn't sure how to do that now. Those boys had taken away her sense of security on her own property. She didn't feel safe inside her own home, even with all the guns and ammo. She couldn't watch every window and door.

For a moment, Savanah considered packing up her children and heading into town. Derek was a scumbag drug dealer, but he was their father. He wouldn't let anyone hurt them. Jason was scraping his plate into the slop bucket by the back door. He'd risk his life to protect her and her kids. Not Derek. If the town was attacked by Jason's family, being Derek's children could get them killed. No, they were safer there on the farm. Somehow, they had to find a way to defend the place. If it took a long time for things to come back on and return to normal, they'd need the food she'd stored and the animals in the barn. She'd stay put, and they'd find a way to defend their home. They were Cajun. She wouldn't back down. She would do what she needed to do.

"Cher, catch me that hammer and that box of nails," Savanah said.

"What are you gonna do?" Kendra asked.

"I'm going to make sure if anyone else wants to come through that gate, they get lagniappe," Savanah said.

"What little something extra?" Jason said from the doorway.

"First, we need to park that tractor against the gate. And then, for a little extra something, I'm going to line the driveway with spike strips. No one is just coming down my driveway."

Jason opened the door. "I'll get the tractor."

THIRTY-FIVE

Will

DAY THREE

Will and the others waded through waist-high water for several blocks, trying to follow the sound of the engines. Will was relieved to reach the dry pavement of the overpass spanning both the South and Eastex Freeways. From there Will could see military vehicles heading north and south for as far as the eye could see.

Isabella waved her arms above her head, attempting to flag them down, but they just kept moving. "Hey," she yelled. "We need help here."

The convoy slowed and eventually stopped, but not for them. Traffic appeared to back up as a large military vehicle shoved stranded cars to the side of the highway, clearing the lanes for the convoy.

Isabella leaned over the rail, waving her hands to get the attention of the young guardsmen in the military truck just below them. "Hey. Hey you. We have an injured FBI agent here." She pointed to Betley. "Show them your badge, Betley."

Betley grimaced as he reached into his pocket. He gingerly pulled out his badge, opened it, and waved it where the men could see.

"I'm sorry. We can't help you," the man yelled from the cab of his truck. He diverted his gaze from them. Will wondered how many other survivors he'd said that to that day. He tried not to imagine all the stranded people who'd been attempting to evacuate the city in advance of the hurricane. What had happened to them all?

Betley leaned against the rail, "Do you have a radio?"

The man said nothing.

"Radio your commanding officer and tell him that FBI Agent James Betley of the Houston field office is on this bridge. I have something from the Chinese Consulate that is of utmost importance to national security."

No reaction.

"They aren't going to help us," Isabella said. "They're really going to leave us to fend for ourselves. How can they do that?"

"Listen here, asshole. This man here is a federal agent. He has information about the plans of the people who took out our power grid. If you do nothing, we might as well learn to speak Chinese real quick," Isabella said. She was so upset, the veins in her forehead protruded.

She attempted to throw her leg over the railing, but Will and Cayden caught her by the arms. "No! That won't help, Isabella."

"Something has to. They aren't listening." She broke free and ran to the opposite side of the overpass. She yelled and yelled until someone poked their head out the passenger side window.

"Please listen. We don't want anything. We have an injured federal agent. He has information about a planned enemy invasion. We've spent the last twenty-four hours guarding a flash drive and a bunch of schematics for the stupid refineries and the power plant from some Chinese gang sent to get it back from a spy named Kim Yang. All we need is for you to get on your radio and tell your commander. Please," Isabella said.

"Let's go, Isabella. They aren't going to listen to us," Will said, pulling her back from the rail.

"What's the agent's name?"

Will leaned over. "Betley. FBI Agent James Betley." Betley suddenly appeared at his side.

"I'm Agent James Betley. I work out of the Houston field office. The special agent in charge is Troy Emerson. I've been working on a case of corporate espionage. My informant worked with the Chinese Consulate. I have reason to believe that information she passed me contains classified information regarding the Texas power grid and refineries."

"Wait there. Someone will be by soon to collect it," the man said as the convoy began to move, and his vehicle pulled away.

"You think he's telling the truth?" Isabella asked. "Will they send someone for us?"

"Maybe." Betley eased himself down on the pavement. "I need to sit a minute."

He looked like he might pass out. That was the last thing they needed. Will didn't have the energy to carry the man.

"Where are they all going?" Cayden asked.

"Likely to secure the port and refineries."

"But they're on fire," Cayden said.

"Maybe not all of them. And at others, it may be only storage tanks. The refineries themselves might be salvageable. The country will need that fuel to recover," Betley said.

"I'm glad the military is here. That means that Kim's countrymen won't be able to pull off their plan, right?"

"Right," Betley said. Will detected something in his voice.

"Where are you going to go?" Cayden asked. "If they can't get things back to normal right away, I mean."

"Well, I'd planned to hole up in my storage unit until the initial phase passed, and then, I planned to head down to Kemah and ride things out on my boat."

"Initial phase?" Will asked. He was interested in seeing what phase Betley thought they were in.

"I figured there'd be several stages we'd go through. The initial would be denial or panic. Those in denial would operate as if it were any other disaster and do what they could to survive in their homes. Others would loot and burn like they always do during natural disasters or civil unrest. And then, when everyone realized that things weren't getting back to normal any time soon, the panic would set in, and people would be pushed to the point of desperation. That is the most frightening stage, in my opinion."

"Why?" Will asked.

"Desperate people are willing to do anything to survive."

"That's scary," Isabella said. "What stage are we in?"

"Denial. Especially here locally. Without communications, many will think that the storm has caused a temporary disruption and that help is on the way. They'll handle this like any other hurricane."

"How long do you think the denial phase will last?" Will asked.

"A week, maybe two. Neighbors will band together and help one another, expecting that the Red Cross and FEMA will arrive any day. But, when help doesn't arrive, those same neighbors will be at each other's throats, stealing whatever they can from the other just to survive."

"That sounds like a very pessimistic view. I choose to believe that people are inherently good and that they will continue to work together to persevere," Isabella said.

"You can choose to believe what you like, but if you are standing between someone's child and starvation, what do you think will happen?"

Will hated thinking about what might play out in neighborhoods all across the city. At least for the ones that survived the storm and made it back to their homes. If they had a home to return to.

A Humvee came into view, headed up the off-ramp and towards them. It stopped fifty yards from the overpass. A soldier stepped out. "FBI Agent James Betley," he called.

Betley waved his hand in the air. "That's me."

"Can you step this way, sir?"

Will grabbed one arm, and Isabella grabbed the other, and the two lifted Betley to his feet. As they began toward the Humvee, the soldier held out his hand to halt them. "Stop right there. Only the FBI agent."

"He can't walk. He's injured," Isabella said.

"Sit him down there and back away," the soldier said.

"What?" Isabella asked.

"It's okay, sergeant. They're with me. They're all right," Betley said.

"I said step away from him," the soldier said, moving his hand to his holstered pistol.

Another soldier stepped out, his M16 rifle trained on them.

Will grabbed Cayden and stepped in front of him. "Isabella, let's do what they say."

"But—" Isabella said.

"It's all right. Betley will get it sorted out. Right, Betley?"

Betley kept his gaze on the soldiers. "Right. I can walk. You guys just wait here. I'll talk to them."

Isabella huffed as Betley slowly limped toward the soldiers.

"You risk your life to save some stupid flash drive that is vital to the security of the nation, and this is the thanks you get," Isabella said, placing her hands on her hips.

"He said he'd get it straightened out with them," Cayden said.

A moment later, Betley was leaning against the front of the Humvee, pointing in their direction. He gesticulated as he spoke. Will could hear raised voices, but not what was being said. It didn't sound promising. The soldier grabbed Betley and spun him around, pinning him against the military vehicle.

"Betley," Isabella yelled, taking two steps in his direction. Cayden and Will both grabbed her and pulled her back.

A second Humvee roared up the off-ramp and stopped behind the first. Two soldiers stepped out. The two from the first vehicle took a step back and saluted them. Betley shook one of the men's hands. He pointed a thumb over his shoulder. The soldier leaned to his left and looked at Will, Cayden, and Isabella.

"He looks important," Cayden said.

"He's an officer," Will replied.

"Now we're getting somewhere," Isabella said.

Betley motioned them over. Isabella shot the two initial soldiers a dirty look as she walked past them and up beside Betley.

"Ma'am," the officer said. "Lieutenant Sharp. We're going to give you a ride. Just tell Sergeant Brown there where you'd like to go."

"We're not going to a shelter?" Cayden asked.

"I'm afraid there are no shelters just yet. Not anywhere near here. FEMA and the Red Cross had people and supplies ready to bring in after the storm passed. But as far as I know, they're stuck up in Huntsville. It could be some time before they're able to get a shelter up and running here in Houston with what has occurred. They may be able to set up something in Huntsville for those that can make it up there. There were a lot of folks on the road when this happened."

"What exactly did happen?" Cayden asked.

"Officially? I really can't say," Lieutenant Sharp said.

"Unofficially," Will said.

"We've been attacked."

"That much we knew," Isabella said.

"I'm sorry, I can't tell you more," Sharp said.

"So, now what?" Isabella asked, turning to Will.

Will looked at Betley. "Cayden and I need to get to Lake Charles. I have a sister north of there.

"That's a bit too far for us," Sharp said.

"I guess I'll go back to my apartment," Isabella said. "You and Cayden are welcome to come home with me. You can rest up, wait for the waters to recede, and then see if we can find you a ride to Louisiana."

"What about you, Betley?" Cayden asked.

"He's going to have to come with us. He'll have to be debriefed," Sharp said.

"I guess this is goodbye then," Will said, holding out his hand.

"For now," Betley said.

Betley and Isabella's embrace lasted an uncomfortable amount of time. Will turned and looked away. Will and Cayden waited while Isabella gave Betley her address. Will doubted they'd ever see the G-man again. He would likely be too busy tracking down spies and insurgents to pay personal visits with all that was happening. Will didn't know why he cared anyway.

Betley ruffled Cayden's hair. "You take care of that old man of yours."

"I will," Cayden said.

Old man? At the moment, Will felt like an old man. They watched Betley ride off with Lieutenant Sharp before climbing into a military transport vehicle.

THIRTY-SIX

Will

DAY THREE

The military transport vehicle let Will, Cayden, and Isabella off two blocks from her apartment to avoid driving through the flooded neighborhood. After wading through knee-deep water, they finally reach Isabella's apartment complex. She stopped in the middle of the street and her head rotated to her left.

"Is that—" Isabella started to ask.

"Music?" Will said. "I do believe it is."

"I'll be damned. I'm going to kill him," Isabella said.

"Who?" Cayden asked.

"Kevin, my boyfriend. While I've been fighting for my life, that f—. Her eyes flicked to Cayden, and she stopped herself mid curse. "He's been in my apartment, drinking my booze and having a hurricane party."

"How are they playing music?" Cayden asked. "Isn't the electricity out at your place?"

"That's live. My boyfriend plays drums. He's in a band. It sounds like they are all still there, in my house."

"Not to defend him, but he might not even know anything other than the storm has occurred. Depending on how much alcohol was involved, they might not have noticed the world went to shit," Will said.

"Knowing Kevin and the boys, there was lots of alcohol involved," Isabella said.

The first-floor apartments had been flooded, but the second and third floors had been spared. The metal had been ripped off the entire length of the covered parking structure. Cars had floated away and were piled up against the side of one of the buildings.

The sound of an accordion, fiddle, guitar, and drums came through a third-floor window as someone sang *The Back Door* with the distinctive southwest Louisiana French vernacular.

"Your boyfriend's Cajun?" Cayden asked.

"No. He just plays the drums in a Cajun band," Isabella said.

"You sure it's okay for us to stay here?" Will asked as they climbed the stairs to her apartment.

"Of course," she said unequivocally.

When they reached the landing at the top of the steps, several people came into view. Each of the doors to the various apartments was open. Lawn chairs and several coolers lined the walkway. Two large trash cans flanked each side of the steps, one half-full of beer, the other filled with empty cans and bottles. At the far end, a band was set up. It had been over a decade since Will had been to one, but this looked like the best hurricane party he'd seen.

Two females dressed in bikini tops and shorts danced in front of the band. One held a beer in one hand and slung Mardi Gras beads over her head with the other. A second later, one of the band members threw out a handful of beads, and the second woman lifted her top. That was when Isabella lost it.

"Hello!" Isabella yelled as she raced toward the band. "Honey, I'm home!"

No Way Out

After all that they'd been through trying to survive the apocalypse, Will just wanted a quiet place to sleep. When they arrived to find a hurricane party in progress, Will knew that wasn't about to happen. But after a heated exchange with her boyfriend, Isabella began filling the partygoers in on the bad news.

For the most part, they took the news that the world as they knew it had ended pretty well. Will didn't know how they'd react once the shock wore off. But after thirty minutes or so of explaining things, most seemed to get that they needed to sober up and take it seriously.

"From this moment on, we need to begin rationing food and water. No one is coming to bring more. The stores aren't going to re-open. Water is going to be our major concern. You can go a few days without food, but in this heat and humidity, a few hours without drinkable water and you could dehydrate and die," Isabella said.

"All the bottled water is gone already. The only thing we have left is some ginger ale and a few beers," one of the women said.

"You can drain your hot water heaters," Cayden said.

Cayden was right. Will wondered how he knew such a thing. He was impressed.

"Is that safe to drink?" someone in the crowd said.

"Yes," Cayden replied.

"I don't even know where my hot water heater is located," one of the bikini-clad women said.

"I'd be glad to come and help you find it," the accordion player said.

No doubt it would be a rough couple of days as he and Cayden waited for the floodwaters to recede. Finding the supplies they needed to make the hundred-and-fifty-mile trip to Calcasieu Parish would mean looting nearby apartments and homes. Whatever he and Cayden took for themselves would leave fewer resources for

Isabella and her neighbors. But, he didn't really have a choice. It could take several days to make the trip to Louisiana. Staying wasn't an option.

Remaining in the city would be a deadly decision. With over two million people competing for scant resources and law enforcement hindered by the lack of transportation and communication, how long would it take for Houston to fall? Weeks? Days? And with the threat of insurgents or a possible foreign invasion, the city was unsafe. He and Cayden needed to take their chances out on the road. Things would be better at Savanah's. She was prepared for something like this. She was used to living off-grid, and she knew how to raise her own food. The only question was, could she afford two more mouths to feed?

Will stared at Isabella. She looked up, and their eyes locked. What chance did Isabella have to survive in the city? She was home, but she wasn't safe. Why did he still feel so responsible for the woman? He could talk to her, convince her to leave. But where could she go? Isabella's boyfriend put his arm around her shoulders, and she moved away.

Cayden nudge Will. "Are we staying here?"

"Just for now," Will said. "We'll leave when the flood recedes."

"What about Isabella?"

Cayden liked her. She was good with him. Good for him. Maybe Savanah wouldn't mind if Cayden brought a friend.

"We'll talk to her in the morning, okay?"

Cayden smiled. It warmed Will's heart to see it. After all the boy had been through, Will had worried that Cayden would withdraw even more, but Isabella had drawn him out. Will felt hopeful for the first time in a long time about his relationship with his son. Whatever they faced out there beyond Houston, he was grateful for that. He'd do whatever it took to make sure that Cayden survived.

Isabella approached them. "Come with me, Cayden. Help me

clean out the guest room so you and your dad will have a place to sleep tonight."

As Isabella and Cayden walked toward her apartment, Isabella glanced over her shoulder. "Coming, Will?"

Will nodded and stepped over an intoxicated man. He gave a sideways glance at Isabella's boyfriend. He didn't look pleased that they were there.

"Right behind you," Will said.

∼

Thank you for purchasing No Way Out, book one in the Fall of Houston series. **The story continues in book two, No Other Choice.** Order your copy on Amazon.com today.

Also I'd like to hear from you and hope that you could take a moment and post an honest review on Amazon. Your support and feedback will help this author improve for future projects. Without the support of readers like yourself, self-publishing would not be possible. **Don't forget to sign up for my spam-free newsletter at www.tlpayne.com to be the first to know of new releases, giveaways and special offers.**

No Way Out has gone through several layers of editing. If you found a typographical, grammatical, or other error which impacted your enjoyment of the book, I offer my apologies and ask that you let me know so I can fix it for future readers. To do so, email me at contact@tlpayne.com In appreciation, I would like to offer you a free ebook copy of my next book.

Have you read my Days of Want series? If not, please check out the sample chapters for Turbulent, book one in the series or order your copy on Amazon today.

Also by T. L. Payne

The Days of Want Series

Turbulent

Hunted

Turmoil

Uprising

Upheaval

Mayhem

Defiance

Fall of Houston Series

A Days of Want Companion Series

No Way Out

No Other Choice

No Turning Back

No Surrender

No Man's Land

The Gateway to Chaos Series

Seeking Safety

Seeking Refuge

Seeking Justice

Seeking Hope

Survive the Collapse Series

Brink of Darkness

Brink of Chaos

Brink of Panic

Brink of Collapse

Brink of Destruction: A FREE Novelette

Desperate Age Series (Coming soon!)

About the Author

T. L. Payne is the author of the bestselling Days of Want, Gateway to Chaos and Fall of Houston series. T. L. lives and writes in the Osage Hills region of Oklahoma. T. L. enjoys many outdoor activities including kayaking, rockhounding, metal detecting, and fishing the many rivers and lakes of the area.

Don't forget to sign up for T. L.'s spam-free newsletter at www.tlpayne.com to be the first to know of new releases, giveaways and special offers.

T. L. loves to hear from readers. You may email T. L. at contact@tlpayne.com or join the Facebook reader group at https://www.facebook.com/groups/tlpaynereadergroup

Printed in Dunstable, United Kingdom

72226745R00152